The BAD MOTHER'S DIARY

SUZY K QUINN

Lightning Books

Published by
Lightning Books Ltd
Imprint of EyeStorm Media
312 Uxbridge Road
Rickmansworth
Hertfordshire
WD3 8YL

www.lightning-books.com

British Library Cataloguing in Publication Data
A catalogue record for this book is available from the British Library

Printed by CPI Group (UK) Ltd, Croydon CR0 4YY

ISBN 9781785631566

Gratitude from Suzy

I still can't believe so many people read my books.
Each and every day, I am grateful for you, dear readers.
Thank you so much.
If you want to ask me any questions about the books
or chat about anything at all, get in touch:

Happy reading,
Suzy xxx

Email: suzykquinn@devoted-ebooks.com
Facebook.com/suzykquinn
(You can friend request me. I like friends.)
Twitter: @suzykquinn
Website: suzykquinn.com

Friday, 1st January
New Year's Day

Back at my parents' house after HUGE argument with Nick.

Am FURIOUS.

Asked Nick to look after Daisy while I went to the supermarket (I always get distracted if I bring her along, and buy random things like special edition brownie Mars Bars).

Got home to find Nick playing computer games, with TEN empty bottles of original Guinness beside him.

TEN BOTTLES! In TWO hours!

I was furious.

'I'm not drunk,' he slurred. 'If I were drunk, I'd never have cracked this part of *Assassin's Creed*.'

I demanded he walk in a straight line, and he fell over.

As I was screaming at him, Nick's mother let herself into the apartment.

She saw Nick on the floor and said, 'You look tired, darling.' Then she asked what all the fuss was about.

I said Nick was getting drunk when he was supposed to be looking after a three-month old baby.

'Oh *Nick*,' said Helen. 'But Juliette, he *has* been working all day. He's *obviously* stressed.'

Working! All Nick's done today is read a two-page script for an online poker commercial.

'If I ever need relationship advice from a divorcee,' I told Helen, 'I'll let you know.'

Then I screamed at Nick a bit more, threw a bag together and said I was taking Daisy to my parents' house.

I would have made a strong, dignified-woman exit, except I had to come back for Daisy's pink waffle blanket, Teddy Snuggles, blackout curtain with suckers and finally her Lullaby Light Bear.

Saturday, 2nd January

Nick just phoned begging for forgiveness.

'I need you, Julesy, I need my little girl. I'm lost without you.'

But I'm not going to start feeling sorry for him. He needs to shape up. It's bad enough all these hangovers. But to be drunk when he's actually looking after her...

Weighed myself this morning on Dad's 1970s scales, because they're usually kinder than the ones at the apartment.

I am 30 POUNDS heavier than before I was pregnant.

And that is standing completely naked on the scales *after* I've been to the toilet.

Blaaaaaah.

Sunday, 3rd January

The trouble with motherhood these days is you're expected to:

+ Be slim(ish), well-groomed and fashionably dressed, with a brightly coloured designer baby bag covered in little forest animals.

+ Have a perfect IKEA home with quirky little child-friendly details, like a colourful chalkboard stuck on the fridge and designer robot toys.

• Be an all-natural, organic earth mother and not use any nasty plastic Tupperware with chemicals in it, only buy organic vegetables, breastfeed, have a drug-free birth, etc. BUT at the same time…

• Be a super-clean chemical spray freak with hygienic clean surfaces and floors at all times, plus wash your hands ten times a day.

All this AND get out of the house without mysterious white stains all over you.

How do women do it?

Nick's been calling and texting all day. Promising he'll never drink again. Begging to see pictures of Daisy.

It's a start I suppose.

Monday, 4th January

Laura visited today, and suggested we go jogging around Great Oakley together.

Like an idiot, I agreed.

Running beside my beautiful, athletic older sister…so not a good idea. Especially with my big, fat, post-baby bottom.

I was a lumbering cow, puffing behind a long-legged, shiny-haired blonde racing horse.

We ended up jogging in the woods by the train track, and predictably I lagged behind.

While I was swearing about 'fucking jogging', I saw a shadow that looked like dog poo. Swerved, stumbled and fell.

The next thing I knew, an iPhone light shone in my face.

'Who are you and why are you blinding me?' I shouted.

A curt voice replied, 'Juliette? It's Alex.'

'Alex who?' I asked.

'Alex Dalton.'

The light went off, and I saw my old friend Alex, wearing the sort of ninja-black running outfit you'd see on a Runner's World model. Alex was frowning as usual, apparently pondering some terrible injustice.

'*The* Alex Dalton?' I said. 'Business magnate and rope-swing champion? What are you doing back here on a weekday?'

'It's a long story,' said Alex. 'By the way, a magnate is by definition a business person.'

Typical Alex. I suppose a sense of humour isn't necessary on the global business scene.

'It's good to see you,' I said, as he helped me up. 'I thought you were based in London now.'

'I am,' said Alex. 'Most of the time.'

'Why are you wearing short-sleeved running gear in winter?' I asked. 'Are you parading your toned physique for the squirrels?'

'Of course not,' said Alex. 'I've just jogged seven miles. I'm hot. Anyway, this arm never feels the cold.' He gave the knotty, burned skin on his left bicep a solid slap. 'Why are you out here alone?'

'I'm not alone,' I said. 'I'm with Laura. What are *you* doing out here alone? A pretty boy like you should be careful in the woods.'

'Pretty boy?'

'OK, fine. Healthy good looks, then. The product of a gymkhana upbringing and excellent diet.'

'I always thought of myself as rugged.'

'If you want to look rugged, you should shave less.'

'And I was never interested in gymkhana,' said Alex, finally managing a smile. 'I always preferred skiing. Where's your sister?'

I said Laura was up ahead somewhere.

'I'll take you to her,' said Alex. 'It's treacherous out here.'

He offered me his arm, and I held the scarred part.

'You don't have to touch that if you don't want to,' he said. 'I know it's fairly repellent.'

'No it isn't,' I said. 'Don't be ridiculous.'

Then I asked if Alex enjoyed running. He said yes, adding, 'It's one of the few times I can be anonymous. I'm totally inconsequential when I run.'

'If you like being anonymous,' I said, 'why do you drive that flashy "I've-made-a-load-of-money" Rolls Royce?'

'To show I'm my own man.'

'I don't think people would confuse you with anyone else,' I said. 'You're Great Oakley's big success story.'

'Some people do,' said Alex. 'They confuse me with my father.'

'If you don't want to be confused with your father, why drive a Mr Monopoly old-man car?' I asked. 'You're in your thirties. Next, you'll be wearing a top hat.'

Alex gave his quirky half-smile and said, 'I like my car. I've never seen you running before.'

Admitted I'd been stupid enough to sign up for the Winter Marathon.

More specifically, Sadie had pressured me into signing up while I was pregnant and sitting around eating cake.

'You're training early, aren't you?' said Alex. 'It's eleven months away.'

I said I needed all the practice I could get.

Conversationally, Alex told me he'd probably run the Winter Marathon this year – and also the London, Tokyo and Berlin marathons. He said this as if marathons were a perfectly normal activity, not gruelling physical challenges.

I told him I didn't think I'd finish.

'That's a terrific attitude, Juliette,' said Alex. 'Forecasting failure before you even start.'

I said I was being realistic, and that Nick had bet I wouldn't finish.

'Don't listen to Nick Spencer,' said Alex. 'Anyone can run a marathon, as long as they train. It's more mental than physical.'

I told Alex I hardly ever listened to Nick. But on this rare occasion, the father of my child could be right.

'Rubbish,' said Alex. 'I'll train you, and we'll prove him wrong.'

I told him there was no point wasting his time. Then we saw Laura up ahead, and Alex said, 'I'll see you at my mother's ball this weekend.'

The Dalton Ball is usually on New Year's Eve, but it's late this year because Catrina Dalton is still in Italy, sourcing a special type of marble.

'I don't know about that,' I said. 'I've just had a baby.'

'Oh come on,' said Alex. 'You and your sisters were there at the beginning. You can't miss one now.'

Said I'd come, as long as Mum could take care of Daisy.

Alex said, 'See you Saturday then'. And off he went, tall, dark and handsome, jogging into the woods.

'Was that Alex Dalton?' Laura asked, as I limped up to her. 'Did he mention Zach?'

Teased Laura all the way home about liking Alex's brother. She took it quite well. Maybe there's something going on there.

I always suspected Zach Dalton had a thing for Laura.

Tuesday, 5th January

Have decided to give Nick another chance.

Got the train home this morning, and Nick met me at the station – just like the old days.

We had a long heart-to-heart, and Nick told me how down he felt.

'But it's no excuse for my behaviour,' he said. 'I'll try to do better.

I WILL do better.'

And then he asked me to marry him.

Cried happy tears, tainted somewhat with annoyance.

All these years together, and he FINALLY proposes after a big row, when I'm carrying 30 pounds of baby weight and have a car-crash vagina.

Wednesday, 6th January

Back in London.

It's nice to be able to buy a fresh croissant 24-hours a day. It's not nice seeing Helen.

The apartment is small enough with me, Nick and Daisy in it, plus all the baby paraphernalia that's slowly drowning us. With Helen always 'dropping by', perching at the breakfast bar, sipping an espresso through pursed lips, I can barely breathe.

Thursday, 7th January

Nick can't make the Dalton Ball. He's got a part up north, playing a cleaner in a soap opera.

He only has one line: 'That can happen if you eat too much chicken pie.'

I'm happy that he's got a part, but Nick always seems to go away when I need him. Which, when you have a three-month-old baby, is every day.

I can guarantee that if Daisy has a temperature or has woken up five times in the night, Nick will be in Manchester.

Spent the afternoon making Christmas thank you letters, supposedly from Daisy. I got a bit ambitious and decided to photograph Daisy with each and every present. Then she fell asleep, and it all looked a bit weird.

Nick's mum turned up and asked me what the hell I was doing arranging a set of bath products around a sleeping baby.

'Helen,' I said, 'for once, could you knock?'

But I don't think she heard me properly, because she said, 'Yes, all right then, I'll have a decaf.'

Friday, 8th January

Tried to de-clutter the bathroom today, in preparation for Dalton Ball preening tomorrow.

I haven't done any preening since Daisy was born, and I'm a little worried about what I might find when I get started. But hey ho.

I divided the bathroom into pre- and post-pregnancy.

Pre-pregnancy

Va-va-voom! mascara, neon eyeshadow, glittery nail varnish, fruit face mask, waxing strips, tampons and general pampering stuff.

Post-pregnancy

Sanitary towels big enough to absorb a bath-load of water, a vaginal toning weight kit, stretch-mark cream, suppositories, a big Velcro belt to help my stomach muscles knit together and surgical underwear made of stretchy netting.

How can something as natural as pregnancy and childbirth mess your body up so badly?

Saturday, 9th January

Too tired to preen. Daisy slept a grand total of three hours last night. Barely have the energy to shower.

Sunday, 10th January

Dalton Ball was awful. Just awful.

New mothers shouldn't be required to go out in public, especially not to fancy places requiring unstained clothes and plucked eyebrows.

Kept glimpsing my tired face in the ballroom mirrors and wishing I'd worn more makeup.

I have an English-rose complexion (pale skin, instant sunburn) that usually looks OK natural, but right now a bit of colour is sorely needed.

My hair (which my hairdresser politely calls 'not quite blonde, not quite brown') could do with some attention too. It's been ages since I had highlights, and my curls are past my shoulder blades and need a trim.

None of my old party dresses fit, so I wore a maternity summer dress with tights and a sort of shawl thing.

I ended up two seats away from Alex, who looked like he'd just finished a Gucci photoshoot – sharp, cleanly-shaven jaw, fitted black suit and tastefully dishevelled black hair.

I asked him how the hotel empire was coming along, and he asked me how the running was going.

'Crap,' I said. 'I don't know how anyone can run twenty-six miles.'

'A marathon is twenty-seven miles,' he said.

I suggested that maybe he could give me a piggyback.

'Listen, Juliette,' said Alex. 'Don't pay any attention to Nicholas Spencer. I'm serious about training you. I'm in London this week – are you still in London?'

I had to admit that yes, Nick and I are still living in his mother's apartment. A glossy bachelor pad in London's financial district, designed for weekday executive sleepovers and microwave meals, not a couple and their new baby.

I mean, we don't live *with* Helen. Obviously. That would just be unbearable. We just pay her rent because she owns the flat. But she comes over pretty often because she works five minutes away at Canary Wharf.

A little later in the evening, when I was coming back from the loo, Catrina Dalton was leaning over Alex's shoulder, all rock-hard white French pleat and fingers loaded with diamond rings.

She was whispering about 'Shirley Duffy's girls', and saying, 'Steer clear if I were you.'

Hopefully, Zach and Laura will get married, and Catrina Dalton will have us all as in-laws.

Including Mum and Brandi.

Ha ha ha!

While I was at the bar, the horrible charity auction began.

Doug Cockett (local businessman and red-nosed drunk) did the hosting.

He owns Cockett Fitness but is fatter than most darts players.

Doug boomed about what an honour it was to be at yet another Dalton charity event, and asked Alex and Zach if they'd be bidding on any 'lovely ladies'.

Zach said he 'certainly would be', and looked at Laura.

Alex slid his hands into his pockets and said, 'No thank you, Doug. Paying for women isn't really my scene.'

When Alex stood up to leave, Catrina clutched his suit sleeve and said, 'Oh Alex, it's only a little fun.'

Alex said, 'Somehow, I don't see it.' And strode out.

A few giggling girls were volunteered by their dates, and Zach walked Laura right up to the stage.

Laura looked absolutely beautiful. Shiny, long blonde hair. Pink, fitted silk dress that stopped mid-calf. It's amazing she comes from a mother who thinks black lycra is formal dress.

Brandi, of course, shot up on stage without anyone having to ask. Her dress looked like it had been shrunk in the wash, then glitter-bombed.

My little sister is a natural blonde, but that isn't blonde enough for her, so she adds platinum streaks and backcombs it to look three times the size.

She is SO much like Mum. Loud. Likes a drink or three. Has been known to fight men and win.

I tried to sneak off, but Doug was too quick for me.

'JULIETTE DUFFY! WHERE DO YOU THINK YOU'RE GOING?'

I said I didn't want to do the auction this year because Nick couldn't make it, but Doug wouldn't take pity on me. Instead, he got the whole room to chant 'Juliette! Juliette!'

So up I went.

I was wearing my big blue maternity dress, and my feet were too swollen for high heels, so I'd settled on brown boots that were a tiny bit muddy.

My cheeks were bright red; my curly hair was frizzy with brown roots – all in all, I felt like I was worth less than five pounds. Quite a bit less.

I ended up standing between Kate Thompson, who plays professional tennis, and Laura whose nickname at school was 'Princess Beautiful'.

Brandi was at the end of the line, back-combing her hair with her fingers.

As usual, loads of men bid on Laura. And as usual, she looked genuinely surprised.

Zach cut out the competition by bidding four-hundred pounds. He said, 'But she's worth a lot more!' And got a round of applause.

Brandi didn't do badly either. Her date bid against some guy Brandi had a one-night stand with. She ended up raising a respectable one hundred and fifty pounds.

When it was my turn, Doug put a sweaty arm around my shoulder and said, 'Now Juliette may not be at her best, with a new baby at home. But her fella couldn't make it tonight, so let's do what we can for her. There's life in the old girl yet. Am I right, fellas?'

Then he asked how long before I'd be a decent married woman.

'Soon!' I said, forcing a silly grin on my face.

In the end, I got three pity bids from some old men.

God, I'm lucky to have Nick. I really am.

Monday, 11th January

Helen came round early today.

We were still in bed when she called.

Nick pulled a pillow over his head and pretended to be asleep, so I had to talk to her.

Helen said, 'Jul-iette. How was the Dalton Ball, darling? I couldn't go – I had a work thing.'

I knew something was wrong then. She never calls me darling.

She fixed me with those manic blue eyes of hers and told me she'd heard something 'disconcerting' about the auction. That Zachary Dalton had bid 'rather a large amount' on my sister Laura.

I said, 'What?'

'*Pardon*', said Helen, closing her eyes like she had a headache.

Then she grilled me about Laura and Zach – whether they were an item, how serious things were.

I told her it was none of her business.

Apparently, *certain* people in the village are talking. Saying how inappropriate it is that Laura and Zach could be together.

'Considering Laura's background,' Helen clarified.

I said Laura's background was the same as mine – she grew up in a nice, big house in the country and wanted for nothing.

Admittedly the downstairs of that big house is a bar/pub…but it's a nice family-friendly place with a garden and good food.

Helen said – almost whispered actually – 'But your younger sister had that teenage pregnancy…'

And then it all came out – Catrina Dalton phoned Helen yesterday. I had no idea they were friends, but apparently, they run a designer-clothing charity together.

Catrina is 'beside herself' with concern that 'poor Zachary' is getting himself distracted when he should be settling down with someone 'sensible'.

Ha!

Laura is the most sensible person I know. She keeps a record of all her expenses, has three different savings accounts and is studying for her second degree.

I told Helen I'm happy that Laura and Zach like each other. I'd never get in the way of that, and nor should anyone else.

'That's what you want for your sister, is it?' said Helen. 'To be gossiped about?'

I told her people always gossiped about our family. With a mum like ours, we're used to it.

'Well you should warn her at least,' said Helen. 'Catrina Dalton is *not* happy. What relationship can work if a mother isn't happy?'

I pointed out that Helen hadn't liked me much at first.

'Um …yes,' said Helen. 'But then there was the mishap. So…'

Sometimes Helen really crosses the line.

I shouted, 'Don't EVER call Daisy a mishap.'

Nick yelled from the bedroom, 'She's right, Mum. That's out of line.'

Helen looked a bit chastised. Then she said, 'What I mean is, I appreciate there are certain things one must accept.'

'So maybe Catrina Dalton will learn to accept Laura,' I said. 'And she could do a lot worse. Laura is beautiful and kind and ladylike.'

Helen's lips did that horrible puckering thing they do when she gets really angry.

She barked that Catrina had made her feelings 'VERY clear'. Then she left, muttering that she was practically planning the wedding for me and got no thanks.

I shouted after her that she could stop bringing round ridiculous pictures of *Vogue* models wearing turquoise wedding dresses and neon, plastic wedding rings.

When she'd gone, Nick crawled out from the bedroom and asked if there was any Coca-Cola in the fridge.

It's always funny when he tries to be serious with his hair all sticking up and duckling-fluffy.

I told him about the ball and how Catrina Dalton had been whispering to Alex about us 'Duffy girls'.

I didn't tell him about Alex offering to train me.

'The Daltons are complete idiots,' said Nick. 'Daisy's asleep, you know.'

I asked if he'd checked her breathing.

He rolled his eyes and said, '*Yes*. Get over here.'

Then he kissed me – just like he used to do.

Suddenly, it was like the old days.

I'd forgotten he's a good kisser.

He whispered, 'I still love you, Julesy. Even with all the baby weight.'

I gave him an outraged punch on the arm, but he just laughed.

He was SO rock-hard.

Before long we were having sex, and I realised how much I'd missed him. It was so nice being close. He was really pounding me into the sofa. Really going for it. So unlike how things have been recently.

I think I would have come quickly – except he came first. And when he did, he moaned and fell on top of me.

Usually, he says 'oh Julesy' when he comes. But he said something else today. I'm not sure what.

Then he turned me around, put his hand between my legs and helped me come too.

We lay on the sofa with our arms around each other.

It felt really nice. But I kept trying to work out what he'd said.

It definitely wasn't my name.

Tuesday, 12th January

Nick wouldn't cheat on me. He *wouldn't*. I mean, he was a player in the past, but we have a baby now.

I should know better than to over-think things, especially when I'm tired and sleep-deprived.

I'm just being paranoid.

Wednesday, 13th January

Phoned Laura to talk about wedding stuff.

She was a bit distracted because she was getting ready for a date with Zach. He's taking her on a London riverboat cruise up the River Thames.

Phoned Althea, and she shouted about weddings being capitalist bullshit.

'But *you* got married,' I pointed out.

'I only did it for the party.'

I told her I had sex with Nick yesterday and I thought he said something weird.

'Men are always weird when they're having sex,' said Althea. 'Just look at the porn they watch. Maybe that's why Nick is such a dickhead right now. You don't have sex enough.'

Which I suppose could be true.

Made it out running, even though it was pretty cold.

I meant to jog for an hour non-stop. But after fifty minutes it was too horrible, and I ended up leaning against my knees, panting and thinking I might throw up. I walked for ten minutes. Jogged another three. Walked a bit more. Then I jogged the last bit back to the apartment in case Nick's mum was looking out of the window.

My whole body wobbled when I ran, including the bits between my legs (that's a new one).

I think you've really got to ease yourself into this running stuff. No point putting yourself through pain and getting injured.

Gently does it.

Thursday, 14th January

Alex came over this evening to take me running.

Was totally shocked to hear his voice on the intercom, and was in no way prepared for exercise, having just eaten chicken in black-bean sauce, egg-fried rice, hot and spicy pork ribs and half a tub of Ben and Jerry's ice cream. But I couldn't really say no with him on the doorstep.

Nick was clearly jealous, but he managed to grunt an 'all right' when I let Alex up to the apartment. He really needs to get over himself. I'm allowed to have male friends. Nick has plenty of twenty-something female actresses liking his Facebook posts.

Was embarrassed, because my running outfit is currently baggy elephant grey joggers covered in weird white marks that no amount of washing will shift. (Where does all that white stuff come from when you have a baby? Is it spit? And if so, how does it get on your legs?)

As I was putting on my running gear, I thought, 'This is going to be an absolute nightmare. Alex is really fit. He'll run at 100mph.'

But actually, Alex was kind, and we did lots of walking as well as running.

Neither of us said much at first – in my case, partly because I was out of breath. But after a while, we got talking.

I asked Alex about his family and the hotel business. Then I asked about the Dalton estate, and whether the rumours were true about him selling his Great Oakley home this year.

He told me I listened to too much gossip.

'I thought the house might hold bad memories,' I said.

'I hardly ever think about the fire,' said Alex. 'Not any more.'

'Jemima visits you a lot,' I said. 'Does she like Great Oakley?'

'She loves the village,' said Alex. 'What seven-year-old wouldn't? All the woods and rivers. She doesn't enjoy her time with our mother much, truth be told. Zach and I are more on her wavelength.'

'You're good big brothers,' I said. 'It's always sweet, seeing you two with her.'

'I love taking Jemima out in Great Oakley,' said Alex. 'It reminds me of growing up here. And I like to be reminded.'

That surprised me because, as a child, Alex never seemed all that happy.

Zach was always as bouncy and cheerful as they come, but Alex was more serious. Not exactly withdrawn, but quite stern. People rarely messed with him. Put it that way.

I suppose he and Zach do have different dads. Allegedly.

I asked how Jemima found her school. She stays away from home at one of those ultra-expensive London private schools. It must be lonely – being apart from her family.

'She's learning independence,' said Alex. 'Just like Zach and I did. Childhood isn't all about fun.'

Alex and Zach went to Windsor College, where they foster confidence, perseverance, tolerance and integrity.

Us Duffys went to Oakley Primary, where they foster a tolerance of chewing gum under tables and powdery mashed potato.

'But didn't you feel lonely as a boarder?' I asked.

21

'Sometimes,' said Alex. 'But it was good for me.'

I asked Alex if he remembered playing in the woods when we were kids.

Alex looked very serious and said, 'Of course I do.'

When we got back to the apartment, Alex crossed his arms and frowned. 'Goodbye Juliette. I'll come again next week.'

And off he went.

Nick was all grumpy when I got in, asking me how 'fancy pants Dalton' could run with a gold watch between his butt cheeks.'

Friday, 15th January

Sadie called round today to train and talk about marathon outfits.

She was pretty annoyed that I'd been jogging without her – especially when she found out it was with Alex Dalton.

'You *know* Catrina runs a modelling agency,' she moaned. 'If I date Alex or Zach…poof! I get a glossy magazine photo-shoot.'

But I wasn't going to give in to Sadie's emotional blackmail. She's let me down for enough training sessions – how can she expect me to phone her last minute?

Sadie looked stunning, but then she always does. She has a big, beautiful face like the moon, and one of those figures that look fantastic in everything.

Nick calls her 'pancake face'.

As we were getting changed into our running gear, I asked Sadie how often she thought a couple should have sex.

'I do it whenever I want a man to buy me something!' she said. Then giggled at her own 'hilarious' joke. Except, in Sadie's case it's only half a joke.

Sadie asked how often Nick and I had sex.

I told her not very often.

'I always thought he'd be weird in bed,' said Sadie. 'He strikes me as the sort of guy who'd watch himself in a full-length mirror.'

But he's only ever done that once.

Saturday, 16th January

Most embarrassing day ever. EVER.

Oh my God. Oh my God! I can barely write it down.

Birthday lunch for Helen today, which was bad enough in itself. But worse, it was at Bill and Penelope Dearheart's house.

Bill and Penelope hadn't seen Nick in 'far too long'. (In Helen's world, Nick needs to be paraded in front of her friends regularly. God knows why. He hardly makes her look good.) So Helen and Penelope arranged a 'simple birthday luncheon' where the parading could take place.

The Dearhearts live in one of those big farmhouses at the end of a muddy tractor path.

It's called 'The Vicarage' and has a huge conservatory and a garden full of lavender bushes.

You can only really get there by Land Rover, so my little car tipped and heaved over the muddy tractor marks like a lame dog.

Penelope Dearheart greeted us at the big oak front door with a forced smile.

She's a shorter, blonde version of Helen – perfectly groomed, perfectly scarfed and perfectly fragranced.

And like Helen, she has those thin twitchy lips that always look a little bit angry.

Bill was his usual loud, rude self, with his big square head and booming laugh.

As Penelope ushered us in, her two crazy, inbred greyhounds, Sergeant and Horatio, bounded in from the garden.

They were the size of small horses and knocked over a bottle of scented fig oil and an antique chair as they leapt around the hall.

23

Sergeant was chewing a gnarled copy of *Period Home*, and Horatio had clearly been eating mud.

If they had human faces, they'd have been cross-eyed and grinning.

Penelope shouted at them as though they were human children. 'How many times have I *asked* you to be careful in here?'

Then she sent the dogs into the garden and announced we'd be eating in the conservatory, 'so we can enjoy the pale spring sun peeking through the clouds.'

I was totally nervous.

Especially when we sat at the table, and Penelope told us the wine glasses were antique family heirlooms.

Daisy was in the sling and kept trying to grab everything. And the more I moved the glasses away from her, the more she wanted them.

I was so busy moving the wine glasses, that I didn't notice Daisy grab a big block of Stilton and stuff it into her mouth. Then she half-coughed, half-vomited blue cheese and dribbled all over the lovely white table linen, the beige carpet and Penelope's plate.

I tried to clear everything up, saying *sorry* over and over again.

Penelope and Helen's lips twitched.

Then (WHY does she always do this at the WORST POSSIBLE MOMENT?) Daisy did the longest, loudest mega-farty poo ever. It sounded like a train rumbling past.

Everyone tried to pretend they hadn't heard. Which made it even funnier.

I excused myself to change Daisy, and Penelope got all flustered.

'NOT in the downstairs lavatory, please. It's being decorated. You can use the upstairs bathroom.'

The upstairs bathroom had one of those free-standing baths with Victorian taps. But it didn't have a bin for the dirty nappy.

Daisy was crying. I got all flustered.

Decided to stash the nappy under the stroller downstairs. Bit disgusting, but I thought I could throw it away at home. Then I went upstairs again to wash my hands.

When Daisy and I got back to the conservatory, the two dogs were going crazy over something in the garden.

'Oh no. Bill,' said Penelope. 'What have those dogs got now?'

I had a bad feeling. Right in the pit of my stomach.

Suddenly, Sergeant galloped up to the glass with Daisy's shitty nappy in his mouth.

Penelope said, 'I think he's got a…'

'It looks like…a *nappy*,' said Bill.

Then everyone was horribly quiet.

Everything was in slow motion.

Horatio chased Sergeant and tried to tear the nappy from his teeth. Sergeant wouldn't let go. The nappy was ripped apart, and shit flew all over the conservatory windows.

There was this terrible, terrible silence.

Brown shadows hung over the lunch table.

Everyone looked politely at their plates. Except for Helen, who was glaring at me with boiling eyes.

We all carried on having lunch as though there wasn't shit on the glass.

Penelope rushed us through the courses (walnut and Stilton salad, beef Wellington, crème brûlée). Then she said there wasn't really time for a cheese course and she and Bill had an appointment.

'What appointment?' said Bill.

Penelope hissed, 'The appointment!' like a fire extinguisher going off.

When we left, Helen grabbed my arm and said, 'I will never, EVER live this down. Do not tell ANYONE about this lunch. Ever.'

Got home, phoned Mum and told her about the lunch.

She laughed for ten minutes without stopping.

25

Then she got Dad, Laura and Brandi on a conference call and told them the story.

They laughed for ten minutes without stopping.

Then Mum ran downstairs and told everyone in the pub.

Sunday, 17th January

Daisy fell asleep on the sofa this afternoon. I didn't dare move her into the stroller – she gets all upset if she's woken. So I was stuck indoors and couldn't get out to do the shopping.

I asked Nick to pick up milk for Daisy on the way home. He bought:

+ A four-pack of Italian beer
+ A large bag of double-fried sour cream nacho chips
+ A Spanish meat platter
+ A pint of semi-skimmed milk

When I asked Nick about *formula* milk for Daisy, he looked at me blankly.

'She doesn't have cow's milk yet,' I explained.

He said he wasn't a 'baby nutritionist' and had no idea what she needed.

Then he sat on the sofa, ate all the nacho chips and the meat platter and drank an Italian beer while bouncing Daisy on his knee.

Helen was lingering in the kitchen, pretending to work on her laptop.

'Nicholas shouldn't have to do the shopping,' she muttered. 'He works hard enough as it is.'

Ha!

All Nick's done today is meet a director friend for lunch.

I told Helen it wasn't the 1950s and Nick should pull his weight. And anyway, Daisy had kept me under house arrest all day, so I couldn't make the supermarket.

'Well, that proves my point once again about routine, doesn't it?' said Helen. 'You let that baby rule this house.'

'No Helen – *you* rule this house,' I said. 'And you don't even live here.'

Right now, I'm past caring about falling out with her. She still hasn't forgiven me for the Dearheart lunch.

God – WE NEED TO MOVE!

Tuesday, 19th January

Miracle of miracles, Sadie turned up for training today.

She was wearing a designer running outfit with go-faster stripes, and colour-coordinated sunglasses.

I think she was hoping to see Alex, because she said, 'Oh – is it just you then?'

Nick snorted, 'What are you auditioning for, Sadie? Least convincing athlete? You're just not believable.'

Sadie fired back, 'No one's ever CGI'd me out, lizard boy.'

Nick's 'big part' in *Star Trek* was 'reworked' last year. The computer animation team turned him into a reptilian soldier, and all his lines were cut.

Sadie knows how to twist the knife.

Nick muttered something like 'pancake face'.

Sadie and Nick hate each other. They went to the same theatre school, and have always been rivals.

In fact, I first met Nick at a party Sadie dragged me along to. She pointed at Nick and said, 'See that pretty boy actor over there? He is the biggest idiot you will ever meet.'

While I was changing into my running stuff, Sadie stuck her bottom out and said, 'You know, I should have been an athlete. It suits me, don't you think? I can run forever. Just forever.'

Then she looked at me and said, 'You really do need a sports bra.'

During our run, we started talking about babies and pregnancy and stuff.

Sadie asked how Nick was at Daisy's birth.

I told her he was terrified and spent half my labour 'out walking' to cope with 'mental female shit'. And after the birth, he took all my prescription painkillers for his hangover.

Sadie said maybe he'd do better with the next baby.

I told her we weren't having another baby. Not unless Nick did some serious growing up.

We ran about a mile in total before Sadie complained about blisters.

'You can *over*-train,' she said, as we walked back to the apartment. 'No sense burning ourselves out before the big day.'

Wednesday, 20th January
Morning

More house-hunting.

Viewed three absolute shit holes in East London.

The last house was so bad that even the man showing us the house said, 'It's a bit oppressive, isn't it?'

I tried to be open-minded and imagine how things could look with different colour walls. But realistically, a fresh coat of paint won't fix a cellar full of water.

This is getting desperate.

We just don't fit in this apartment any more. It looks like a jumble sale.

Cot, changing table, baby wardrobe, bouncy chair, baby gym, stroller – none of these things are small.

Thursday, 21st January

Alex called round again to take me running.

Nick was annoyed, but he had no reason to be.

Anyway, Sadie is so unreliable.

Alex and I did more running and less walking this time.

We jogged along the River Thames, all the way to Tower Bridge.

A man on the deck of a river cruiser shouted: 'Alex Dalton! I don't believe it. Just the man. Jump on board – I have some killer news about Maverick.'

Alex shouted, 'Not right now, Ben.'

The man looked at his cocktail glass, pretended to rub his eyes and said, 'Did you just say, "not right now"? This is about *Maverick*.'

'We'll talk tomorrow,' said Alex.

We ran on, and I asked about Maverick.

'It's a Swedish hotel chain,' Alex told me. 'We're taking them over.'

'So isn't that important?' I said. 'Do you want to go back?'

'It's not important,' said Alex. 'Not right now.'

Friday, 22nd January

Phoned Laura to ask about Zach, but she said nothing much was happening. They've been on a few dates, but that's it.

I was hoping they were secretly engaged or something. That would irritate Catrina Dalton and Helen no end.

After watching *One Born Every Minute*, I realise I might still be traumatised about Daisy's birth.

She came out OK in the end, but they had to use some big metal barbeque tongs.

Before I had Daisy, I wanted a natural birth. Now I know the truth.

Nature is cruel and awful, and we're lucky to have things like morphine and haemorrhoid cream.

Saturday, 23rd January

Dad came round this morning to discuss alcohol for the wedding.

He made detailed notes about guests and drinking habits, worked out the amount of wine bottles we'd need, then fixed the leaking sink in the bathroom and replaced a blown fuse in the kitchen light.

Thinking about wedding logistics and guest numbers (or any numbers) was a nightmare.

What's happened to my brain? I used to know whole phone numbers. Now I can't even find my bag in the morning.

How do women manage with two children? Or three?

My old school friend, Mandy Hughes, has FOUR children. She looks like the walking dead – all blank-eyed. She can't even match up her kids' names – she cycles through all four until she gets the right one.

Sunday, 24th January

Laura turned up unexpectedly and forced me off the sofa.

She threw away my tube of Pringles and wouldn't let me finish my Double Decker until I'd got my running gear on. Then she dragged me out in the rain.

Now we're back I'm glad I went running. I feel great, actually. Really great. I should so make this a habit, even after the marathon. Not just for losing weight, but for feeling good too.

Monday, 25th January

Alex and I went running again this evening.

Nick was furious. I think he's getting worried that I might win the bet. He said he'd buy me a whole new wardrobe if I finished the marathon (a subtle criticism, because I'm still wearing my maternity clothes).

When unreliable Sadie was my running partner, the odds were much more in Nick's favour.

I have to admit, it's very pleasant watching Alex running. He sort of glides along, barely touching the floor.

His body is also extremely toned and athletic. And he's so *tall*.

I suppose it's no wonder Nick is jealous – every girl we ran past turned to stare at Alex.

On the way back, it started raining. Actually, pouring down.

At first, it was just cold, horrible rain. But then it became ridiculous. Sheets of water. Rain splatters hissing on the hard ground and bouncing up to our knees.

It was so ridiculous it became funny – running in such a downpour.

By the time we reached my apartment, we were both laughing.

'My nana has a saying about this kind of weather,' I said, as we sheltered under the porch. 'Life isn't about avoiding the storms. It's about dancing in the rain.'

Alex moved wet hair from my face.

It was nice. The way he was looking at me. Sort of too nice.

I told him I had to go up, and he said, 'Goodnight Juliette. Don't sit around in those wet things. OK?'

I was glowing when I came through the front door – it was the very first time I actually thought, yes, I could have a chance of finishing this marathon.

Tuesday, 26th January

Went to Regent's Park with Althea and baby Wolfgang today.

Wolfgang is eleven months old, but he looks much older. He has one menacing front tooth and can snap a bundle of twenty coffee stirrers in half.

I love Althea. She's the most laid-back parent I know. Not many first-time mums would drive their baby around on a moped.

Althea lives in a big, rambling Victorian house in Bethnal Green. It's worth a fortune, but you'd never guess because Althea has decorated it in what she calls, 'kindergarten fusion style'.

All the original fireplaces have been spray-painted neon, and one wall of her kitchen has empty paint cans nailed to the wall. There are also a lot of sprayed silver egg boxes and Wolfgang's handprints around the place.

Today, Althea wore her big Afghan coat, Jackie O shades and bright red cowboy boots. Her curly gypsy hair was tied with a fluorescent yellow ribbon.

Althea's laugh is just brilliant. It could break plates. She sort of goes, 'Nah, nah, nah!' and shows all her teeth.

From some angles, Althea looks a *tiny* bit like a frog. But a pretty one. With a temper.

Wolfgang was dressed in a little blue mod suit. God knows where Althea found that. It gave him a slightly sinister 'Brighton Rock' air – especially when he was pulling kids off the swings.

When Wolfgang bit one of the other children, Althea laughed and said, 'Aw, bless him. He's having such fun.'

Then she tried to put him in his sling, but Wolfgang clung to a swing, and neither of us could budge him. Eventually, Althea lured him away with beef jerky.

I told her about my diet, but Althea shouted about diets being sexist crap.

'You were a measly size twelve,' she barked. 'Now you're a measly size sixteen. I weigh far more than you, and *I* don't care. The universe made us all perfect. So get over it.'

I told her that Nick had finally proposed.

'So fucking what?' said Althea. 'He's no bloody prize pigeon, is he? Has he got himself a decent job yet? He should be crawling over broken glass to marry a girl like you.'

We talked about me and Nick's meal on New Year's Eve, and I asked if she thought it was anything to worry about.

'That he drank six bottles of beer in two hours?' she said.

'No,' I said. 'That we couldn't agree on where we wanted to live.'

'You're different,' she said. 'So you're bound to want different things.'

'They say opposites attract.'

Althea said, 'Hmm.'

Wednesday, 27th January

Mum came round to help with Daisy this morning.

She'd bought me some bits from the wholesale supermarket, where she does shopping for the pub. Her bag contained:

+ 2,000 teabags
+ Five giant tubs of liquid hand soap
+ A lemon torte that said 'serves 50'.

The torte wouldn't fit in the fridge, so Mum cut us a big slice each for 'a snack', then sawed up the rest and filled every fridge shelf and half the freezer.

After that, she showed me how to clean the toilet with her 'Wonder Woman technique' (squirting half a bottle of bleach over everything and blasting it off with the shower), threw Daisy around and sang 'YMCA' with all the hand movements.

Quite a few passersby stared through the big glass window at her dancing, but Mum never cares what people think. If she did, she wouldn't wear leopard and zebra prints at the same time.

Mum had to leave after lunch. She was heading to Camden to buy an electric pink feather boa. She and her old school friends are dressing up in '70s clothes to watch the *Mamma Mia* musical.

Mum absolutely can't wait. She's already ordered silver platform boots from eBay.

Thursday, 28th January

Went round Helen and Henry's today for more wedding planning.

I hate Helen and Henry's house.

They live in a modern, gated complex for people who think they're too good to mix with the rest of the village.

I quite like Henry, though. How he ended up with Helen, I'll never know. Maybe because she's quite slim and looks good for her age. It blinded him to the fact that she's a total harpy.

Henry owns Great Oakley Plastics Factory (which makes toilet roll holders, but Helen says it makes aeroplane parts), and is your typical jolly man who looks a little bit like Toad from *The Wind in the Willows*.

Helen's always bossing him around.

'Tuck your shirt in darling. Goodness, you look like a truck driver. You smell revolting darling, do go and have a shower…'

He's always running around trying to make her happy, but that's impossible.

They can't have much of a relationship because Helen is always round our house. She has her evening meal at ours half the time – some horrible fishy salad she eats standing at the breakfast bar.

Helen had a list of 36 wedding things to 'discuss urgently'.

Colour scheme, wedding favours, blah blah.

I told her she'd forgotten something. 'Item number 37. Mind your own business.'

Friday, 29th January

Found the best TV program ever!

It's called *Cheaters*. A TV crew film people cheating on their partners, then confront them with the damning footage.

Nick went mad when he found me watching it. Went on about my low-brow taste in television.

I think he's in a bad mood because it's the Actors' Guild party tomorrow and he's promised to take me along.

He hates me going to his acting things because I'm too honest.

When other actors ask Nick what he's up to, he says he has some interesting projects in the pipeline. I tell the truth and say he's giving out flyers dressed as a spicy potato wedge.

While Nick was tweezing his eyebrows and nose hair, he told me not to show any baby pictures at the party.

I asked why not.

'For all anyone knows I could be in my twenties,' he said. 'The family-man image adds ten years.'

'Fine,' I said. 'I won't show any pictures. As long as you don't wear your sunglasses indoors.'

Nick did his theatrical sigh and said, 'I've told you a thousand times. Sunglasses are a *look*. Speaking of which, don't you have anything that makes you look…less mumsy?'

Fucking hell. I've carried his baby for the best part of ten months and then had acid poured into my insides – aka labour.

I shouted that I was a *mother* so looking *mumsy* was part of the deal.

'Fine, OK,' he conceded. 'Forget it. If you're just going to get crazy.'

It's OK for men. They stay exactly the same after they have kids. Women age ten years overnight.

I keep catching glances of myself in the mirror and having unnerving flashes of Mum staring back at me.

Saturday, 30th January

Squeezed myself into pre-pregnancy grey skinny jeans for what turned out to be a horrible night.

Couldn't bend down all evening without making a weird, creaky groaning noise. When I tried to kiss Daisy, I let out this 'wheeee!' sound.

I couldn't even do the jeans up without an elastic band around the button.

With high heels on I thought I looked all right.

But the effect was lost on Nick.

He said, 'Why are you walking like a robot?'

While I was getting ready, Daisy managed to pull the toilet roll into her Moses basket. God knows how – I moved everything in our bathroom to eye level ages ago. The shelf is like a game of Jenga – toilet brush, bathroom bin and scales all on top of each other.

I don't know if Daisy ate any toilet roll, but she was definitely giving it a good chew.

Panicked about toilet roll in her digestive system.

Phoned Mum.

'Toilet roll?' Mum said. 'You used to chew your dad's fishhooks. And you turned out just fine.'

I asked Mum what she thought about Helen babysitting Daisy.

Mum said, 'As long as Daisy's asleep, what difference does it make who's there?'

'But if she wakes up…'

'She won't wake up,' Mum insisted. 'It'll be just fine.'

But still, I didn't like leaving Daisy with Helen. She reminds me a little of the child snatcher from *Chitty Chitty Bang Bang*.

The party was really bad.

It was full of flashy, beautiful people with bleached teeth. They all shouted, rather than spoke.

'Oh, BABY CAKES! I haven't seen you in FOREVER!'

All the men boomed at each other. 'Ra Ra! Jonathan! Ra, ra ra!'

And all the women clutched champagne glasses, tossed their hair and admired themselves in the shiny windows.

Just as I was coming out of the loo, I bumped into Sadie. She goes to Actors' Guild events sometimes, but I didn't know she was going to this one.

'Why didn't you warn me you and Nick were coming?' she hissed. 'If I'd have known lizard boy would be working the room wearing his sunglasses I would have stayed away. Good lord! Are you wearing *jeans*? *Why?*'

She wore a huge peacock-blue ball gown and held a feathered masquerade mask.

Then Helen called my mobile saying I needed to come home.

Daisy was wailing like a fire engine in the background.

I felt like my heart was being yanked down the phone line.

My little girl! My little girl!

I shouted that I needed to get home *right now*.

Sadie put on her sympathetic face. 'The perils of motherhood. But how will Nick wipe his bottom when you're gone?'

Nick appeared behind Sadie and said, 'Speaking of bottoms, Tony Rice had to Photoshop yours for that *Elle* shoot. He'd never seen a backside with acne before.'

Sadie shouted, 'I *told* my agent that was CONFIDENTIAL!'

Got the tube across London and ran to the apartment like a crazy person.

Somewhere on the way home, the rubber band on my jeans snapped.

Helen opened her front door to find a frizzy-haired, red-faced maniac with her jeans undone.

I knew I looked bad, because Helen said, 'Christ almighty!'

Poor little Daisy was on her shoulder, totally red in the face, screaming her head off.

Daisy reached out her arms when she saw me and fell straight to sleep on my shoulder.

'If you had a routine, this wouldn't have happened,' Helen said.

'Go fuck yourself, Helen,' I replied.

Then I started crying. I don't know why.

Sunday, 31st January

Got a massive telling-off from Nick about being rude to his mother.

He's such a hypocrite! He talks to her like the hired help.

I tried to explain what happened, but he wasn't having any of it. Just went on about how lucky we are and how grateful we should be for everything his mum does for us.

I blew my top.

I shouted that I wanted a place of our own. That we shouldn't be relying on his mum like we do.

And then it was same old, same old. Any day now. My break is coming. It's SO hard being an actor. Blah blah blah.

While we were rowing, Alex turned up to go running.

Nick said, 'Oh that's very mature Juliette. You're quite literally running off with another man, while we're trying to have an adult discussion.'

But frankly, I wanted to get out of that apartment and be around someone who wasn't an actor and didn't turn everything into one huge drama.

I think Alex sensed something was up, because he said, 'Bad day?'

I admitted Nick and I had been arguing.

He asked me if I had pre-wedding nerves.

I told him no – I'm looking forward to getting married. It will be a clean slate and a new beginning.

'What a romantic sentiment,' said Alex. 'And here was I thinking you get married because you love someone.'

'I do love Nick,' I insisted.

'I know that,' said Alex. 'I've just never had a clue why.'

Monday, 1st February

Pretty sure Daisy is teething.

It's early, but she's showing all the signs.

She keeps dribbling and smashing her head against things.

The book says this goes on for months. *Months?*

Mum says not to worry because when the tooth comes through another problem will take its place.

She made a big long list of all the problems I had to come:
+ Separation anxiety
+ Night terrors
+ Molars (then I'll wish it was the little teeth again)
+ Opening cupboards
+ Climbing stairs
+ Pulling nappies off and throwing them across the room

She added, 'And it doesn't necessarily stop when they're grown up. They could be like Brandi and have a baby at sixteen. Then you're stuck with them forever.'

Tuesday, 2nd February

I am an AMAZING mum! Daisy slept ALL night last night.

ALL NIGHT!

And I jogged TWO miles today! Two whole miles without stopping. For the first time, I actually have hope that I might be able to finish the marathon.

Of course, when I phoned Sadie she said, 'It's easier to train now the weather's warmer. The real marathon will be freezing. You've got a long way to go.'

I said it would be easier if my so-called running partner actually showed up.

'Look, you know me,' said Sadie. 'I'm terrible with time.'

If she's terrible with time, how come she's never early?

Wednesday, 3rd February

Fucking hell.

Daisy woke up FIVE TIMES last night.

So tired I've lost two cups of coffee today.

Found one in the bathroom, but where's the other one?

I've never loved anything as much as Daisy. She is the best thing I have ever seen, heard, touched or smelt. But sometimes – especially at night-time – I want to kill her.

I used to judge those mums who scream at their kids in supermarkets. But now I don't. Because they're only saying what I think in my head sometimes.

Couldn't be bothered to go for a run today. There's no way I'll finish this marathon.

Just no way.

Thursday, 4th February

Oh my God, I am totally fed up. Daisy woke up at 2 am, 4 am, and 5.30 am – at which point she cried until 7 am.

I mean, it's not like I'd give Daisy back or anything. I am totally in love with her. But when does it end? It's so gruelling. Every night, not knowing if she's going to sleep or not. And not being able to stop the crying. And not knowing WHY she's crying.

What am I doing wrong? WHY WON'T SHE SLEEP!!!

Ate a jumbo bar of Cadbury's Whole Nut chocolate for lunch.

Didn't mean to, but it was half-price at the bookshop.

I went in to buy *The Big Book of Baby Sleep*, and they'd put giant bars of chocolate by the cash registers. It's like they know sleep-deprived mums go in there.

Friday, 5th February

Bought more sleep books today. Apparently, a baby Daisy's age (four months) should be sleeping all night without waking.

Well it's all right to SAY that, isn't it? But how do you make them do it? I mean, what if offering cooled boiled water doesn't work at 3 am?

Feel very alone today.

I'm a mother. I'm supposed to be the one who fixes things.

But I don't know what I'm doing.

Alex called round for training, but I couldn't face it.

I was way too tired.

He came down hard on me, saying I mustn't give up and that difficulty is part of every victory.

I know he's right, but I just don't care about victory right now. Survival will do me just fine.

Saturday, 6th February

7 pm

Daisy has a fever!

I am so worried.

Can't get hold of Nick, and there's no way I can bother Mum tonight. She has her *Mamma Mia* thing.

Dad's running the pub, Brandi has Callum and Laura has classroom training tomorrow.

I am totally alone and terrified.

Why does Nick never answer his phone when I need him?

Called NHS direct, and they told me to 'keep an eye on her'. As if I'd do anything else! My eyes are *glued* to her.

8 pm

Daisy's temperature is even higher! I can't take her to accident and emergency on a Saturday night – it will be full of shouting drunk people.

Will try NHS direct again.

8.30 pm

NHS direct refused to send a doctor. They said it wasn't serious until Daisy's temperature goes over 100 Fahrenheit.

Not serious? She is boiling hot!

9 pm

Mum just phoned from the theatre. She had a 'sixth sense' that something was wrong.

Told her I was fine. Then burst into tears and admitted Daisy was ill.

Mum said she'd get a taxi straight over, but I told her not to ruin her night.

Nick will be home soon.

9.30 pm

Mum just turned up in platform boots and a feather boa, holding a bottle of baby fever medicine. It was so nice to see her that I cried.

I said, 'What about your night out?'

'Abba can wait,' Mum boomed. 'My little girl needs me.'

10.30 pm

Thank god!

Daisy's temperature is back to normal. Mum's insisting on staying until Nick gets home.

12 am

Nick just got back. He found me, Mum and Daisy asleep on the sofa.

He's going to stay up all night now and take Daisy's temperature every hour. Just in case.

Sunday, 7th February

Daisy's fine today.

Nick and I took her to the emergency doctor anyway, just in case. We had to wait with a load of nervous-looking teenage girls, all wanting the morning-after pill.

Felt quite angry with them for wasting precious NHS time.

Nick reminded me I'd taken three morning-after pills in the early days of our relationship.

I shut up then.

Monday, 8th February

Sadie came round tonight – not to train, but to show me her new coat. It was a red soldier's jacket that she thought would go perfectly with leather jeans.

While I was putting Daisy to bed, she said, 'Christ! Are baby's ribs supposed to stick out like that?'

It made me worry because there are several genetic deformities in our family. Dad has a weird lump on his ear, and Mum has giant boobs that she can balance a pint between.

Also, Callum had big bulging eyes when he was born. Like he was on a Coca-Cola high (which is totally possible – Brandi drank a lot of cola when she was pregnant).

Sadie asked where my 'loser boyfriend' was, and I had to admit I wasn't sure. He should have been home hours ago.

'He's just got a new role,' I told her. 'He's probably working late.'

'Nick's actually got a job?' said Sadie. 'Since when?'

'He *does* work you know,' I insisted.

'Yeah, right,' said Sadie.

I told her it was a very insecure life, being an actor.

'I know,' said Sadie. 'Maybe he should get a real job.'

Was too tired to defend Nick yet again.

Have spent all evening worrying about Daisy's ribs.

Tuesday, 9th February

3 am

Googled 'baby ribs'.

All that came up were BBQ rib recipes.

Actually quite fancy some Chinese food now.

9 am

SO tired. But promised I'd see Nana Joan today, so have whizzed up Brandi's 'wake-up special' – four spoons of instant coffee blended with milk and a chocolate Boost bar.

1 pm

I love my nana! She refuses to age gracefully. When I got to the care home, she was doing boxercise with the other old people.

I held punch pads for Nana's new boyfriend – a kindly-faced man, who Nana boasts has 'real teeth'. He really likes Nana, but she was eyeing up a new resident – a man with his own electric wheelchair.

After boxercise, we made pancakes, which Nana covered in maple syrup, Nutella and hundreds-and-thousands. Then I took Nana food shopping. The care home offers three meals a day, but they're too healthy for her taste.

The bulk of Nana's shopping consisted of toffees, white-sliced bread and Bailey's Irish Cream.

When we got back to the care home, Nana showed me a 'cracking dress' she'd bought on eBay.

It was fluorescent pink, Lycra and skin-tight.

She's always buying me clothes like that.

I said thanks, but I don't really have the figure for that kind of thing any more.

Nana said it wasn't for me – it was for her.

To demonstrate, she put the dress on and said, 'See? Perfect for the next séance. Your granddad always shows up when I wear bright colours.'

Then she told me I shouldn't put my figure down, and I was a 'stunner' and that she'd kill for a body like mine.

Mum and Nana love their figures, wobbles and all.

I used to be more like that. Before I had Daisy. But then, I had a better figure back then.

Nana and I talked about the wedding flowers, and the fact Nick hasn't bought them yet.

Nana said, 'Don't wait around for a man to buy you flowers. Plant your own frigging garden.'

Wednesday, 10th February

Helen has got us a 'present' – a cleaner called Juan.

He's coming once a week to 'help out'.

It's Helen's way of saying I don't clean the flat properly, but I really don't care what she thinks.

Juan works part-time as a masseur, which means his hands are very strong.

After he'd cleaned this morning, the kitchen tap was loose, and the oven clock was hanging off by its wires.

He also likes to fan things out. Takeaway leaflets. Remote controls. My sanitary towels on top of the toilet.

It's weird having staff. I'm just not cut out for it. I spend the whole time apologising. 'Sorry, it's not very tidy. Sorry, I'm in the way. Sorry, Daisy keeps trying to climb on the vacuum cleaner...'

45

Thursday, 11th February

Got a text message from Helen today. She always writes her text messages like letters:

Dear Juliette,

Nicholas tells me you STILL haven't chosen wedding flowers, so thought we should meet up. You MUST ONLY go to Perfect Petals nr Dalton Road. The owner and I are old friends, and she'll be very offended if I go elsewhere.

What's your agenda today?

Regards,

Helen Jolly-Piggott

When Nick first told me his mum's surname, I thought he was joking.

Then he got annoyed, and I realised he wasn't joking at all.

He said the Jolly-Piggott name was very famous in the right circles.

I told him I didn't move in the right circles.

He said, 'That's what I love about you. You don't pretend to be something you're not.'

Nick's surname is Jolly-Piggott too, but he goes by his stage name – Spencer – after his dad. Henry Piggott is his stepdad.

When we get married, Helen wants us to carry on the family name.

So we'll be Nick and Juliette Jolly-Piggott.

I texted Helen back:

Dear Helen,

I am busy today because Daisy has shat all over the sofa.

Regards,

Juliette

Friday, 12th February

Met Althea at Great Oakley library today for Little Tiddles Story Time.

Wolfgang kept trying to grab the storybook from the librarian.

The librarian laughed at first. Then it turned into a bit of a struggle.

Wolfgang ended up sinking his big front tooth into her hand. He wrestled the book from her, and no one could get it off him.

Althea was very proud.

'He's so confident, isn't he?' she boasted.

Saturday, 13th February

Lunch with the family today.

We ate downstairs in the pub, because Dad is using the dining table to clean his *Lord of the Rings* figurines.

I actually prefer eating in our family pub restaurant. Daisy gets bar-snack packets to rustle, and the regulars make such a fuss of her that she forgets to cry.

Mum asked me what sort of thing she should say in her wedding speech.

She's already been googling jokes.

'Mum,' I begged. 'Please don't make a speech. Let Dad do it. He'll make a speech straight out of *Talking at Christian Occasions*.'

Mum snorted, 'But it'll send everyone to sleep.'

'Look, Mum,' I reasoned. 'If you HAVE to make a speech, please, please don't say anything bad about Helen.'

'But I've got all these brilliant jokes about her nose!'

I told her she couldn't tell any of them. No – none of them at all.

She got all huffy then and asked if Helen was making a speech.

I said Helen hadn't mentioned it.

'Well, she'd better not make any jokes about you,' said Mum.

'That's my job.'

'Don't be silly, Mum,' I said. 'Helen won't make a joke. She has absolutely no sense of humour.'

Sunday, 14th February
Valentine's Day

Nick tried to cook a romantic Valentine's Day meal today. I say 'tried', because Helen ended up doing it.

She 'popped round' mid-afternoon and micro-managed Nick's cooking for the next three hours.

'No darling, that's not how you use a tin opener. DON'T PUT THAT IN THE SINK! I don't care what the recipe says, ketchup has no place in bolognaise sauce.'

It should have been a good opportunity for Nick and me to talk about the wedding and our future. But it was a bit hard with Helen hovering over us, asking if we wanted more parmesan.

Tuesday, 16th February
2 am

Daisy just won't sleep.

Thank God Nick's still out – he'd be so stressed by now.

Am going to sleep on the living room sofa and do controlled crying.

Ten minutes at a time, they say. I can manage ten minutes of crying. It's just ten minutes.

2.05 am

God, she sounds REALLY hungry. Maybe she's having a growth spurt? Or maybe she's thrown up her milk.

Oh my God, WHAT IF SHE'S THROWN UP AND IS CHOKING?

This level of crying just can't be normal. There must be something really badly wrong.

I'm going in.

2.25 am

The little con artist.

As soon as I opened the door, Daisy was all smiles.

I cuddled her, but she would not go back to sleep, so I ended up giving her milk.

3 am

She's awake AGAIN!!! She can't be hungry now – I only fed her half an hour ago! PLEASE STOP CRYING!

Please, God, help her sleep.

Please, please, please.

3.10 am

Just realised why God lets famines and earthquakes happen. It's because he's distracted by millions of mothers begging for their baby to sleep.

3.30 am

Gave in and let Daisy have more milk. She fell straight to sleep.

Wednesday, 17th February
SOOO tired.

Thursday, 18th February
Alex called round to train, but I told him I really couldn't run this marathon.

Daisy woke up four times last night. The last time she just cried and WOULD NOT stop.

In the end, I got three hours sleep. It's not enough.

I can't train for a race. I just can't. I need to plan a wedding and move house and care for a sleepless baby.

I let Alex up to the apartment, expecting a big, angry lecture. But he just looked disappointed – which felt even worse.

He gave me a stoic hug, kissed me on the head and told me to take care. Then he asked if there was anyone around to look after me this evening. I assured him Nick would be home soon.

In the end, Nick didn't make it back until midnight. He was out 'comfort drinking' because he's realised the movie he's just signed up to, *Dead Stars on Mars*, 'lacks artistic integrity'.

I mean, for goodness sake! He read the script. How much integrity did he expect in a love triangle between Marilyn Monroe, Elvis and an alien?

Friday, 19th February

Wow – the wedding is REALLY soon now. Barely a month away.

Nick seems to be getting grumpier the nearer we get to it. I think it's a money thing because I'm forcing him to budget.

He likes wasting money on super-duper toys for Daisy, Thai takeaways, beer and *Star Wars* gadgets. But we can't do that now we have a wedding and a house deposit to pay for. Plus, Daisy really doesn't need any more animatronic teddy bears.

Saturday, 20th February

Me and Nick's anniversary today.

We've been together five years.

I know Nick forgot, because when I said, 'happy anniversary' he went white and rushed off to the supermarket to 'buy milk'.

When he got back, he gave me an old-lady card and a bottle of red wine.

Sunday, 21st February

Lovely day!

Tea and scones with Laura and Brandi at the Bond Street Dalton.

Laura arranged it – I think because she thought Zach might be there, which he was.

She looked all glossy and lovely in black jeans, knee-high boots and a blouse.

Brandi wore a sexy secretary outfit – tight black pencil skirt, tight white blouse and lots of gold jewellery and red lipstick.

I tried to smarten up my saggy leggings with a Chanel jacket that Helen was throwing out and a big necklace.

The jacket was a snug fit. And the arms were too long. But you know…it's Chanel.

I asked Laura if she'd seen much of Zach, and she went all red and mumbled that it was early days.

Then I moaned about looking fat in my leggings.

'You're not even overweight,' Laura insisted. 'Just a tiny bit curvy in all the right places.'

I told her that Nick didn't think so. And then I started to cry.

Laura and Brandi both put their arms around me and said I was beautiful.

Then Brandi said I should call off the wedding.

She really hates Nick.

Sometimes, in my lowest moments, I think about what life would be like on my own. Some parts would be better. I could move back to Great Oakley and live in a house where Nick's mother doesn't come over every night.

I wouldn't have to deal with Nick's depression or grumpiness, or recycling bins full of beer bottles. In some ways, I'd have one less child to look after.

But we have a baby together. I owe it to Daisy to make it work.

I went to clean myself up in the loo, but it had one of those toilet attendants.

I always panic when there's an attendant because I never know what to do.

Do you tip depending on what you've done in the toilet?

I'd only been for a wee, but I got all flustered and ended up dropping a five-pound note on her plate. So she must have definitely thought I'd been for a poo.

When I came back through the lobby, there was Alex Dalton. All dark hair and long limbs, striding across the thick carpet.

He stopped dead when he saw me and said, 'Juliette. What are you doing here?'

I told him I was having afternoon tea with my sisters.

'You should have mentioned it,' he said. 'I could have got you the private sitting room.'

Then he said, 'Hang on. Laura's in there, is she? I wondered where Zachary disappeared to. Tell him to get a move on.'

Alex was right. Zach was in the dining room, leaning on the back of Laura's chair.

Laura and Zach were looking at each other like I look at Daisy.

Brandi was tapping at her phone with long, sparkly fingernails, looking bored.

I told Zach I'd just seen his brother.

'Christ – I should go,' said Zach. 'He tears my ears off if I'm late.'

Just as Zach was leaving, a bottle of Champagne arrived at the table, 'compliments of Mr Dalton'.

We all gushed and smiled and thanked Zach.

But Zach said, 'Not from me. It must be from Alex.'

I looked out at the lobby, and Alex was there, arms crossed.

I asked Zach why Alex would send us Champagne.

'Why wouldn't he?' said Zach. 'Three beautiful ladies from our village. Whose parents run a fabulous pub. Christ – I really should go. He hates me being late.'

After the afternoon tea, I wanted to thank Alex for the Champagne. But he was nowhere around. So I wrote him a thank you letter on the hotel headed paper.

Behind me, Alex said, 'If that's a complaint letter I can give it straight to the manager.'

I said it was a thank you. For the Champagne and for taking me out training all those times.

'A gesture worth five kisses it would seem,' he said, eyebrow raised.

Then Brandi came running up saying our cab was here.

Alex said, 'Goodbye Juliette.'

When we left, Alex's Rolls Royce was parked outside the hotel. I felt myself smiling at it.

I didn't tell Nick about Alex buying us Champagne.

It would only have caused an argument.

Monday, 22nd February

Wedding flower-shopping today.

Helen is furious that Nick hasn't done it already.

She was even more furious when I said I wanted to go all natural and pick daisies from a field.

'No son of mine is getting married in a church full of grubby daisies,' she said. 'Look – I'll pay for it, all right?'

I said it had nothing to do with money. I just like wild flowers.

Helen put on her horrible false smile and said, 'Would you please let me help you with this, Juliette? The church looks grubby enough as it is.'

'It's my wedding, Helen,' I shouted. 'If I want it to look grubby, that's up to me.'

In the end, I decided to be kind and let Helen drive me to Perfect

Petals in her big black Land Rover.

The flower-shop lady was one of Helen's old school friends – another heavily-perfumed Helen clone.

Helen asked me which flowers I liked. Then she told me why I was wrong to like them.

I tried to pick flowers that looked natural and beautiful, but the flower-shop lady said they were funeral flowers.

Eventually, I chose giant white daisies that Helen hated. But it was sort of a compromise because at least they were paid for and not picked from a field.

Tuesday, 23rd February

Disgusting fact of the day – my poo weighs two ounces. I know this because I weighed myself before and after. My weight is getting a bit obsessive now. But I really would like to be slimmer for the wedding.

Mum and Dad had very different analogies about two ounces.

Dad said it was the same as a Swiss Army knife, two AA batteries or a large letter for posting.

Mum said it was roughly one bag of peanut M&Ms or a share size bag of Doritos.

Wednesday, 24th February

Daisy only woke up once last night.

Not too bad. And she went straight back to sleep after I fed her. Why can't she do that every night? Once is totally bearable.

The trouble was, *I* couldn't get back to sleep.

I kept thinking about the wedding.

It's not as though I think Nick will back out. But it took him so long to propose…

Of course, it doesn't help that Nick is so miserable about the wedding. I wish he could at least *pretend* to be happy. I know this is all girly stuff. But it's supposed to mean *something* to him.

Thursday, 25th February
HAEMORRHOIDS!!!

And with the wedding only a month or so away!

Just as I'd made my peace with my boobs dropping an inch, wee coming out for no reason, and a disaster downstairs area, now my backside as well. And don't even get me started on the weird spots on my arms…

I've learned something important.

Never, EVER Google the word 'haemorrhoids' and look at the image page.

Went back to the village to see Doctor Slaughter because getting a doctor in London is impossible.

Doctor Slaughter gave me a prescription for suppositories. He also gave me phone numbers of three other women in the village that had them and suggested we meet up. Doctor Slaughter doesn't believe in patient confidentiality.

The village chemist was closed 'due to a problem with our tills'. (Meaning the owner is having an all-day lie-in).

None of the London chemists could read Doctor Slaughter's handwriting, so couldn't get proper medical suppositories.

Googled home-remedy pile treatments. Smashed up a garlic clove and applied it to the area.

Have never known pain like it.

Screamed. Did a weird, grunty dance around the breakfast bar.

Helen came round and asked me if I'd been making guacamole.

Friday, 26th February

Started a new diet today – the 5:2 diet. It's basically starving yourself for two days a week.

After no breakfast or lunch, I felt all sick and faint and light-headed. Decided that with a baby, it wasn't responsible to starve myself.

So had a big bowl of pasta and pesto.

Maybe I'll try the diet again tomorrow.

Saturday, 27th February

Nick is working in Leeds for the rest of the week, so Daisy and I are back at Mum and Dad's.

Great Oakley is only a half-hour train ride from London, but it's like a different planet.

Flowers.

Trees.

People who don't hate children.

Such a relief to be away from Helen's now nightly visits. She's getting crazier the nearer we get to the wedding.

Yesterday, she came round with *Vogue Wedding* and showed me a rail-thin, pouty model bride wearing a lion's mane.

'*So* stylish, don't you think?' she said, stroking the glossy page. 'Viv West at her best.'

I told her it looked absolutely fucking ridiculous.

She got all huffy and started polishing the stainless-steel kitchen cupboards.

(One of the many problems with living in a fancy executive pied-à-terre is that shiny stuff shows up everything. I fried an egg once. Never again.)

While she was frantically polishing, Helen asked me what Mum would wear to the wedding.

I said probably something ten years too young for her.

Helen blinked her manic eyes and said, 'Please persuade her to wear something *tasteful*. Maybe with a shawl? For the pictures...'

I had a good laugh about that. *My* mother! In a shawl! I suppose Helen can dream.

The idea of *anyone* persuading Mum to wear something that isn't skin-tight is hilarious.

Mum Facetimed me a few weeks back to show off her '70s *Mamma Mia* outfit. It would have made Christina Aguilera blush.

Sunday, 28th February

Went to the play park with Daisy.

Alex and Zach's little sister, Jemima, was there.

As usual, she was the best-dressed seven-year-old in the park, with a jaunty orange scarf tied perfectly under her pretty face.

Thought the Dalton brothers might be there too, but Jemima was with her nanny.

Jemima and I had a nice play together. She's so polite and didn't even laugh when my bottom got stuck on the slide.

She was also really good with Daisy and helped me push her on the bucket swings.

I think Jemima's nanny was pleased. She was sitting at the far end of the park, drinking a takeaway coffee and watching YouTube on her phone.

Jemima asked if I'd play with her again some time.

I said of course I would.

Then Jemima said, 'I wish I had friends my own age to play with.' Poor little thing.

It makes me realise how lucky I am to have sisters.

I mean, Brandi and I used to fight a fair bit, but we still had loads of fun.

I asked Jemima if she was still staying on the Dalton Estate on the weekends. She said she was. With her big brothers and Nanny Charlotte.

She told me how fun Alex was and how he always played with her. She said he let her toot the horn in his Rolls Royce.

Then she whispered, 'My nanny isn't a real nanny, you know. Mummy only hired her because she's the daughter of her old school friend.'

I couldn't think of anything to say to that, so I said, 'That's nice.'

'It's not nice,' said Jemima. 'I don't like her.'

Monday, 29th February

Babies grow so quickly!

It feels like yesterday that I bought Daisy 0-3-month clothes. And she's already too big for them.

The 3-6 month ones are too big, so it's either squashed toes or great big long legs.

Keep meaning to adjust the stroller straps too. They're getting a bit tight, but they are so FIDDLY! I can't work them out. And what the fuck are those extra squashy black bits for? An eternal mystery. I know as soon as I throw them out, I'll realise they're essential.

I can't work out the bottle warmer or the car seat either.

I used to be GOOD at practical stuff. What happened? Are all baby devices just stupidly complicated? Or have I lost a lot of brain cells?

Tuesday, 1st March

Went wedding dress shopping today and found THE DRESS!

Nick told Helen where I was going, so she turned up uninvited with a load of fabric samples and magazines.

She criticised every dress I tried on and, while I was changing, criticised the shop carpet and the fitting-room curtains (you'd *never* see TASSELS in a London bridal boutique…)

'DIAMANTE Juliette? For the love of God, no. Classy. Think classy. You're not marrying a footballer.'

Fortunately, three free glasses of Prosecco softened the edges, and I resisted the urge to swear.

Brandi was whispering, 'That old witch. She thinks it's her wedding.'

When the girls tried on bridesmaids' dresses, Althea shouted, 'Don't say a fucking word, Helen, or you'll be wearing this Prosecco.'

After that, Helen was full of compliments.

Then Nick turned up.

I shouted at him that it was bad luck to see the dress. He rolled his eyes about 'all that traditional bollocks' and told me we'd be fine because we had true love.

I actually got a little fluttery at the thought of marrying him then – for the first time since he proposed.

Nick laid on the charm, telling us 'ladies' how beautiful we all looked. Except for Sadie, who he said looked like a dinner plate on a stick.

Sadie picked a different dress from everyone else. It was a bit *white*, but that's Sadie. She always has to break with tradition.

My wedding dress was low-key in the end. This long, silky thing. Pretty. Kind of plain, but as Nick says, you shouldn't be over-the-top when you've just had a baby.

Wednesday, 2nd March

Keep trying on the wedding dress.

It is a *bit* tent-like.

59

But I think if I lose weight it will become the flowing, ethereal princess gown it's supposed to be.

Thursday, 3rd March
Very hungry.

Friday, 4th March
Lost a pound since the weekend! Not bad.

Saturday, 5th March
Did the wedding dress rehearsal today. In the church.

Mum was very good. She only said, 'Oh be quiet, Helen' once.

Since Nick pretty much chose my wedding dress, I thought I might as well rehearse in it. The more I practise wearing it, the less chance I have of falling over.

All my bridesmaids were there, except Sadie. She met some theatre director last night and ended up on a yacht in Richmond.

Brandi was hung over, but she held it together pretty well. She picked the wrong underwear for her bridesmaid dress, though – it really showed through.

When Helen saw that Brandi had rolled up her dress into a mini-skirt, her nostrils flared.

I thanked Helen for helping with the wedding flowers.

She snorted, 'Lucky I helped. Or this church *could* have looked like your sister's underwear.'

Brandi twiddled her neon-pink bra strap and said, 'What's wrong with a bit of colour?'

Then Helen got distracted because one of the pew cushions had 'an unidentifiable brown stain'.

Sunday, 6th March

Mothering Sunday

Laura did a lovely thing – she booked me a facial in Kensington as a Mother's Day treat.

I think she guessed Nick would forget. He's not great with dates. He often forgets his own birthday, so I don't take it personally.

Nick got all panicky when he realised he'd be looking after Daisy alone.

Phoned Mum to ask how long she left us for as babies.

'As long as I could bloody well get away with,' she bellowed.

Decided a few hours would probably be OK.

After going through Daisy's routine with Nick (she will ONLY sleep with her Teddy Snuggles, her pink sleeping bag and her waffle blanket), I made a break for it.

Facial was lovely. And I stayed awake for most of it too.

When I got home, Daisy was red-faced and screaming the place down.

Nick had put her to sleep without her Teddy Snuggles, pink sleeping bag or waffle blanket.

After shouting at Nick, I spent an hour walking and shushing, trying to calm Daisy down.

When she finally fell asleep, she sprang awake five minutes later like a manic devil child, and I had to go through everything all over again.

Nick tried to help. He sang 'Strangers in the Night' in Daisy's ear. But it just made her worse.

When she finally fell asleep, I shouted at Nick for a full half hour.

He admitted he'd panicked and forgotten my instructions. And that I probably should have written them down.

God – I can't even trust him for one afternoon!

Monday, 7th March

I've PUT ON A POUND!! Ugh.

Laura pointed out that I've lost a quarter of an inch around my waist and thighs, and I know that should cheer me up. But it doesn't.

'What would you prefer?' said Laura. 'A flatter tummy or numbers on the scale that no one sees but you?'

The stupid truth is I'd prefer numbers on a scale.

Told Laura in a sad voice that I'd never wear a midriff top again.

Laura said, 'But you never did wear midriff tops.'

True. But I'd like the option…

Tuesday, 8th March

Made the wedding invitations today.

Helen found me trying to scrub PVA glue off Daisy's baby gym.

She gave me her 'you've displeased me' look and said, 'This is a wedding, not make-do-and-mend. For heaven's sakes, *buy* the invitations. I gave Nicholas three hundred pounds yesterday – you can't have spent it already.'

When Nick came home, I asked him about the money.

He said he'd taken a theatre director for a meal at Claridge's, and the director had drunk a lot of wine.

Then he sang, 'The Circle of Life' right over Daisy's cot, waking her up.

It had taken me nearly an HOUR to rock and shush her to sleep, so I was furious.

Hitting Nick around the head with a pillow only made me feel marginally better.

Wednesday, 9th March

Decided to try the Atkins diet today.

Had a plain omelette for breakfast with vegetables and lots and lots of oil.

It was all right.

By lunchtime, I was absolutely crawling the walls with hunger. I so did NOT want bacon or eggs or butter.

Then I made the mistake of going round Mum and Dad's house so Mum could help me do the last of the wedding invites.

The fridge was full of last night's 'double takeaway' (A Duffy family tradition) – egg-fried rice, sweet-and-sour prawn balls, slices of Domino's pizza.

Decided I'd switch to calorie-counting instead. I have no idea how many calories were in that omelette this morning, so I'll have to start again tomorrow.

Ate egg-fried rice, sweet-and-sour prawn balls and the last few slices of Domino's pizza.

Thursday, 10th March

Started stupid, boring calorie-counting diet. Now my head is full of numbers.

It turns out a tube of Pringles has THOUSANDS of calories in it. Which would account for a lot of Mum's extra weight.

Friday, 11th March

Weighed myself today, thinking all that calorie-counting has probably shifted...ooo, I don't know, at least seven pounds in time for the wedding.

But no. I have lost absolutely no weight at all. If dieting doesn't work, what hope is there for me?

Phoned Laura.

She said that muscle weighs more than fat and I shouldn't weigh myself until I've dieted for at least a week anyway. That made me feel better.

Phoned Brandi and she said, 'That muscle and fat thing is a load of bollocks. Google it.'

I Googled it, and she was right. Muscle and fat weigh the same.

I asked Brandi if I looked any thinner to her. And she said, 'You *could* look thinner if you let me straighten your hair. It's not a good idea to have curly hair with a round face like yours.'

Then she suggested I come to her pole-dancing class tomorrow, claiming that one student lost 14 pounds in 'like a week'.

I told her that in my wobbly, fat, post-baby state, the idea of me dancing around a pole makes me think of an elephant in fishnet stockings.

But Brandi promised I definitely wouldn't be the fattest one there.

Saturday, 12th March

POLE DANCING!!!!!

What was I thinking?

I definitely WAS the fattest. The mega-sized pole dancer Brandi promised me didn't show up. If she ever really existed.

The instructor was a bright orange girl with muscles on every part of her body. She drank two bottles of Lucozade, then bounced and jiggled non-stop for a full hour. She was like a blurry line.

'And step, step, spin, squat, LEGS!, spin, drop – HAIR FLICK!'

We were also supposed to *climb* the pole. The combination of my weedy, chicken arms and my big fat bottom meant I could barely get myself an inch off the ground.

When it was over, my muscles ached so badly I could hardly get my coat on.

Brandi bounced along beside me talking about how energised she felt and saying we should get a drink.

I said I couldn't because of Daisy.

Brandi looked all confused and said, 'But isn't Mum looking after her?'

'Yes, but Daisy might wake up,' I pointed out.

'So?' said Brandi. 'Mum will handle it.'

'Didn't you worry?' I asked. 'When Callum was a baby?'

'To be honest, I've blotted out that first year,' said Brandi. 'It was so awful.'

I asked if Callum was sleeping better now, and she said not really.

She counted her gold-ringed fingers and said he still wakes up three or four times a night.

I asked what she did when he woke up.

She said she hides under the duvet, adding, 'I love Callum to bits, but I wish I'd waited until I was a bit older. It definitely puts a crimp on things. I mean, I have, like, NO social life.'

Then she Facebooked her friends and arranged to hit a few clubs.

Sunday, 13th March

Wedding SO soon now.

But I think we're pretty much on top of everything. Helen can worry about all the frills – I don't care if the table placeholders coordinate with the napkins.

There's this thing going around Facebook called a 'no make-up selfie'. You're supposed to take off all your make-up and do a selfie looking rough.

Brandi volunteered me, but there's no way I'm taking a close-up of my baby-worn face. No way.

Monday, 14th March

Made Nick promise to go on a family picnic tomorrow.

Ended up having to watch some boring war film as a bribe, but it will be worth it because tomorrow we'll have a lovely family picnic at Hyde Park, and talk about our wedding day.

I've even bought a wicker picnic hamper with chequered cloth inside and little elastic loops for cutlery.

Tuesday, 15th March

Baguette, wheel of Brie, Kettle Chips, a bottle of elderflower water – all packed into our new picnic hamper.

And it poured with rain.

Nick thought this was hilarious.

He sat on the sofa all day eating Kettle Chip and Brie sandwiches, watching the *Wizard of Oz* and saying, 'Whoever cast the Tin Man is a *dickhead*. He so can't act.'

Wednesday, 16th March

Had another big row with Nick.

I just can't stand Helen coming round any more.

If I have to spend another day watching her criticising, moving and wiping things that look completely perfect, I will go mad.

Helen is one of those women who has everything but is never happy.

She is skinny as a rake, incredibly rich, and works as a hobby. And yet everything is wrong. The shade of granite in the kitchen is 'a total disaster'. Her new cashmere cardigan makes her look 'disgustingly fat'. Henry, her husband, is going 'horribly bald'.

When Helen's here, the flat isn't a home at all. It's a showroom.

There can't be so much as a cushion out of place.

Living here is like a 24/7 job interview. It's constant stress.

One of Daisy's socks was on the shag-pile rug this morning, and Helen stared like it was an unexploded bomb.

'Jul-iette. (It's never Ni-ck.) This shouldn't be here.'

I said if she was offering to do the laundry for me, that would be a great help.

She gave me her Helen glare. Then she checked her slim, solid-gold watch and said, 'I have twenty minutes to talk last-minute wedding details.'

She stood in perfect ballerina posture, one hand on the granite work surface, stomach held in and said, 'You've put on weight.'

I said, 'Nice of you to be so supportive, Helen. Dieting is hard with a baby.'

Helen told me she had 'a few ex-ballerinas tips' to get slim. They were basically, 'Drink only Diet Coke, and if you feel *very* faint have a spoonful of honey.'

Then she went on about the wedding photos and said maybe she should talk to Mum about the dress code.

I told her there wasn't a dress code, and that Mum had already bought her dress.

Helen asked where from.

'Forever 21.'

Helen squeezed her eyes tight shut and said, 'Heaven help us.'

Thursday, 17th March
St Patrick's Day

Mum and Dad are doing their usual Paddy's Night party at the Oakley Arms this evening.

I really wanted to go, just for an hour or so, but Daisy wouldn't settle.

Called Dad to let him know.

The pub sounded pretty lively.

I could hear an Irish band and the 'stamp! stamp! stamp!' of people dancing on the bar. Mum was drunkenly singing 'The Irish Rover' in the background, and yelling at Brandi for drinking Guinness straight from the tap.

Friday, 18th March

All my friends keep nominating me for a no-make-up selfie.

Saturday, 19th March

Had a brainwave! Put up a picture of Taylor Swift as my no-make-up selfie.

Hopefully, everyone will think it's funny and not bother me to do a real one.

Sunday, 20th March

25 comments on my Facebook page telling me off for my Taylor Swift picture.

Put up a real picture of my tired face.

Got a load of lovely comments telling me how beautiful I look without make-up. Awwww…

Monday, 21st March

I am pretty sick of being a mother today.

The worst thing is just not knowing what I'm doing.

Daisy just wouldn't sleep last night.

I think she was over-tired. The only way I could get her to nod off was walking around the room making Darth Vader breathing noises and bending my legs in time to the Hokey Cokey.

Tuesday, 22nd March

The wedding is creeping up, and I haven't lost any weight since last Saturday.

Am trying the PureLife milkshake diet.

Had one for breakfast and lunch, but by teatime, I was absolutely starving. So I cooked spaghetti bolognaise and ended up eating Nick's portion because he was late home.

Then I took Daisy to the 24-hour supermarket and bought a melt-in-the-middle fondant chocolate pudding and a bag of toffee popcorn.

Will carry on the diet tomorrow.

Maybe strawberry milkshakes will taste better.

Wednesday, 23rd March

Tried the PureLife strawberry milkshakes. They taste like chalk mixed with women's deodorant.

Nick came home with another huge toy for Daisy today – a swinging chair with disco lights.

He was all excited, saying it would teach her to be a musical genius.

'If I'd grown up with toys like this,' he said, 'I'd get way more parts.'

It turns out he got rejected for a musical today for not being able to dance. Which I think is unfair, because Nick is a pretty good dancer. He's the only person I know who can properly vogue.

I told him it didn't matter and that I loved him no matter what. And that Daisy loved him too.

We're a family. Together for richer or poorer. For better or worse.

Friday, 25th March

Feel like I should be doing something with Daisy – taking her on an Easter egg hunt or something. But I'm just too exhausted.

Did manage a small bit of normality though. Made it to the village supermarket, and bought Callum a Cadbury's Buttons Easter egg. Daisy's too young for chocolate (although Mum says we had Easter eggs 'practically from birth'), so I bought her socks with little chickens on them.

I won't give Callum his egg until Easter Sunday.

Dad always insisted we didn't have our Easter eggs until then, and it taught us patience and self-control.

Saturday, 26th March

Did a bad thing.

Ate Callum's Easter egg.

Luckily the village supermarket was still open, so I bought him another one.

9 pm

Did a bad thing again. Ate the replacement egg.

Supermarket closed now.

Sunday, 27th March
Easter Sunday

Snuck out early to buy a replacement egg, but the village supermarket was closed.

Ended up taking Daisy to London and buying a giant chocolate bunny rabbit from a 24-hour off-licence.

It was enormous – almost as big as Daisy.

Of course, Callum ate the whole thing at once. Then he jumped on every bouncy surface in the house and put his foot through a wicker coffee table.

Monday, 28th March
Easter Monday

Bit sick of chocolate. But Mum has made a double-chocolate Easter cake covered in chocolate frosting, chocolate chicks, and chocolate bunnies. There's also a surprise in the middle – chocolate fondant.

Tuesday, 29th March

Have decided to hit the gym, pre-wedding. I know one session isn't going to make a lot of difference, but a bit of toning won't hurt.

Found a special-offer coupon for Fitness Factory and signed up online.

Will go tomorrow.

Wednesday, 30th March

Made it to the gym to do a pre-wedding workout.

Put Daisy in the crèche, and she cried and cried. Thought I might have to take her home, but then the crèche ladies put her in a bouncy swing, and she was instantly happy. So I had to exercise.

I spent ages walking around the gym, touching equipment and then being too scared to actually get on it.

Eventually, I worked up the courage to sit on a weight machine. I pulled at some handles. Then this Lycra bicep man said, 'Let me show you how to do that *properly*.'

The proper way absolutely killed my arms. So I did some jogging on the treadmill and watched *Eastenders* on the mini telly.

Everyone wears Lycra at the gym these days. How can fashion be so cruel?

Thursday, 31st March

Was too hungry to sleep last night, so typically Daisy slept perfectly.

Ended up squirting cream on Oreo cookies at 1 am, and suddenly Helen appeared like some pale, big-nosed ghost.

After I'd stopped screaming, Helen explained that she'd had an 'all-nighter' in the city and decided to stay on the guest mezzanine without telling us.

She looked at my cookies and said, 'Children have midnight feasts, Juliette. Grown women watch their weight.'

I said I hardly saw the point of dieting any more, what with the wedding being so soon. Nick would just have to accept me for me, baby weight and all.

I asked Helen if she'd put on any weight after Nick was born.

She stroked her bony hips in skinny black jeans, pulled her cashmere cardigan around her bony ribs and said, 'No, I *lost* weight actually. The whole experience was so traumatic. The hospital staff were worried I was just *too* slim.'

Then she went on about how perfect her wedding day had been.

I asked how Henry had liked it.

She said, 'Not my wedding to *Henry*. My wedding to *Nicholas's* father. Marrying him was the best day of my life.'

Often, Helen makes me think of a raven bobbing its nasty head around the insides of an animal.

When she smiles, she looks like Mr Punch.

'What about the day Nick was born?' I asked.

'Oh *that* day was awful,' she said. 'Absolutely awful. Being handed this scrawny, ugly little thing covered in... God, I don't even want to say it. I seriously wanted to complain to somebody. But I really *did* love Nicholas's father. From the moment I met him.'

Then her eyes went all sharp and Helen-like, and she said, 'Men are imperfect creatures. You mustn't forget that. Don't love a man too much. He'll only let you down.'

Friday, 1st April
April Fool's Day

Nick's stag party tonight.

Ugh. I do not even want to THINK about what Nick will be up to.

I'm not exactly having a hen night, but Mum, Laura and Brandi have 'something planned'.

Helen turned up unannounced again, and said, 'Christ – don't have one of those hideous L-plate bingo heavy-drinking affairs, will you? *So* tacky.'

I told her we'd probably just go for a nice meal somewhere in Great Oakley. I'm a mum now, after all. No more wild nights for me.

Daisy played an April Fool's joke on me. I thought her nappy needed changing, but it was a false alarm.

How we laughed.

Sunday, 3rd April
Morning

Gala Bingo!

Learner plates!

PINK TUTUS!

We hit the West End and danced on the stage until 3 am.

Must remember though – fluorescent lights show up white stains. How had Daisy managed to wipe her nose on my back?

Had SUCH a laugh.

Mum did her party trick of drinking a bottle of Original Guinness from her cleavage.

We were so drunk by 3 am that we all sang 'Let it Go' on the tube home.

Tired this morning, but it was worth it.

Of course, as soon as I passed out, Daisy woke up. And then again. And again.

It's like she knew I'd gone to bed late and was telling me off.

Afternoon

Eeek!

Brandi Facebooked pictures of me dancing on tables at the hen night.

Nick saw them this morning and went mad.

'You need to grow up, Juliette,' he said. 'You're not a teenager any more.'

I told him to go fuck himself. When he had his stag do, HE didn't roll in until 4 am and spent the whole day in bed, while Helen brought him iced teas and Alka-Seltzer.

Was hungover and bored, so took Daisy to Mum and Dad's.

When I arrived, Mum and Brandi were still in their dressing gowns, drinking Monster Energy cans.

Laura was at the library.

Callum had covered himself in toilet roll and was running around shouting, 'POO MONSTER! POO MONSTER!'

I asked Mum if it was OK for her to be drinking Monster Energy, what with her diabetes and everything.

'What's wrong with it?' she asked.

I told her it was full of sugar and caffeine.

'Do you want one?' she offered.

I said, 'Yes please.'

Callum got more and more mental as the afternoon went on.

74

It turns out Brandi had put a bit of Monster Energy in his Incredible Hulk cup.

She said, 'Who'd have thought he'd be so sensitive? He has Coca-Cola ALL the time, and it hardly affects him.'

Hung out at Mum and Dad's house drinking Monster Energy.

Laura came over in the afternoon with a homemade wholemeal banana cake. She'd spent the day studying *and* baking. Even though she stayed out until 3 am too.

I don't know why she bothers making healthy stuff for Mum. If it doesn't say 'Birdseye', Mum doesn't want to know.

We started talking about the wedding and Dad got all misty-eyed, saying his wedding was the best day of his life.

Mum said it was her second best – Brandi being born was her best. She apologised for not liking the days Laura and I were born, but apparently, painkillers weren't as good back then.

Was a nice day in the end.

Dad took Daisy out for a bit.

I always feel safe when she's with him. He's so sensible. He writes her a schedule and sets the alarm when she needs milk.

Monday, 4th April

Daisy is officially old enough to have food, which means that she MUST sleep better from now on. Right?

The books all say start with baby rice, but it just looks so gluey and boring.

I phoned Althea for advice, and she said babies couldn't digest grains until they're at least a year. And that I should give Daisy a soft-boiled egg yolk.

Apparently, she did it with Wolfgang.

So. Here goes.

12 pm

OMG – nearly had a heart attack.

Daisy has just retched and retched until nothing more would come up.

Was so close to phoning an ambulance. Phoned NHS direct instead, and they told me off for giving Daisy semi-raw egg.

I phoned Althea, and she said, 'Oh yes, Wolfgang threw up too.'

I said, 'Why didn't you tell me?'

She said it only lasted the first couple of days. Then he was fine. Although he hates eggs now.

Tuesday, 5th April
Tried baby rice.

Daisy loved it.

Wednesday, 6th April
Worst night's sleep ever. I think the baby rice gave Daisy wind. Or something. She was up every two hours and just would not settle.

I thought when babies had food things got easier.

Thursday, 7th April
Funny how life changes. I used to love bars, vintage clothes hunting, bingo nights and music festivals.

Now one of my greatest joys is squeezing Daisy in just the right way, so she does a massive burp.

Friday, 8th April
Wedding so soon now.

Excited and nervous.

I know Nick isn't perfect. But I suppose it's good that I know all his imperfections before we're married. Otherwise, I'd be horribly disappointed.

Went to Mum and Dad's today so Brandi could practise doing my hair.

I ended up looking like Dolly Parton.

'But you *love* Dolly Parton,' said Brandi.

Even Dad, who thinks I look lovely in everything, said, 'Blimey, you want to be careful. There'll be naked flames in the church.'

I had a bit of a bridezilla moment and told Brandi I didn't want to be a foot taller than Nick on my wedding day.

She got a bit grumpy and said she'd 'have another go' after she'd had a cigarette.

'Don't smoke near Juliette's hair,' said Dad. 'It could go up.'

Finally, after a lot more teasing and combing and a picture of Ellie Goulding, we got there, and my hair really did look quite nice.

But I think I'll do my own make-up.

Saturday, 9th April

Baby book says Daisy should be rolling over by now.

Bit worried.

I keep trying to show her how to do it, but she just isn't interested.

She looks at me all happy like I'm doing a funny trick.

Althea says Wolfgang rolled over at three months. Probably there was some beef jerky nearby.

Monday, 11th April

Took Daisy to 'Baby Singing' at Great Oakley library today.

All the mums sang with gusto, 'Little Peter Rabbit has a fly upon his nose!' in perfect Judy Garland voices.

I mumbled along, like when I have to sing hymns at a wedding.

Daisy loved the songs and chewing the cymbals.

ALL the babies Daisy's age were rolling over. I'm a bit worried. What if something's wrong?

When we got back to London, I thought I should continue Daisy's musical education.

I put on 'Bangin' Club Anthems' and did animated rave dancing.

Helen appeared, arms folded, while I was jumping up and down with Daisy and shouting 'TUUUNE!'

I wish she wouldn't sneak in like that.

She raised a skinny black eyebrow and said, 'Age-appropriate?'

I told her all music helped with developmental brain stuff.

Helen winced and said I'd teach Daisy to be 'a terror' if I wasn't careful. Then she dropped an Yves Saint-Laurent bag on the sofa, saying she'd bought Nick a new suit.

She looked around the apartment and said, 'Christ, what a state. Hasn't Juan been this week?'

I have to admit the place did look a mess.

I'd taken all the cushions off the sofa and made a sort of nest for Daisy. There was mashed-up rice cake all over the floor too.

I wanted to say to Helen, 'You were a mother once, weren't you?'

But Helen is one of those hideously organised control-freak women who lie and say their baby never gave a moment of trouble.

According to Helen, Nick slept through the night at two months old, ate everything he was supposed to, never cried and 'appeared to understand concepts far beyond his young years.'

If I didn't know Nick, I'd imagine him to be a neat-haired child prodigy. Not a heavy-drinking bit-part actor.

Tuesday, 12th April

Daisy's learned to roll over!

Finally! FINALLY!

The only trouble is she hasn't learned to roll back again.

So she rolls onto her stomach and cries until I put her back. Then she rolls over again.

I preferred it when she just lay on her back. Don't know what the rush to roll over was, really. Like Mum says, they all do it in their own time.

Thursday, 14th April

Getting a bit nervous about the wedding now.

I know it's only one day, but it's a big deal.

So close.

Friday, 15th April

Evening

Am staying at Mum and Dad's tonight.

I don't want Nick to see me before the wedding.

I think the way things have been going between the two of us, I need all the luck I can get.

Has been a lovely evening, actually.

Laura came over, and we all played Monopoly.

It's hilarious playing games with my family.

Dad and Laura always stick EXACTLY to the rules.

Mum and Brandi always cheat.

I got all teary at one point, saying I'd be getting married and leaving them all behind.

Mum said, 'What are you talking about? You haven't even got

your own place yet.'

We ended up playing Monopoly, drinking tea and eating custard creams until really late. Too late for Laura to get the train back to London, so she's staying in our old bedroom – me in the bottom bunk, her in the top. Daisy in the travel cot.

(I can never get the hang of putting that thing up. It always collapses on me like a knock-kneed giraffe.)

Mum, Dad, Brandi and Callum are down the hall. Just like old times. Nice being a family again. All cosy and warm.

Saturday, 16th April
Wedding day.

I can't write today. I just can't.

Sunday, 17th April
Oh, diary. Diary, diary, diary. I have never known pain like this.

I will never get over this. Never, ever, ever.

Monday, 18th April
Laura told me it was sunny today, but who cares?

Spent all day in bed with the curtains drawn.

Daisy cries, smiles and sleeps just like always. Like nothing has changed.

She doesn't understand our whole world has just been ripped apart.

Tuesday, 19th April
Stayed in my bedroom with Daisy again today, sobbing.

Mum bought me a McDonald's breakfast.

'Get some food down you, and then we'll go out,' she coaxed.

But the thought of food made me feel sick. And the thought of going out anywhere – even sicker.

Mum told me she'd punch Nick's lights out if I wanted her to.

'What's the point?' I sobbed. 'It won't change anything.'

'It might make you feel better,' said Mum.

'Nothing will make me feel better right now.'

'You'll feel better one day, love,' said Mum 'I promise.' Then she bounced Daisy on her knee and said, 'No matter what you're going through if you've got kids you've won the lottery.'

Wednesday, 20th April

Text message from Althea today:

'The greatest pain brings the greatest growth. The universe is looking down on you and smiling because it knows this is all part of a greater plan. Life is beautiful and so are you.'

Thursday, 21st April

Brandi came storming into my bedroom this morning and ripped the curtains open.

She said, 'You've done enough wallowing. Daisy needs some sunshine. So do you. It's time to get up and show up. Never give up.'

She forced me to get dressed; then we went out for a walk.

We stuck to places where no one could see my haggard, cried-out face. I never knew I had so many tears in me. They still keep coming.

If I didn't have Daisy, I don't know what I'd do. She is my only light right now.

When I moaned to Brandi about having nowhere to live, she said, 'Don't be stupid. You'll live at the pub with Mum, Dad, Callum and me.'

Oh, God. A single mum. Living with my parents and my teen-pregnancy sister.

Brandi still has her youth.

I'm old and on the shelf.

I asked Brandi if this happened because I got fat and didn't wear scarves.

'Don't be stupid,' said Brandi. 'Mum gets fatter every year. And Dad still loves her. And ANYWAY, you're not *that* fat.'

Which is a pretty big compliment for Brandi.

'Why would he do this to me?' I cried.

Brandi said, 'Because he's an idiot, Jules. An idiot.'

Friday, 22nd April

Dad knocked on my bedroom door today.

He tried to cheer me up by showing me his 1950s maroon-coloured Hornby switchable locomotive.

'You're worth ten of him, love,' he told me. 'You know that, don't you?'

Then why did it happen?

Saturday, 23rd April

Nana Joan visited today.

She'd borrowed her new boyfriend's mobility scooter. Typical Nana Joan – she turned off the safety switch so it would go over 15 mph and nearly ran over a dog.

I told Nana off for coming all that way on her own, but she said, 'Nothing's more important than my Julesy right now.'

She took my hand in her gold-ringed fingers and said, 'I reckon I gave Nick a black eye on your wedding day. Maybe worse.'

Apparently, she'd attacked Nick with her crutches after I left the church. It had taken two people to restrain her.

Realise I haven't even written about my wedding day.

God – I'm SUCH a mess.

Sunday, 24th April

OK. My wedding day.

Here goes.

Mum made us sausage sandwiches for breakfast in the morning (probably the last decent meal I've eaten, now I come to think of it).

I let Brandi do my hair.

Laura stood over her (No Brandi! Don't backcomb it. PUT THE HAIRSPRAY DOWN!), and it came out as we'd planned.

Laura sent Brandi to the corner shop for cans of Red Bull, and then we quickly did my make-up all nice and natural.

I put the wedding dress on... I mean, it never made me feel 'wow' or anything. But it was pretty. A little bit of a tent, but pretty.

Mum kept making me drink Red Bull for my nerves. But I didn't feel nervous. I didn't feel anything. Just sort of flat.

I kept telling Daisy, 'It's my wedding day. My WEDDING day. Me and Daddy are getting married.'

But nothing.

Even in the black Mercedes (Helen insisted on that car – I wanted to go in Brandi's pink Mini), I didn't feel anything.

I was squashed in there with my bridesmaids (except Althea – there wasn't room for her and Wolfgang) thinking, 'This is it. I really am getting married.'

But it still didn't feel real.

Sadie kept fidgeting and saying she felt sick. Which was just typical Sadie – she hates the attention being on anyone else.

We were a bit late getting to the church.

I didn't feel worried or anything. Just...ready to get the job done.

83

Laura and Brandi helped me fluff out my wedding dress, and Sadie paced around with her hand on her stomach.

Then Sadie grabbed my hand and said, 'Jules. I need to talk to you. RIGHT NOW.'

I said, 'Sadie, are you OK?'

'I NEED TO TALK TO YOU!' she hissed.

It was all so weird.

'Look – let's get the wedding out of the way,' I said. 'OK?'

Sadie did this sort of big gulp and said, 'I know something about Nick.'

I went a bit bridezilla then. I think it was all the Red Bull.

I said, 'Sadie, I know you hate Nick. But he's Daisy's dad, and I love him, and WE'RE GETTING MARRIED. Now get out of the way.'

I started walking down the aisle, and I saw Nick ahead.

He turned around, and I thought, 'Wow, he looks really hung over.'

He was sweating. Proper, proper sweating, on his forehead and down the front of his shirt.

But he wasn't looking at me. He was looking at Sadie.

I carried on walking, sort of on automatic pilot. I even think I might have been smiling.

Everyone in the church had weird looks on their faces. Maybe they'd heard Sadie saying she needed to talk to me. Or maybe they all knew what was going on.

When I got to Nick, he smiled. But it was a scared smile. And he kept glancing at Sadie.

I could see Helen in the front row – huge navy hat on – sort of glaring and smiling at the same time.

The vicar cleared his throat and said some stuff I can't remember.

I kept thinking, *What's going on? Nick looks weird. He keeps looking at Sadie...*

Then the vicar said the part about, 'Any persons here present have any lawful reason why these two shouldn't be joined in matrimony...'

And Sadie said, 'SHE SHOULDN'T MARRY HIM AND IF HE WON'T TELL HER WHY THEN I WILL!'

Nick looked really scared and sort of muttered to Sadie, 'Let's not do this now.'

Sadie said, 'Nick. She needs to know about us.'

She didn't need to say anything else.

I knew then. I just knew.

Sadie and Nick...*Sadie and Nick...*

They're better actors than I realised.

I felt like I was going to pass out. The big tent dress felt so tight all of a sudden. I couldn't breathe.

All I could see were disappointed faces – people I knew. People I didn't. People who loved me. All of us together in this horrible train wreck. And Daisy with Mum...wearing a little flower-girl dress.

I seriously thought I was going to have a heart attack or pass out or something.

I grabbed Daisy and ran down the aisle.

Then I sat in the wedding car, holding onto Daisy for dear life while she chewed the silk on my wedding dress.

Dad got in beside me, put his arm around me and told the driver to take us back to the pub.

Then I sat in my dark bedroom, watching Daisy sleep and thinking, 'Her life is ruined.'

Monday, 25th April

Nick still hasn't called or texted. He hasn't seen Daisy since the wedding.

It's not like I want to speak to him. I never want to see him again.

But I want him to *try* to get in touch. And I know he must be desperate to see Daisy.

Althea said it's always the betrayal that hurts the most. But it's not the betrayal. It's the fact I didn't have a clue. And I really should have done...

Tuesday, 26th April

All the bills went out today, and I watched my bank account sink a little lower.

It made me realise that there are loads of practical things to sort out. Money and living arrangements. And (this makes me feel sick to think about) visitation.

I can't keep paying for a flat I'm not living in.

But where *am* I going to live?

A part of me wishes I'd never found out about Nick and Sadie. That everything could just carry on as before. Things weren't good with Nick. I knew that. He knew it too.

But I still thought we had a chance.

What an idiot.

Wednesday, 27th April

Took Daisy to see Nana Joan today.

A bit of normality amid the chaos of my life right now.

At Nana's care home, there was a big sign on the visitor's notice board:

<u>*VISITORS – PLEASE BE AWARE!*</u> *DORIS JENKINS CHASES ANY VISITOR WEARING RED.*

Nana was so pleased to see us. She hugged me for ages and talked to Daisy in her funny pigeon voice. 'Ooooeee! Coo coo coo!'

After taking photos of us with her new selfie stick, Nana said I looked 'gaunt' and was getting 'skinny with all the worry'. She warned me not to 'catch an eating disorder' and forced me to eat half a tin of teatime biscuits.

I never trust her views on weight, though. She's lost most of her teeth because of all the Walnut Whips she eats.

Nana was especially happy because her toenails hadn't been cut in ages. I'm the only one who can do it without breaking the clippers.

She asked if I'd seen Nick, and I told her he hadn't been in touch.

After I'd done Nana's bath, I washed her hair and helped dye it 'Vibrant Cherry'. Then I showed her how to play Angry Birds on her phone.

'That Nick is a useless idiot,' she told me. 'You're better off without him.'

But he's still Daisy's father.

Thursday, 28th April

Still no call from Nick.

Maybe he's gone into his actor's wallowing pit and thinks everyone hates him (we do) and that he wouldn't be welcome if he called round (he wouldn't).

But he should see Daisy. He's her dad, after all.

Friday, 29th April

Told Althea I was thinking of calling Nick.

I've never heard so many swear words in one sentence.

After Althea had calmed down, she said, 'Don't start feeling sorry for him. He's a cock-head. You're too nice. Why hasn't he called *you* for fuck's sake?'

She's right.

Totally, completely right.

'When life gives you lemons,' she said, 'add rum and coke.'

Saturday, 30th April

Cracked and called Nick today.

I suppose I just wanted to get some clarity. Some answers.

For a horrible moment, I thought he wasn't going to pick up. That would have been the ultimate humiliation. But he did. On the tenth ring.

He sounded gravelly and tired.

I told him he should arrange to see his daughter.

He said, 'Yeah, I know, I know. I miss her so much. I just didn't want to make anything worse.'

I said things couldn't get any worse. Then I asked if there was anything else he wanted to say.

He said he hoped there were no bad feelings.

Like we'd had a row over the electricity bill or something.

I told him there was nothing *but* bad feelings. And that he was a disgusting human being who'd ruined Daisy's life.

In a village as small as Great Oakley, everyone will know that Daddy slept with Mummy's bridesmaid.

'You're staying in Oakley then?' Nick said.

I said I'd be at the Oakley Arms until I'd sorted things out.

'When will you and Daisy next be in London?' he asked. 'I really miss her.'

I told him I didn't know.

There was silence. Then Nick said, 'Sorry about all this, Jules. Sadie and I – we just fit. You know how I am. I just go with my heart.'

I didn't think he could hurt me any more.

Bastard.

Bastard, bastard, bastard.

I shouted a load of abuse at him, hung up, then thumped the phone on the pillow.

Sunday, 1st May

Too embarrassed to go out in the village today.

I've been hiding at Mum and Dad's, stuffing my face with comfort food. It's not difficult. The fridge is full of cheesecake, dips, sausage rolls, pork pies and Coca-Cola.

But food isn't working. I'm too far into my depression hole. It's not making me feel even the tiniest bit better. Everything is so empty. Hollow. Hopeless.

Everything except Daisy.

If I didn't have her, I don't know what I'd do.

The pub downstairs is full of people celebrating the early spring bank holiday. It's so weird, hearing people enjoying themselves.

Don't they know the world has just ended?

Monday, 2nd May
Early May Bank Holiday

Pretty much everyone in the village is hung over today.

I suppose that's the bonus of suffering a big trauma.

I'm too antisocial to drink too much.

Tuesday, 3rd May

What a mess my life is.

Dad asked me today if I'd thought about the legal side of things. I hadn't.

But I suppose I should.

Like Dad says, I should make sure I get custody of Daisy. And make Nick pay maintenance. I doubt Nick will give us much though. Unless he borrows money from Helen.

Wednesday, 4th May

I can't get what Nick said out of my head.

'I just go with my heart.'

Does he love her? I mean, what else could that mean?

All I can think about today is Nick and Sadie.

Some crazy part of me wants to know all the details. How many times did they do it? When? Where? Does he love her? Does she love him? How long has it been going on?

Althea has turned spy for me because she's friends with Sadie's gay make-up artist friend, Rylan.

Apparently, Sadie and Nick have been seen together loads of times around Soho.

Ugh. To be so brazen about it…they must have so little respect for me.

Sadie told Rylan that she and Nick had sex at her apartment because Nick's mother was always dropping in at his place. No mention that the mother of his child was there too.

How could she do this to me? After everything I've done for her.

Althea says she'll try and find out more. But she warned me I might not want to know.

I told Althea what Nick has said.

Sorry about all this Jules. I just go with my heart.

She exploded and said he was always a thoughtless, tactless bastard.

'But do you think that means he loves her?' I asked.

'Nick doesn't love anyone but himself,' Althea replied.

I said, 'What about Daisy?'

'He loves her,' said Althea, 'but only because she's half of him.'

Thursday, 5th May

Keep thinking that Daisy doesn't have a family any more. And bursting into tears.

Friday, 6th May

Helen came round today.

Mum shouted, 'Get off my doorstep you nasty cow.'

I told Mum it was all right. I wanted to hear what Helen had to say.

Dad tactfully asked Mum and Brandi to help at the pub and said if Callum was a *very* good boy he could play 'ice cream van' with the beer taps.

So Helen and I had the upstairs to ourselves.

While I was making us a cup of tea, Brandi came up looking for Callum's sunglasses.

'Is that tea for her ladyship?' she whispered.

I said yes.

Brandi spat in the cup.

It's the first time I've laughed since the wedding.

Then Helen appeared.

I had to give Helen the cup of tea then – it would have looked suspicious if I'd got rid of it.

Brandi said, 'Do enjoy your *lovely* cup of tea.'

Helen went on about the garden and how it was lovely for families. Or something.

Mum's got all these wind chimes, gnomes and wishing wells out there, amid picnic tables and beer parasols. Not exactly the slate flowerbeds and lollypop hedges in Helen's garden. But nice for children.

It was very weird – Helen trying to be nice. A bit unsettling.

Luckily it didn't last long.

Helen said she wanted to arrange 'visitation' for Nick and that she was happy to act as a 'go-between'.

I asked why Nick couldn't sort things out himself.

Helen talked about how sensitive Nick was and what a failure he felt.

She said, 'You know how men are – when they feel low they often look to the baser comforts.'

Then she put her nasty, bony hand over mine and said, 'Nicholas is like his father. A lover of women. A charmer.'

'Didn't you divorce Nick's dad?' I asked.

'Yes,' she said. 'But I shouldn't have done. Men cheat. I should have forgiven him.' Then she told me that Henry cheated on her with one of his factory workers – a woman who presses the toilet roll dispensers.

I asked her if Henry had ever slept with her bridesmaid.

She went quiet then, and asked if I'd seen Sadie.

I told her I never wanted to see Sadie or Nick ever again.

'Perhaps if you talked to Sadie you might be more sympathetic,' said Helen. 'She's…vulnerable right now.'

I asked her what she was talking about. Sadie is about as vulnerable as an armoured tank.

Helen said, 'Given her…condition.'

'Condition?' I said. 'What condition? The condition of being a complete backstabbing bitch?'

Then Helen said, 'The condition of being *pregnant*.' In this low, calm voice. She put a hand on mine and said, 'Nick is the father.'

OMG, OMG, OMG.

I just freaked out, shouting and swearing. Sobbing.

I kept saying over and over, 'How could they do this to Daisy? How could they do this?'

Then Helen left.

I was really glad Brandi had spat in her tea.

Saturday, 7th May

I can't believe it. I just can't believe it.

Sadie's pregnant.

PREGNANT.

Since when? Was she pregnant on our wedding day?

I thought I couldn't be any more humiliated than I already am.

What next? Will I find dog shit on the bottom of my wedding shoes?

Is Sadie keeping the baby?

Actually, that's a stupid thing to wonder. Of course she will. She's an actress. A baby is nine months of drama.

I wonder what Nick said when he found out?

I'll never forget the night I told him I was pregnant.

I did the pregnancy test while he was watching *Game of Thrones*.

I shouted, 'Nick. NICK! I think I might be pregnant.'

'Even if she is,' he yelled back, 'I think she dies in this episode.'

'No. I'M pregnant,' I bellowed.

'Christ,' said Nick. 'As if I haven't got enough to worry about.'

What did he say when Sadie told him?

God, I feel so sick.

Sunday, 8th May

I am totally fat, horrible, unlovable. No reason to lose weight any more. Who cares?

Pigged out on Chicago Town pizzas, sour-cream dip and

Pringles – all the usual stuff round Mum and Dad's.

I ate so much even Mum was worried. Well – she told me to slow down anyway. I think because there were no Pringles left and she likes to eat a tube while she's watching *The Apprentice*.

No one seemed surprised that Sadie was pregnant. I even wondered if everyone knew already, but I think Brandi at least would have told me. She's rubbish at keeping secrets.

Mum said she hoped Sadie would have triplets with huge heads.

I keep having niggling thoughts about Sadie.

I mean – yes, I hate her. She's ruined my life and Daisy's chance of a happy family. But if she's pregnant and alone…I mean, that's pretty awful.

Monday, 9th May

Grilled Althea about the pregnancy.

But she had nothing more to report. Her gay make-up artist friend is doing a 'dance spectacular' act on a cruise ship and has no phone reception.

Tuesday, 10th May

ARG!!!

Got a letter today from the Jolly-Piggott family solicitors. They're asking for a DNA test for Daisy.

The BASTARDS!!!

I rang Nick twenty times, but he didn't (wouldn't) answer.

Drove round to Helen's house and thumped on the door until the stained glass rattled.

When Helen answered, she looked down her long bird nose at my Ugg boots and pyjamas and said, 'You'd better come inside before anyone sees you.'

Helen is having the kitchen redone, so there were tile samples everywhere with her manic pen scrawl on the back:

Dreadful.

Ghastly.

Christ – looks like a Manchester council estate.

I raged about the letter and the DNA test.

Helen put on her serious glasses and pretended to look at the letter. I could tell she knew exactly what it said, because after a two-second glance she said, 'Just standard legal procedure. Nothing personal. Our solicitor thought it best.'

I told her it didn't get more personal than questioning my *virtue*. Not sure why I used that word. Think I've been watching the TV remake of *Pride and Prejudice...*

'You have to understand,' Helen said. 'Nicholas could have *two* children to support soon. We need to make sure things are clear.'

I asked whether Sadie would do a DNA test when the baby came.

Helen said she was 'fully on board'. Which I suppose means yes.

Sadie won't care about her honesty being questioned. She's very at peace with being a liar.

I roared at Helen that Nick would have to pay for his daughter.

She said, 'As long as Daisy *is* his daughter.'

I think I swore quite a lot then because I remember Helen wincing and saying something about bad language.

I made it all the way to the car before I burst into tears.

I cuddled Daisy. She chewed on a tile sample.

Then I phoned Laura. She was in the uni coffee shop with Zach.

In the background, I could hear Zach saying, 'Excuse me, I'm *terribly* sorry but is this fair-trade tea? Don't want to shit all over the farmers. Thank you.'

It's sweet that those two are getting along, but also bad timing.

Why couldn't Laura get a wonderful boyfriend years ago when I was happy with Nick?

Wednesday, 11th May

Had five voicemail messages today. Thought they'd all be from Nick, but they were all blank ones from Althea. She's never figured out how to hang up if someone doesn't answer.

Thursday, 12th May

SO sick of checking my phone for Nick to call or text. I've decided to block his number. That way I won't drive myself mad running to my phone whenever it bleeps.

Saturday, 14th May

Laura's birthday today. I feel terrible – I forgot all about it.

Brandi forgot too, but she forgets everyone's birthday. As the youngest in the family, she gets away with everything.

Phoned Laura to beg forgiveness. She didn't mind. She said the health and happiness of her family and friends was the only gift she wanted.

Zach is taking her out to some fancy restaurant tonight.

Laura's panicking that she won't understand the menu.

She's been studying upper-class food words. Apparently, lardon is just another word for bacon.

Sunday, 15th May

Still no news about Nick and Sadie.

Daisy has another cold. The poor snotty little thing. It's agonising listening to her gasping for breath. I feel so worried.

Mum said, 'She's fine. Look at the size of those nostrils. You three were always getting colds as babies. And you turned out just fine...'

I ended up buying a contraption to suck snot out of Daisy's nose.

It goes on the pile of baby devices that are supposed to make life easier but don't actually work.

I have a whole box of them now, including:

♦ A nursery thermometer that always says the room is dangerously hot.

♦ A cot-death prevention sensor that goes off every time Daisy falls asleep.

♦ A car bottle warmer that takes half an hour to heat a bottle.

♦ A warmer for wet wipes.

♦ Various teething products – amber teething necklace, teething powder sachets, chunky plastic teething keys.

I wonder how far along Sadie is? Is she sick? Was she pregnant on my WEDDING DAY? I wish I didn't keep torturing myself with these questions. But it's sort of impossible not to.

Monday, 16th May

Mum said she would 'take Daisy off my hands' today so I could have a rest.

I told her about Daisy's routine.

Mum did her usual, 'Stop telling me how to do it, Jules, I've had three kids.'

Yes. In the Eighties.

Mum's philosophy is, 'As long as the baby's not dead, everything's fine.'

She still doesn't know how to use disposable nappies. Daisy ALWAYS comes back with her nappy on back-to-front and the sticky bits stuck to her clothing.

Still. It was nice to have an hour to myself. Although Daisy was so upset when she came back that I had to spend a good hour and a half calming her down.

Tuesday, 17th May

Althea phoned today.

She asked if I was still planning on running the Winter Marathon. I said no way.

I never wanted to do it in the first place.

Althea said Sadie has pulled out.

Felt pretty happy about that.

'Look, you're already signed up,' Althea pointed out. 'And you've raised hundreds for Children's Aid. Why pull out because of that nasty moon-faced cow?'

I said I'd think about it.

Meaning no.

If being dumped on my wedding day doesn't give me an excuse not to run a marathon, what does?

Wednesday, 18th May

Everyone always says what a happy baby Daisy is, but I really wish she was a sleepy baby.

I am so jealous of Althea, who says Wolfgang falls asleep all over the house. Apparently, all she has to do is give him some beef jerky to chew, and he drifts off.

Thursday, 19th May

Took Callum to McDonald's today, while Brandi studied for her beauty exams.

The McDonald's server just COULD NOT understand that I wanted carrot sticks for Callum's Happy Meal.

'Cheeseburger Happy Meal with carrot sticks please,' I said.

'So, fries, yeah?' said the server.

'No,' I said. 'Carrot sticks *instead* of fries.'

He said, '*Carrot* sticks?' Like I'd asked for grilled lobster.

'No Aunty Julesy, I want fries,' moaned Callum.

'So, fries, yeah?' said the server.

'NO. Carrot sticks.'

The Happy Meal came with fries.

While we were eating, Callum said, 'Do you hate Uncle Nick?'

'I don't hate him,' I explained. 'I just feel very, very sad when I think about him.'

'Mummy says Uncle Nick is a right busted,' said Callum.

'Yes Callum,' I agreed. 'Uncle Nick *is* a right busted. But he's still Daisy's dad.'

Callum said, 'I never see my dad. And I don't care. Daisy won't care either.'

Sometimes Callum is wise beyond his years. Maybe it comes of having a mum who's still a baby herself.

Friday, 20th May

Got a handwritten letter from Nick.

Unusual for him. He prefers computers.

At first, I wondered why he hadn't texted or called. But then I remembered I'd blocked his number.

The letter said,

Juliette,

Baby. I know I've fucked up. The DNA test – so not my idea.

I miss my little Daisy boo. Is she saying daddy yet? Does she still look like me?

Can I see my little girl? Pretty please? I know I've been a bastard, but I'm still her dad.

Can we talk?

Nick.

He'd put a big flourishy signature under his name, like when he signs his autograph.

I couldn't stop crying.

I've read and re-read the letter all day.

I still can't forgive Nick, but...maybe I'm being too harsh... Maybe we really can make a go of things. For Daisy's sake. We're supposed to be a family.

Saturday, 21st May

Mum and Brandi both took turns in shouting at me today re the Nick letter.

Apparently, I'm not under any circumstances to consider going back to him. He is a shit bag. Plain and simple.

Simple to them. But not to me.

I thought you were supposed to get married, have kids and live happily ever after.

Where did I go wrong?

Monday, 23rd May

It's Nick's birthday today.

I wonder what he's doing right now.

Probably out shopping on his Helen-funded credit card, buying clothes at Abercrombie and Fitch and hitting another bar from his favourite coffee-table book, 'London's 100 coolest bars.'

Bastard.

Tuesday, 24th May

By the time I had a baby, I had thought we'd live in a proper house with tasteful wooden board games and a vegetable patch.

I also thought I would own a rolling pin and be able to fold up a stroller without slicing my fingers open.

Yet here I am, living in my old bedroom with '80s stripe wallpaper, my baby in a collapsing travel cot, while my ex-fiancé has sex with my ex-best friend.

Funny how life turns out.

Wednesday, 25th May

Spoke to Laura and Althea about Nick's letter.

They both shouted at me too. Even Laura, and she never shouts.

Althea said Nick was a horrible, nasty piece of theatrical shit, and me and Daisy were better off without him.

She'd got through to Rylan, Sadie's gay make-up artist friend, on the cruise ship. Rylan said Sadie 'fell pregnant' after the wedding. That's something at least.

But Nick has been having sex with her since January.

What an idiot I am.

Nick *is* a shitbag, and I'm better off without him.

But he's still Daisy's dad. He has to see her eventually.

Thursday, 26th May

Daisy was eating Dad's massive bible while I was on the loo, and it opened on a passage about forgiveness.

And I thought – could it be a sign? A sign I should forgive Nick? Maybe even take him back?

Everyone makes mistakes. I can't throw away Daisy's family just because I'm feeling angry.

I'm going to the flat today, and maybe we can talk.

Friday, 27th May

Those B******s!

Sadie's stuff was all over our apartment.

She's LIVING with him!

Nick had the decency to look embarrassed, but only for a minute. Then he spun Daisy around and asked if she liked his new beard.

Daisy giggled and cooed and grabbed at his chin. The little traitor.

Nick asked if I wanted to pick up the rest of my things, like my running gear. He'd put it all in a bin bag for me.

I lied and said he should get ready to pay his bet, and buy me a new wardrobe when I finished the marathon.

Brave talk, I know.

I stalked out with my head held high.

Then I burst into tears in the lobby.

Saturday, 28th May

Dark curtains and sobbing again. It didn't last all day though because I had a play date with Althea. She hammered on my bedroom door and wouldn't stop shouting until I got dressed and came out.

We ended up in the Great Oakley pottery café.

It's one of those places where kids get to paint their own plates.

Daisy and Wolfgang were way too young in my opinion, but Althea insisted they should express themselves.

Wolfgang's plates were very *intense* – all angry slashes, deep purples, blacks, and reds. He's either going to be an artist or need therapy.

He only smashed two things. He would have smashed a third, but the pottery lady wrestled it out of his hands.

She didn't exactly throw us out, but she made it clear we wouldn't be getting any more cups of tea.

Told Althea about my trip to Nick's apartment.

She boomed, 'That SHIT bag.' Then she offered to slash Nick's tyres.

Althea is a good friend.

Sunday, 29th May

Laura and I had a chat about 'next steps' re Nick and Sadie.

She said, 'Sort out maintenance quickly. Because it looks like she's getting her claws in. How pregnant did she look?'

I told her I didn't know. Sadie had been under the duvet when I went round.

I confessed my bravado speech about running the marathon, and Laura said, 'Why not run it? Show them both what you can do? Make Nick pay that bet.'

'But I *can't* do it, Laura,' I moaned. 'I can barely manage two miles. And that's in warm weather.'

'Of course you can do it,' said Laura. 'You know what they say in my martial arts class? A black belt is a white belt who never gave up. We can start training again. Whenever you like.'

I said I'd think about it. Meaning no.

Monday, 30th May

Spring Bank Holiday

Heard from mutual friends that Sadie has been 'sort of living' with Nick for a few weeks.

So, pretty much since the wedding.

I didn't think I had any tears left, but I do.

Poor Daisy. Poor, poor Daisy.

Tuesday, 31st May

Desperate to find out more about Sadie and Nick, but nothing on Facebook. Just the usual daily selfies from both of them.

I keep checking Sadie's relationship status.

She's single. Like Nick.

Maybe they're not *actually* living together. Maybe she just came round to see him that one day. And threw her stuff everywhere...

Wednesday, 1st June

Brandi's birthday.

Her favourite present was a T-shirt from Mum. It was skin-tight, bright pink and said, 'I'm a Mum, not a Nun'.

I used three different pots of glitter to make Brandi's birthday card.

Brandi said, 'What's that big sparkly splodge on the front?'

'Your niece's handprint,' I explained.

'My niece?' said Brandi. 'Who's my niece?'

'*Daisy* is your niece.'

She nodded slowly like it was all suddenly making sense.

Then she said, 'So is Daisy *Callum's* niece too?'

No wonder she failed all her exams at school.

Thursday, 2nd June

Daisy had a cold last night.

She woke up every two hours, all snuffly.

I was so worried I couldn't sleep – I just lay next to her, checking she was still breathing.

I know I should nap today, but I just can't seem to nod off. Plus I've nearly cracked level 50 on Candy Crush Saga.

5 pm

Sooooooo tired. But can't sleep.

8 pm

Daisy has woken up.

11 pm

Daisy still awake! Desperately looking for sleep apps on my phone.

11.30 pm

Found an app that makes hairdryer noises. Seems to have done the trick. Daisy asleep. My turn now, thank goodness.

Friday, 3rd June

3 am

Daisy just woke up!

I woke Mum in sleep-deprived tears.

'The Duffy family have never been good sleepers,' Mum said. 'Remember Brandi? She used to suicide dive out of the cot.'

I broke down, sobbing, 'Why doesn't she have an off switch? Why are there no answers?'

Mum reassured me that, 'Feeling confused is what motherhood is all about.'

Then I remembered the iPhone app that makes hairdryer noises. I shouted, 'I need my phone, Mum. I can't find it! I've lost my phone!'

Mum pointed out that I was holding my phone.

I am so sleep-deprived!

Then Dad suggested I put cinnamon in Daisy's milk.

I sobbed that we didn't have any sodding cinnamon.

Mum said she'd drive over to the all-night supermarket. Then she remembered she'd lost the car keys.

While she was looking for them (and arguing with dad), Daisy fell asleep.

SO tired.

4 am

Can't sleep! Keep thinking that Daisy will wake up any minute.

5 am

Still can't sleep.

6 am

Daisy just woke up.

Thank God for Dad – he's giving her milk and singing 'Food Glorious Food' from *Oliver!*

Afternoon

The health visitor came round today.

She was a big, busty, clucky lady called Pam Fairy who had a lot of strong opinions about the right and wrong way to look after babies.

I could tell Mum was itching to disagree with her. Having 'got through' three kids of her own, Mum can't stand it when anyone else has opinions.

Pam pulled her notes out and asked lots of questions about my sudden change of address.

Then she said, 'You had a nice arrangement, didn't you? Fancy apartment in London. Daisy's father on hand. Any chance of a Mummy-Daddy reunion?'

I said, 'I don't think so.'

Mum added helpfully, 'He slept with her best friend, Mrs Fairy. They broke up on her wedding day.'

Then Pam said, 'Oh, *you're* the Great Oakley Runaway Bride!' And looked all pleased like she'd met a celebrity. Then she remembered herself and started asking about Daisy's diet.

Mum told Pam that Daisy loved Cheesy Wotsits.

Pam went all serious and asked about vegetables.

Mum said, 'She likes potato smiley faces. And tomato ketchup.'

She didn't bother to mention all the organic vegetables I puree!

Pam gave us a long lecture about nutrition and pulled out leaflets about healthy baby food.

Then she told us to ring her if we needed anything else. Apparently, health visitors offer a sort of 'fourth emergency service' and are always on hand if we have any worries or concerns.

Saturday, 4th June

Looked at houses on Rightmove today.

The only ones in my budget are 'in an up-and-coming area' (shit area), 'delightfully cosy' (shit size), 'priced to sell' (massive shit hole) or 'remarkably energy-efficient' (shit-smelling basement).

I'll keep trying though.

It's time I started rebuilding my life. Seeing Sadie's stuff all over the flat…things will never be how they were. It hurts, but I have to move forward, for Daisy's sake.

Like Althea says, pain closes the door. It helps me let go of my old life and look to the future.

Sunday, 5th June

Morning

Sunday lunch with the family today.

Dad has 'spring cleaned' the pub, scrubbing the Tudor beams and whitewashing the walls, so everything looks sparkly and clean. The pub really is a beautiful building. A piece of village history, with its latticed windows and oak doors.

Shame Mum's neon-pink fairy lights are strung around the bar – she has no sense of tradition.

At lunch, Mum tried to give Daisy a teaspoon of Guinness for her runny nose.

I literally had to wrestle the spoon away.

How does she not get that alcohol isn't good for a baby?

'Don't be so paranoid,' Mum bellowed. 'You had spoons of Guinness when you were her age. And you turned out just fine.'

Brandi started bad-mouthing Nick, saying what a lucky escape I'd had. That I didn't have Helen coming round any more, checking my windowsills for dust. And that Nick was a total waste of space.

Little Callum said, 'What does fuck-up mean?'

I told everyone I didn't want to hear about Nick any more, so we talked about their news instead.

Laura is thinking of becoming a vegan.

Brandi has (another) new boyfriend.

Dad saw a meteor in the sky last night.

Mum's been teaching next-door's dog to sing 'Let it Go'.

I told everyone I was determined to lose my baby weight, and Mum said, 'Righty-o. Just four potatoes for you then. Don't you worry. I've cooked this whole roast in olive oil.'

I showed her the calories on the Aunt Bessie's roast potato packet.

'Two hundred,' she read. 'Is that a lot?'

Yes – if you add olive oil when you're cooking them. And eat four.

Considering Mum is overweight and has type II diabetes, it's pretty shocking she knows nothing about calories.

She had eight roast potatoes on her plate, a mountain of buttery mash, oven chips and three huge slices of beef.

One time she asked me if coffee beans counted as one of her five a day.

I worry about her (we all do) but I've given up nagging. Mum just calls me 'obsessive' and warns me about getting an eating disorder.

'Men like a bit of something to hold onto,' Mum said. 'Isn't that right Bob?'

Dad replied, 'It certainly is!'

Mum still dresses in skimpy tops and skin-tight leggings. And

Dad still wolf-whistles at her. If anyone criticises Mum's weight, she says, 'I'm a complete original. Which makes me absolutely fucking priceless.'

Afternoon

Just had nice country walk with Laura, Brandi and little Callum (Daisy bobbing along in the sling), and afternoon tea at Mary and John's Family-Friendly Farm Café.

Mary and John hate children though, so we had to sit outdoors by the pig pens.

Evening

Thinking about Nick's letter.

I am fed up and tired and depressed this evening.

Motherhood is SO gruelling. It just doesn't stop. Feed, change, wash clothes, Daisy sleeps when I don't want her to, wakes up when I don't want her to, feed again…and on it goes.

And I don't want to do it alone. Of course Nick never really helped (in fact, I have more time now I don't have to do his washing). But I'm still technically a single mum, and everyone knows single mums have it hard.

Monday, 6th June

Pam forgot to write Daisy's weight in her red book, so I gave her a ring.

There was no answer. I left a message, but she hasn't called me back.

Tuesday, 7th June

Daisy has had three twinkly pieces of glitter on her scalp since Brandi's birthday.

It only shows up in direct sunlight, but I'm worried people will think I don't wash her. No matter how many baths I give her, the glitter just won't shift.

I wonder if the health visitor noticed? Did *she* think I never wash her? Better ring and explain.

4 pm

Rang Pam Fairy three times and left urgent voicemails. She still hasn't rung back.

Wednesday, 8th June

No call from Pam Fairy.

Mum laughed when I told her about the glitter. She said, 'Health visitors are looking for neglect. A sparkly baby is a happy baby.'

Thursday, 9th June

Did postnatal depression test online. Just in case.

I have an unhealthy fixation with Coldplay and salted caramel. Plus I'm just so miserable whenever I think about Nick and Sadie.

But the test came back fine.

Phoned Althea and she said, 'All mothers feel sad sometimes. I mean, our lives are ruined aren't they?'

Friday, 10th June

Weighed myself today for the first time since the wedding.

When I saw the scales, I couldn't believe it.

I thought Mum must have broken them.

I'm EVEN HEAVIER now than when I had Daisy.

Took off all my clothes and viewed my wobbly post-baby body in a full-length mirror.

If I were being kind, I'd say I look like a Renaissance nude. If I were being unkind, I'd say I looked plump and saggy.

OK. Enough is enough now.

I want to be some of what I was before. Not all, but some. It's not just about the weight. It's about taking control. Taking charge of my life.

Time to move forward.

I want to show Daisy just how strong her mother can be.

Saturday, 11th June

Diet-book shopping with Laura and Brandi.

We had coffee at Barnes and Noble – skinny decaf for me, espresso for Laura and a big frothy whipped strawberry thing for Brandi (bloody twenty-one-year-olds – Brandi is skinny as anything and eats exactly what she likes).

Then we looked at diet books (well, Laura and I did. Brandi browsed magazines, then moaned that bookshops were BORING).

There were so many diet books to choose from:

• *Fat Around the Middle* (But I'm fat *everywhere*!)

• *The 5:2 Diet* (tried starving myself before and frankly I just don't have the willpower.)

• *The Atkins Diet* (There's that bad breath rumour…)

• *Weight Watchers* (Sarah Ferguson did it and, without sounding horrible, she's still fat.)

• *The Slow Carb Diet* (Ugh, who likes beans?)

Bought the *Food Guru* book in the end.

Healthy, sensible eating. No fads or false promises. But you *could* lose ten pounds in a week…

Sunday, 12th June

Bought all the stuff for the *Food Guru* diet.

The Food Guru guy says you can't put a price on health. But you can. It's about two hundred quid.

Bought stuff like steak, salmon, asparagus, and a load of things I've never heard of like chia seeds and psyllium husk.

Dad took me to the supermarket because he's the only one who can work Daisy's car seat.

He was such a proud granddad, telling any shopper who'd listen Daisy's age, birth weight and toilet habits.

Monday, 13th June

10 am

So far today I have eaten:

+ Two boiled eggs (no toast or anything – wheat is the work of the devil).

+ A handful of nuts.

+ Celery with pumpkin seed butter.

11 am

Must be lunchtime by now?! I'm going to eat my own leg if I don't have lunch soon.

11.30 am

Early lunch.

Cooked stir-fry without any soy sauce or flavour of any kind.

Feel pretty good.

Tuesday, 14th June

Althea phoned me at 6 am to remind me to count my blessings.

She's just been on some Buddhist retreat with Wolfgang.

Apparently, they had to count their blessings at 6 am every morning, and she reckons it's changed her life.

Today her blessings are:

+ Her confident little boy who expresses his feelings. (No one else thinks it's a blessing that Wolfgang expresses his feelings, which are generally anger and outrage. But a mother's love is blind.)

+ Fabulous purple furniture.

+ The mystery flowers (weeds) that grow in her garden.

I told her my biggest blessing was Daisy.

I wanted to add, 'And friends who know not to call before 7 am.'

Wednesday, 15th June

A bad, bad day.

Went into town to buy stuff for Daisy and my bank card didn't work. The lady in the bank said, 'Your account has been frozen, Mrs Jolly Piggy.'

I told her I wasn't Mrs Jolly Piggy. I was Mr Jolly-Piggott's ex-girlfriend. And the money in the account was mine.

After a bit of wrangling (well – shouting), she got the manager – a spotty teenager in a suit three sizes too big for him.

He said there was nothing they could do. The account was frozen four days ago, and no one could access funds until 'assets are divided'.

'But it's *my* money,' I said.

'The account was in his name,' said the manager, over and over again.

In the end, he asked if I could accept a Smedley's Bank teddy bear as an apology.

I told him if he could give me five thousand bears and let me sell them outside the bank, we could talk.

Thursday, 16th June

Spent all day in the bank shouting at people and trying to call Nick.

When Nick finally answered the phone, he sounded all suspicious.

'Ye-es?'

Like he didn't know why I was calling!

I shouted at him about the bank account and needing to buy things for Daisy.

He said his mother and the solicitor had made him freeze the account.

When I asked him what happened to the money, he said no one could access it until 'legal shit is sorted out'.

As I was screaming at him, I heard a woman in the background at his end.

'Who's with you?' I asked.

A horrible silence.

And *then* I heard Sadie's loud, clipped voice. *'Nick darling, how do I look in this dress? Pregnant and stylish or pregnant and fat?'*

Before I knew it, I'd thrown my phone at Smedley's Bank window.

A guy in an army jacket shouted, 'Yeah! Smash the fat cats!

Friday, 17th June

Told Mum and Dad about the bank account.

'What am I going to do?' I said.

'Your mum will take you out this afternoon,' said Dad, 'and get everything you need. Just write a list.'

I started crying. I said, 'You already look after Brandi and Callum. It's bad enough I'm living with you.'

Dad said it was fine. He said it would be a good opportunity to economise and re-evaluate their spending.

He put on his reading glasses, got out his household expenses notebook and crossed out 'Cable TV' with his Guinness pencil.

Mum shouted at him to fuck off.

Then a big argument blew up about what was important and what wasn't.

It got really nasty when Mum threatened to sell Dad's *Lord of the Rings* figurines.

I told them no one needed to sell anything.

Dad said I'd always be his little girl and he'd sell the clothes off his back if he had to.

I cried even more then.

In the end, Mum and Dad insisted on transferring money into my bank account.

I promised to pay them back, but they said, 'You just worry about Daisy.'

Althea's right.

I should remember to count my blessings.

I have the best family in the world.

Saturday, 18th June

Althea has signed me up for 'Sing and Splash' at the fancy sports club just outside the village.

It starts next week.

I found out this morning when Althea face-timed me at 6.15 am.

'Come on Jules!' she said. 'Embrace the day. Get your bra on. Wipe all that crap out of your eyes. We're hitting Oxford Street to buy you a swimming costume.'

Then she waved a leaflet in front of her phone.

It said:

Sing and Splash
Help your little ones with their social and cognitive development.
Shallow water – low risk of drowning.

'I know, I know,' Althea conceded. 'It's all a little bit establishment. But fuck it – the kids will love it.'

When I told Althea about all the bank account stuff, she waved her turquoise-ringed fingers at the camera and said, 'Don't be stupid. I'll pay.'

I tried to argue, but there's no point arguing with Althea. She's like a steamroller.

So off we went into London.

Althea banned me from Topshop, New Look or River Island.

'You're a mum now,' she said. 'You need padding and wire.'

So we went to old-lady shops like Marks and Spencer and Laura Ashley.

The ones that sell clothes for women who don't have sex any more.

I found myself in a world of black one-pieces with ruched bust lines and old-lady flower patterns.

I still looked four months pregnant in all of them.

Then we went to John Lewis.

Althea suggested I try a bikini, but I don't want my wrinkly stomach on display.

'Posh Spice has a wrinkly stomach,' Althea pointed out.

'That's why she never wears a bikini,' I replied.

As we were walking through the make-up department, Althea shouted about make-up being 'one big establishment con.' She talked about the pressures of being female and how every woman is beautiful without 'any of this crap'.

Then a make-up lady told Althea she had beautiful eyelashes. Althea went all giggly and agreed to try a new mascara, 'just for a laugh'.

The make-up lady shone a bright light in my face and told me I should try a light diffusing powder for fine lines.

As she was dusting my face, I saw Nick walking through the perfume department. With Sadie.

My stomach dropped to my knees.

I tapped Althea on the arm, and we both stared.

Nick was his usual swaggering self.

Sadie looked amazing. Glowing I suppose is the word. Showing a little bit, but not much. Slim too – especially around her face. Shiny light-brown hair like ironed silk.

She was wearing skinny jeans and brown knee-high boots, a loose blouse and an expensive-looking chiffon scarf wrapped around her neck.

She looked more like a mum than I did, as a matter of fact. All classy and mature.

She picked up some designer sunglasses, tried them on and looked at Nick with a 'don't I look great?' expression.

Althea whispered, 'That *bitch*.'

We watched as Nick's hand slid down to Sadie's toned backside.

Sadie threw her head back and laughed her horsey laugh.

I don't think I've ever felt so small. I started sobbing.

I'm fat...

I have a weird stretchy, wobbly stomach...

My baby still wakes up at night...

I have spotty upper-arms...

And I don't wear scarves...

Althea crushed me into a big bosomy hug and said, 'You're a million times more beautiful than that big-faced cow. Come on. I'm buying you some chocolate cake.'

When I got home, I went straight to my room.

At about eight o'clock, I heard a soft knocking on the door.

It was Mum.

She'd brought me a pint of Guinness on a silver tray.

Then she told me about an old boyfriend of hers, Brian Tuck, who went off with her best friend on Christmas Eve. Worst of all, she'd already bought his Christmas present – a Lovett-green jumper. But she said it all worked out for the best. Because the shop took the jumper back, and then she met Dad.

'But what about Daisy?' I sniffed. 'Nick has hardly seen her.'

'Kids accept life for how it is,' said Mum. 'We should learn a thing or two from them and stop crying about what can't be changed.'

We looked at Daisy, sleeping in the cot.

She did look very contented.

Maybe Mum's right. I mean, Callum doesn't see his dad, and he's the happiest little boy there is. Perhaps because of all the Coca-Cola he drinks, but still…

Sunday, 19th June
Father's Day

For some stupid reason, I thought Nick might call today.

Father's Day and everything.

But no.

I bought him a present months ago (supposedly from Daisy). Solid-silver cufflinks with tiny prints of Daisy's feet on them.

I gave the cufflinks to Dad, and he got all teary and went on about what an idiot Nick is, and how he loved being a granddad.

He's right. Nick is an idiot. I'm better off without him.

Monday, 20th June

When I woke up this morning, the sun was shining.

I looked at Daisy – all smiles, chewing her blanket.

I thought again about Althea counting her blessings.

And I counted mine.

I have a beautiful, healthy baby.

I have amazing family and friends.

I can help myself to Guinness and bar snacks whenever I want.

I told Daisy, 'Let's open up those curtains and welcome the day.'

When I did, this old man jogged past in running gear. He was probably seventy years old, but he was bounding along.

'Do you know what, Daisy?' I said. 'I'm going to run that marathon. I'm going to train, and I'm going to finish it.'

I stuck Daisy in her stroller and ran all the way to the woods and back again.

And for the first time in ages, I saw the sunshine.

Wednesday, 22nd June

'Song and Splash' with Althea today.

It took ages to get Daisy into the car with her swim nappy, swimsuit, water wings, rubber ring, rubber duckies, baby goggles, snacks, nappies, wet wipes, stroller, rain cover, change of clothes, teething ring and warm jumper just in case.

When I parked at the sports club, the car cut out. It wouldn't start again, but I was so late I ran into the club.

Then I found a text message from Althea:

Can't get Wolfy out of the bedroom. He's wrapped himself around the cot leg and won't let go. Don't want to upset his power centre by being too brutal. Sorry baby cakes. See you soon. Kisses!

Considered going home, but Daisy looked so happy to be in the shiny, fancy sports centre I thought – oh well, we're here now.

Wore the new black-sequinned swimming costume Althea bought me yesterday.

Even before we got into the pool, Daisy had eaten two sequins.

In the swimming pool, I noticed three more stuck to her face.

The teacher had a big smile, pigtails and a swimsuit with cupcakes all over it.

It must be nice to be happy all the time.

As soon as the singing started, Daisy started splashing like a maniac, kicking her arms and legs around and getting water all over the other mums and kids.

By the end of the class, there was three feet of space around us.

As we were leaving, I noticed one of the mums looking at me. Then, as we all walked to the changing rooms, I realised who it was.

Clarissa Fielding.

God, I haven't seen her in years.

Not since the school sports day, when she stopped being my best friend – I think because Mum turned up in a see-through purple vest. No one knew where to look when she ran the Mother's Day race.

Clarissa looked great, actually.

Even with soaking wet hair, you could tell she had lovely caramel highlights.

I tried to catch her eye in the changing room, but she just gave me an embarrassed, 'I don't know you. OK?'

After I'd changed, I went to the Sports Centre café and phoned Dad. He must have been in the beer cellar because the call went through to answer machine.

As I was trying to get tea from the vending machine, Alex Dalton walked past.

By the way he was swinging his racquet, I guessed he'd just pummelled an opponent.

He was wearing black shorts and a T-shirt like a sporty hitman.

Alex noticed me, frowned and said, 'Juliette. You're not a member here.'

I said I was just here for 'Sing and Splash'.

Alex replied, 'Daisy has a sequin on her cheek.'

And then out of nowhere Clarissa appeared at my side. She did the whole, 'Juliette!' (Big fake pretend laugh.) 'It is you, isn't it? I wasn't sure…'

She kept glancing at Alex and smiling.

There was a beautiful blonde baby on Clarissa's hip in a spotless dress and frilly white socks.

'This must be your little one?' I said.

Clarissa said yes. Then she looked at Daisy and said, 'And she must be yours.'

Daisy gave a big half-tooth grin, snot running out of her nose, wet hair plastered to her little head. She tried to grab Clarissa's scarf.

Clarissa took a step back.

'She likes to grab things,' I said. 'I should train her to go for jewellery. She could make a fortune.'

Clarissa, still with half an eye on Alex, told me about all the things she'd been up to. The sailing club socials and how her husband had just reached 'the next level' in his banking job.

She asked me where Nick was, and I told her we'd split up.

'Oh,' she said. But it was three syllables long. 'Oh-hh-hh.' Then she added, 'You weren't married then? Before you had Daisy…'

I said that we'd nearly got married. But we'd fallen at the last hurdle, i.e. saying 'I do' in the church.

'Oh wait.' Clarissa put a hand to her face. 'My God. It wasn't you…who was stood up at the village church?'

'I wasn't stood up,' I said. 'I was the one who left.'

Clarissa gave me a pitying smile. 'Oh *dear*. Very sad. Especially for Daisy. That you couldn't make a go of it…'

I felt myself nodding. Then, out of nowhere, I started crying.

Alex's black eyes went all serious. He snapped at Clarissa, 'Do you make a habit of upsetting people?'

Clarissa said I was obviously having 'an emotional day'. She rummaged in her Burberry bag and thrust a business card at Alex, saying, 'Jonathan and I have been meaning to catch up since the Granger thing. *Do* give us a call.'

Alex didn't take the card. He marched me away from Clarissa and asked me how I was getting home.

I said my car had broken down so I'd probably end up catching the bus.

Alex frowned at my stroller, laden down with water wings and soggy swimming towels.

'You're not taking the bus,' he said. 'I'll drive you back.'

I told him that Daisy needed a car seat.

'We can take the car seat from your broken-down car,' he said. 'Obviously. Unless you drove her here without one.'

And then the stupid tears came again, and I couldn't talk any more.

When we got to Alex's Rolls Royce, he had a bit of trouble folding up the stroller. He kept kicking at the folding mechanism like he was trying to start a motorbike. But he managed it eventually.

Then he took Daisy from me and put her in the child seat, testing all the straps to make sure they were secure.

He even winked at Daisy and made her smile.

'You're just like Jemima,' he said. 'When she was a baby. Very alert.'

The car seat looked a bit weird in Alex's fancy car. If the Rolls Royce could have talked, it would have said, 'This indignity must never be spoken of.'

Alex told me to get in the front seat.

I was such a mess that Alex had to reach over and do my seatbelt for me.

'I really don't mind getting the bus,' I sniffed.

'Don't be ridiculous,' said Alex. 'You have a baby with you.'

'They do let babies on buses,' I replied.

'Still,' said Alex. 'A bus with children…'

'Some people *have* to take the bus,' I said. 'Not everyone is handed a hotel chain.'

'I wasn't *handed* a penny,' Alex snapped. 'The Dalton hotel chain wasn't given to me – I had to fight for it. I was never given any money by my family. Everything I own, I earned myself.'

I said, 'Including this flashy car?' Trying to make a joke, sort of.

'It isn't flashy,' said Alex. 'It's elegant.'

'But a Rolls Royce sends a message though, doesn't it?' I insisted. 'You know – that you've done well in life.'

'I don't drive a Rolls Royce to show off how much money I have,' he said. 'I drive it, so people know I'm Alex Dalton. Not Harold Dalton. My father hates this car.'

'Why?' I asked.

'Because Mr Dalton Senior owns car manufacturing plants in China, India…all over the world,' said Alex. 'He could have given me any number of brand-new cars for free. Yet I bought British. And just to rub it in, bespoke British.'

As we got nearer the village, Alex said, 'Just so you know, I think Nicholas Spencer is an idiot.'

'Why?' I asked.

'Because he let you get to the church without marrying you,' he said. 'Zach told me about the wedding.'

'Don't you have more interesting topics of conversation?' I asked. 'Like the New York stock market or the best marble for your hotel floors?'

'He thought I'd want to know,' Alex replied.

I said what a big mess everything was. Daisy not living with her dad.

'From what I heard, she never had much of a dad anyway,' said

Alex. 'You can do much better than Nick Spencer.'

I said that I didn't want to do better. I wanted Daisy to have two parents.

'Would you take him back?' Alex asked.

I said it was seriously unlikely. The door had pretty much closed – what with him getting Sadie pregnant and everything. But I couldn't say I *never* would. Not yet. Not with him being Daisy's dad. But if we ever did get back together, things would have to be very different.

'The man's a train wreck,' said Alex. 'Don't throw your life away.'

I asked Alex what made him an expert on relationships with us simple folk.

'Simple?' said Alex. 'You think that's a word I'd use?'

I said yes.

'Just because I drive an expensive car doesn't mean I look down on people,' he replied.

'You do though. Don't you?' I insisted.

'Only men like Nick Spencer,' said Alex. 'And that's because of who he is. Not where he comes from.'

'What about people who take the bus?' I said.

'I don't look *down* on them,' he replied. 'You have me wrong there. Are you still training for the marathon?'

I told him I'd quit for a while. But I was back in training now.

He smiled and said, 'Good. I'm glad about that.'

We were a few roads from the Oakley Arms, and I said, 'Just here will be fine. We can walk from here.' Like I was talking to a taxi driver.

'Don't be ridiculous,' said Alex. 'I'll drop you outside your mum and dad's pub. You're staying there, aren't you?'

I asked him how he knew that.

He shrugged and said, 'I noticed.'

When we pulled up outside my parent's pub, I caught myself

wondering what Alex must think of the place.

To most people, our house is quite big. Fancy, really. Well – big and flashy. Lots of bedrooms. Tudor beams. Great big garage and garden.

But to Alex, it must look a bit tasteless. What with the big neon sign that says 'Bob and Shirl's Place'. And all the gnomes in the garden.

Alex helped me with the stroller and baby swimming stuff.

Then he took Daisy out of the car while I got the stroller ready.

I thought Daisy would cry when he took her, but she didn't.

Alex held her against his chest and stroked her downy little head.

Daisy gave him an unexpected gummy half-tooth smile – something she hardly ever does for strangers.

I was a bit worried that Mum might come running out in her see-through dressing gown and offer to help unload. But luckily she didn't.

Alex lowered Daisy into the stroller and strapped her in.

He stood for a moment, watching her. Then he said, 'She's a beautiful baby. Goodbye Juliette. Take care.'

And then he was gone.

Thursday, 23rd June

Gorgeous blue sky today.

Lovely big yellow sun.

I love my mum and dad. But they're so LOUD.

'Bob. BOB! I'm going into town. One or TWO PACKETS OF SAUSAGE ROLLS?'

'SHIRLEY! WILL YOU KEEP YOUR VOICE DOWN!'

Mum only has to walk past my bedroom, and Daisy wakes up.

Dad tries a bit harder to be quiet. But in a way, he's louder when he's trying to be quiet. He does all this exaggerated, 'SHHHUUUSSH! DAISY'S SLEEPING!'

Of course, Daisy isn't the easiest sleeper.

It takes half an hour of shushing and rocking and patting to get her dozing off. Then I gently lay her down in the cot. Take a few careful steps back like she's a bomb that could go off. Careful… careful…don't creak the floorboards…

And Mum's voice will come bellowing up the stairs, 'I've got TWO FROZEN PIZZAS! Bob? Shall I cook both of them?'

Still. It's nice being home.

It's especially nice not having Helen walk in at any moment.

But I do need a place of my own.

I just don't want to live alone. Daisy doesn't really count as other people. I mean, she's lovely. But she can't tell the difference between carpet fluff and food. It's not like we have long conversations.

She does make me laugh though.

Friday, 24th June

Went running today and did four miles!

Amazing!

Even though I haven't trained for ages.

I can't believe it.

I mean, fair enough, it took nearly an hour to run those four miles. But I didn't stop or anything. I just kept running and running.

Saturday, 25th June

Took little Callum out for a walk today.

How does anyone cope with two kids?

The second we got to the woodland path, Callum hurtled off towards the lake.

I ran after him, stroller bumping over sticks and mud, shouting, 'Callum! Callum! You'll ruin your flashing trainers!'

Before I knew it, he'd jumped in the lake.

He splashed around shouting, 'Aye, Aye Captain Birdseye!'

I shouted at him to get out.

Then I offered him a biscuit.

He said, 'I want a Magnum Chocolate Infinity.'

(How has he even HEARD about those? I blame Mum.)

Thank God, an old man with a fishing rod shouted, 'Come on out now sonny, and I'll show you my fishing line and maggots.'

Callum loves anything disgusting.

The man showed Callum a patch of daisies too and picked one for him to take home.

Callum seemed quite interested in the daisy. But as we walked back through the woods he said, 'That flower tasted horrible, Aunty Julesy.'

How am I going to cope when Daisy can run around?

Monday, 27th June

Took Daisy to baby group today.

She did a Mega Poo while we were singing 'head, shoulders, knees and toes'.

It was so massive that it went right through her stripy tights and ra-ra skirt.

I put on her spare outfit, but then she did a second Mega Poo and ruined that too.

Luckily the other mums lent me stuff. Women are so nice.

Tuesday, 28th June

Lunch with Laura and Brandi in London today.

Laura suggested some healthy vegan place.

Brandi wanted to go to Burger King.

We compromised on Subway, although Brandi moaned because there was lettuce in her sandwich.

When I told them my running was going well, Brandi said, 'I can't believe you're doing the fucking *Winter* Marathon. That's *mental*. I mean, even top athletes struggle in those conditions. Don't you remember that Danish runner who slipped on ice at Tower Bridge and broke her coccyx?'

Laura offered to go running with me when she can, although her studying is getting more intense.

Brandi pulled her skinny jeans around her tiny waist and said, 'Maybe I'll run it too. I could do with losing weight. How many miles is it?'

I said, 'Twenty-six.'

'No, it's twenty-seven,' said Laura.

Brandi said, 'Fuck that.'

Wednesday, 29th June

Still feel guilty about not breastfeeding.

It's hard being a mum. I'd wanted Daisy to have the very best of everything, but the milk just didn't happen.

It was like my boobs were broken.

In the hospital, they strapped me to this 1970s pump the size of a Ford Fiesta, but no milk came out.

Mum said, 'Oh sod it, Jules, give her a bottle. You and your sisters had bottles and turned out just fine.'

Althea said I had a lucky escape.

She said, 'Breastfeeding makes you fucking thirsty all the time. You wake up in the middle of the night with weird Indian takeaway BO. Your sheets smell of sour milk. And you're like a sodding human dummy. It's bullshit.'

When I asked her why she was still doing it, she said she hates washing up.

Friday, 1st July

Sadie turned up at Mum and Dad's today.

Brandi opened the door and screamed at her to 'FUCK OFF AND DIE'.

But I said she could come in.

Sadie was SO nervous. Shaking, actually.

Mum took Brandi, Callum and Daisy out into the garden.

The pub was pretty empty, so Sadie and I grabbed a corner booth.

Sadie started gabbling and crying, 'I'm so, so sorry. I know I've fucked up. I've ruined everything. I love you more than anything in the world. You're the only one who ever accepted me. My only true friend. And I did this to you. I know I'm a massive selfish bitch. But all that's going to change. I promise you. I'm having a baby. A baby!' Her eyes were all crazy. 'I need you in my life, Jules. I can't do this alone.'

'You're living with Nick aren't you?' I said. 'Won't *he* be in your life?'

'But I need *adult* support,' she said.

Things aren't going well with Nick apparently because he doesn't pay any bills or flush the toilet.

I told her she and Nick deserved each other.

Her eyes went all wide, and she said, 'I'm not that bad, am I?'

Then she went on about how her boyfriends always fancied me

and it had been nice for once that it was the other way around.

I laughed and said, '*Your* boyfriends fancied me?'

Because she goes out with football players and male models from toothpaste adverts. When she's not sleeping with directors.

She said yes, and that I didn't notice because I was 'too nice'.

Then she said we should go for a drink. Just us two.

'It'll be like old times,' she said. 'Before you had Daisy and everything got messed up.'

I asked how she could move in with Nick. After ruining my wedding and Daisy's life.

She said she thought it was to do with hormones.

Helen has been very nice to her, apparently.

'It just feels good to have a stable home,' she said, with seemingly no understanding that she'd wrecked *my* stable home.

After an hour of banging on about herself, I realised that Sadie is a lost cause. Selfish to the core.

I actually felt a lot better for seeing her. Because now I know I haven't lost a friend after all. Sadie was never my friend to begin with.

When she left, Brandi said, 'You need to unwind. We're hitting some clubs. I've got a silver Lycra dress that you can cram yourself into.'

I pointed out it was only 4 pm.

'So?' Brandi said. 'Mum will babysit.'

Saturday, 2nd July

What is it with babies? It's like they KNOW when you've stayed out late.

After weeks of perfect sleep, Daisy woke up every two hours.

I gave her baby paracetamol, milk, water…everything. But she wasn't having it. Actually spat everything out.

130

Waaaaa! WAAAAAH!

It broke my heart seeing her crying. But at the same time, I REALLY wanted to sleep.

Far too tired to write about me and Brandi's night.

Sleep now.

Sunday, 3rd July

Somehow Brandi and I ended up in the West End the other night. At this fancy nightclub.

Brandi is a bad influence on me. Mums should NOT go clubbing on a Saturday.

I swore I'd only stay until nine, but Brandi made the DJ put on 'Independent Woman', and we ended up dancing on the tables and shouting WOO!

Suddenly it was midnight.

I suppose I did need to let go, really. I've been carrying around a lot of stress.

We got talking to some girls who went to school with the Daltons.

They said 'gorgeous' Zachary is rumoured to have a 'mystery' girlfriend.

It was hysterical when they found out the 'mystery' girl was our sister.

They wanted to see photos of Laura like she was a celebrity or something. And they all said she was 'rather lovely'.

I asked if they knew Alex, and they all said how gorgeous he was too.

When the girls left, Brandi said, 'You always fancied Alex, didn't you? Shame you didn't go for him instead of Nick.'

I told her I hardly had a choice. Alex runs a major hotel dynasty. I'm not heiress material.

'Well, he's always staring at you,' Brandi said.

'What, Alex Dalton?' I said. 'I don't think so.'

But just for a moment, thinking about the lift home from the sports club and the running training and the Champagne at afternoon tea, I thought… Wouldn't that be amazing?

Monday, 4th July
American Independence Day

Mum's done the pub out in American flags and bunting.

She's also made a red, white and blue meringue. It's so big it fits a sparkler for every US state.

It put me in a good mood, hearing Mum whistling *American Pie*.

I was looking pretty tired after a sleepless night with Daisy, but I washed my face, dabbed some cover-up around my eyes and did a Skype link-up with Uncle Ralph in Los Angeles.

Uncle Ralph, Aunty Yasmin and little cousin Lolly were in their giant, sunny house, waving American flags.

Uncle Ralph has done well for himself in the US. He's got a big house on the beach, a blonde lingerie-model wife and one of those American fridge freezers that make ice cubes.

I really thought I was moving forward, re the whole wedding-day horror story.

But Uncle Ralph, who's always pretty blunt, asked me if I'd sold the wedding dress yet to try and make some cash back.

I burst into stupid tears and ran out of the room.

Tuesday, 5th July

Told Althea about crying over Skype.

She suggested I go to baby meditation with her and 'chill out'.

Somehow, Wolfgang broke the Buddhist prayer bowl.

I've never seen a Buddhist monk get angry before.

Wednesday, 6th July

Ugh. One pound heavier this morning. How?

Must remember to weigh myself BEFORE I drink any water or eat breakfast, but AFTER I've been for a poo.

Thursday, 7th July

Trying the Nutri-Soup diet today: soup for every meal, no white carbs, no caffeine, no alcohol, etc.

The plan is to be all puritanical and wonderful and cleanse my body with lovely nourishing vegetables.

By eleven o'clock I was starving.

Lunch was parsnip and ginger soup.

In the book, it looked really nice. A lovely white bowl of bright orange soup with a single parsley leaf floating in it. But after boiling the parsnips, all this scummy stuff appeared. I couldn't be bothered to clean the blender AGAIN. So I just mashed everything up with a fork and got this lumpy brown stuff that looked like a muddy puddle.

Friday, 8th July

What happens to your brain when you have a baby? Simple things, like reading bottle-warmer instructions or finding a complete pair of shoes are completely impossible.

Saturday, 9th July

Brandi is dating someone she met on Facebook called 'Spider'.

She can only meet him at his house because he has an electronic curfew tag on his leg.

Dad asked why she couldn't find a nice man like 'Laura's Zachary'.

Brandi said, 'BLURG! Vomit city! Those two are soooo soppy. Oh, *you* go first, Laura. No, *you* Zachary.'

Mum said it would be lovely if Laura and Zach got married.

Brandi told her to 'get real'. She said, 'Zach knows Prince Harry and walks like he's being held up by string. He's very nice, but he's from fancy land. There's no way he'd marry Laura.'

Mum roared about Laura being drop-dead gorgeous *and* having a university degree.

'They *so* could get married,' she shouted.

Brandi said, 'If you believe in fairy tales.'

Sunday, 10th July

Had the BEST idea today. String! I tied a piece of string to the stroller, and then sat on the sofa and pulled it back and forth.

Brilliant!

Got to watch all of *Downton Abbey* while Daisy slept. Why didn't I think of this before?

Monday, 11th July

Daisy has got wise to the string. She cries and tries to eat it.

Shit.

Tuesday, 12th July

Nick came over today to see Daisy.

It was pretty awkward.

He was supposed to come at 1 pm but didn't turn up until 3 pm.

He'd been rowing with Sadie, apparently. She's being 'pregnant and mental', to use Nick's words, and wasn't happy about him seeing Daisy.

Nick spent twenty minutes chucking Daisy into the air and saying, 'Say Dadda! Say Dadda!' But then Daisy got tired and started grizzling. He panicked and asked what was wrong with her.

I said she was just tired.

'How do you *know* things like that?' he said as if I was some magic oracle.

Then he gave me his puppy-dog eyes and said, 'I miss this, you know. You fix things.'

I remained all aloof and snooty and asked when he'd be coming to see his daughter again.

Nick did his guilty head-scratching thing and said he couldn't commit because of 'Sadie's hormones'. But he'd be in touch soon.

Wednesday, 13th July

Whenever I think of Nick, I get this sort of aching in my chest. It's not exactly that I miss him. But…we were together so long.

It's weird not having him around. It feels a bit like having a leg missing. Except it turns out that leg was kicking me up the backside this whole time…

Thursday, 14th July

The paternity test arrived today.

Mum tried to smash it up with a beer-tap wrench, but I stopped her.

The instructions made the test sound sophisticated, but really it was just a giant cotton bud.

I suppose at least it's over and done with now, and my virtue won't be called into question again.

Saturday, 16th July

Woo!

Mum won the bingo last night and wanted to buy a 'family memory'.

So she's taking us on an all-inclusive holiday.

She told Dad, 'See. It pays to gamble.'

Dad put on his glasses, got out his calculator and added up everything Mum's spent on bingo over the last ten years. It was enough to buy three holidays.

But Mum's mood wouldn't be dampened. She told him his calculator was always getting things wrong, and reminded him of the cherry brandy miscalculation that's still propping open the cellar door.

A holiday will be lovely, but going away with my parents has downsides.

For a start, Mum is so LOUD. And she wears teeny bikinis and fluorescent hot pants.

Also, Mum and Brandi don't believe in sun cream. They think turning slapped-face red proves they've been on holiday. So everyone knows we're British and tries to sell us things.

Dad always reads up on the local culture and bores us to death with a load of pointless facts.

('Did you know that feta is a native Greek cheese?')

Brandi is very happy about the trip. She ran right out to buy spray tan and travel miniatures.

Laura wasn't sure at first. But Mum and Dad are booking an extra suitcase for her study books, so she said OK.

Mum is already talking about holiday clothes. She's packing her Day-Glo pink dress from Cyberdog – the one even Brandi tells her off for wearing.

Dad said, 'Oh that'll look a treat at the disco.'

It's like neither of them knows she's fat.

I suppose it's quite sweet in a way.

Sunday, 17th July

AWESOME news!

Laura told Zach about the holiday, and he'll put us up at any Dalton hotel free of charge. All we have to do is choose a location.

Mum and Brandi spent hours on the Dalton Hotel website 'oohing' at pictures.

They've decided we should go to Dubai because it is 'hot as f***' and we can go on a camel ride.

Dad was happy because he wants to find out more about the history of cinnamon.

I'm a little bit nervous.

I have visions of Mum in pink Lycra, barging into the fancy hotel restaurant and asking if they have tomato ketchup.

Still. We'll have a laugh. And a fancy hotel will be nice.

Last time we went away, it was to an all-inclusive resort, and it was a bad idea.

Mum and Brandi started drinking at 11 am every day.

And Mum got in trouble for filling her handbag with chocolate chip cookies and apple strudel from the buffet.

Monday, 18th July

Googled Dubai today.

Getting a bit nervous. Apparently, Arabic people dress very conservatively.

I tried to tell Mum, but she just laughed and said, 'If you think you're getting me in a one-piece swimsuit you've another think coming. I'm only fifty-five. I'm not dead yet.'

Tuesday, 19th July

Saw a documentary last night about wheat, and now it ALL makes sense.

Wheat is the reason I weigh so much! It's been bloating me and stopped me digesting properly.

Decided to go wheat-free today so that I won't look bloated on holiday.

Althea's going to do it with me. She says she's known for a long time about how damaging wheat can be for the digestive tract. 'Not to mention the fucking *planet*.'

Had a vegetable omelette for breakfast. No toast with it.

Mum was cooking chocolate croissants, but I stayed strong.

11 am

It's amazing how many foods have wheat in them. Even that squeezy yellow mustard.

7 pm

Had a wheat frenzy.

Ate a Warburton's thick-slice cheese sandwich, two packets of Iced Jems (feel bad about that because they're for Callum's packed lunch), a Findus crispy pancake and a bowl of super noodles.

I've decided that denial isn't the way forward. As soon as you can't have something, you want loads of it.

Phoned Althea and she's decided the same thing. She'd just eaten a cream-cheese bagel and a packet of chocolate bourbons.

Flying to Dubai TOMORROW!

Can't find my new swimming costume.

Wednesday, 27th July

Back from holiday.

A week gone, just like that!

Great trip.

Bit of a shame it was Ramadan, and all the restaurants were closed.

Lucky Mum bought enough Pringles and Toblerone from duty-free to see us through.

Spent a lot of time on the beach, being sprayed with Evian water. That was nice.

Daisy ate a lot of sand. She loved playing in the shallows, giggling and slapping the water with her hands.

Wish I'd found my swimming costume before the trip though.

I had to borrow one of Brandi's costumes – a sheeny silver G-string bikini that cut big grooves into my hips and back.

We did manage a trip to the old town, but it got too much – everyone staring at Mum and Brandi in their bikini tops and denim cut-offs.

I tried to tell them about the modest Muslim culture, but neither of them was prepared to risk their suntan (meaning sun*burn*) by covering up.

Zach flew out for a day to see Laura!

Awwwww...

Thursday, 28th July

Unpacking.

It's taking quite a long time.

I shouldn't have packed so much stuff for Daisy – I hardly used any of it. Those baby goggles were a waste of time. And she didn't touch any of the water learning toys, rubber beach books or the water baby walker.

Friday, 29th July

Althea phoned today to moan about her sex life. She's seeing some twenty-year-old guy who lives on a canal boat. But apparently, he has 'no sexual energy' and can only do it once a night.

She asked me how many times Nick and I used to do it.

I told her that after Daisy, our sex life was pretty much non-existent.

Daisy slept in our bed half the time, and Nick was always getting home late.

Then I got to thinking, was that why Nick cheated on me? Because we never had sex?

Althea tutted and said, 'Don't start down that road. You didn't do anything wrong. Nick is a teenager in a grown man's body. He needs to grow the fuck up, and you need to find someone better.'

I told her my weight loss was going well, even after the holiday, and she said, 'If it's making you feel good, then I won't knock it.'

Saturday, 30th July

Real Ale Festival at the pub this weekend.

Dad spent all morning lugging ale kegs around, while Mum drank half pints from each of them.

After lunch, I picked up Nana Joan. She loves the Real Ale Festival.

I set her up in the shade with a pint of cloudy cider and Daisy on her lap. But she wanted to be nearer the band.

So Dad showed Daisy how well his raspberries are growing, while Nana sat by the stage stamping her feet.

When I took Nana home, she was a tiny bit worse for wear, but happy. I had to help her to bed, and got covered in sparkles from her party dress.

Sunday, 31st July

The pub is PACKED.

The whole village is downstairs, drinking beer with funny names like Rat's Piss and Bishop's Foreskin.

Mum tried every one of the thirty on offer. Then she got all shouty and called the vicar a 'massive fucking hypocrite' for drinking on a Sunday.

The vicar started swearing back, and Dad had to intervene. After years of running a pub, he's good at calming people down. Even the vicar, who has major anger-management issues.

Monday, 1st August
Summer Bank Holiday

Mum claimed she wouldn't drink any beer today.

Then Dad put out a new keg out called 'Morning Sparkle', and she said, 'Oh go on, I'll try it then.' And had a big tankard full with her cornflakes.

I've lost six pounds!

It must be the running. Because it's certainly not my diet.

Not after a weekend of beer and sausages.

Tuesday, 2nd August

Read the Ferber controlled-crying book today and realised I could be overfeeding Daisy at night-time. Maybe *that's* why she wakes up so much – because the poor little lamb has too much food in her tummy.

The book says babies need to learn to self-settle. And that parents need to help them self-settle by ignoring them.

Daisy woke at 10 pm as usual and cried for nearly an hour.

For the first three minutes, I was strong and serene (I am teaching her to self-settle). Then I began to panic (what if she's *dying* in there?).

Phoned Althea, and she told me I was being very cruel, and that Daisy was just expressing herself.

Then I phoned Laura, who told me to take it ten minutes at a time.

After three more minutes, I cracked and went in to cuddle her.

She howled, even more, when I left. It actually turned into ear-splitting screams.

So I fed her. And then she *still* wouldn't stop crying.

I thought, 'Oh my God, I've broken her! Now she'll *never* stop crying!'

She did, eventually. After half an hour of shushing and rocking. At which point I was way too stressed to sleep.

I kept going over and over the Ferber technique in my head like a madwoman. Then I obsessively Googled 'controlled crying' and read a load of mums who said it didn't work. Although plenty more said it worked brilliantly.

I just want to do what's best. But there are a million different opinions on what 'best' is.

Why are there no answers! No instruction manuals! Why are babies so confusing?

Wednesday, 3rd August

Just saw Nick with Sadie in Great Oakley.

Feel violated, like they've broken some unspoken pact.

Great Oakley is MY place. They should stay in London.

They were having lunch with Helen, and holding hands over the table.

It's bad enough knowing they're living together in London. But to have them flaunting their relationship on my own doorstep...

They were even brazen enough to be on the patio outside, where everyone walks past. It's like they wanted to be seen.

I know they saw me because they suddenly got really interested in their salads.

I walked past, head held high.

Dignity, dignity, dignity.

Then I saw Nick's car parked across the street and squirted one of Daisy's apple and banana pouches all over the windscreen.

Ha ha ha!

Thursday, 4th August

Lost four more pounds!

Whoop whoop!

I can never get my head around weight loss. It seems to me the weeks I'm really good, I don't lose much weight at all. And when I let the apron strings loose…poof! It all comes falling off.

Laura reckons it's the running.

And she's probably right – it can't be what I'm eating.

After I saw Nick and Sadie at the restaurant, Mum and I shared a box of Milk Tray, then ordered Domino's pizza.

I've been doing crazy over-thinking since I saw them.

I guess deep down I've always expected Nick and Sadie to split up.

But what if they stay together? What if he's a proper father to her baby and not to Daisy?

Helen must be over the moon. For all Sadie's faults, she comes from the 'right background'. She knows about cutlery. And sitting up straight. And I doubt she'd ever let a dog get hold of a shitty nappy.

Friday, 5th August

Dad's birthday.

He said he didn't want any fuss, but Mum arranged a surprise party.

It's not much of a surprise these days since Mum does it every year. But Dad was as delighted as ever, hugging all of us and saying he's the luckiest man in the world.

Dad is easy to buy presents for. He likes anything practical, so I gave him a special rack for arranging his spanners.

He got all teary and kept saying, 'How did you know? How did you know?'

Mum gave everyone at the pub shots of her homemade butterscotch vodka to 'get the party started'.

I only drank fizzy water, though. I can't drink much these days. Not now Daisy is moving around. She's a little demolition machine. It takes her less than a minute to unwind a whole toilet roll or pull the bin over and eat whatever she finds inside.

Saturday, 6th August

Daisy would NOT nap today.

I spent twenty minutes rocking and shaking her, swaying back and forth, humming 'Like a Virgin' and making sea noises in her ear.

Mum kept popping her head into the bedroom, asking if I 'had everything under control'. So I kept having to start all the shushing and rocking all over again.

Monday, 8th August

Got a call from our solicitor, Ted Grunty, today.

The paternity results are back. They show Nick is Daisy's dad.

Of course.

'Fancy Nick putting you through all this,' Ted said.

I told him I didn't care any more. Then I burst into tears and asked why Nick was doing this.

Stupid pregnancy hormones. Shouldn't they be gone by now?

Tuesday, 9th August

Visited Dr Slaughter today for my maternity health check-up.

He ranted about Nick and what a 'nasty piece of work' he was.

The whole village thinks so, apparently.

'If it makes you feel any better,' Dr Slaughter said, 'Nick was in here three weeks ago, and his blood pressure was through the roof.'

Then he ranted about Mum 'not respecting' her diabetes – apparently, he saw her in Tesco's, loading up with sugary two-for-ones.

I asked Doctor Slaughter whether he'd seen Sadie recently.

He said no. Her family are paying for private care.

I hope she gets varicose veins. And haemorrhoids. Really massive haemorrhoids.

Wednesday, 10th August

Mum and Dad's wedding anniversary.

I found Dad in the garden with a big mug of tea this morning, flicking through his wedding photos.

He was looking adoringly at all the pictures of Mum, his eyes all misty and happy.

Mum and Dad's wedding photos are postcard-sized and printed at the Kodak booth. They didn't go in for 'all this professional-photographer nonsense'.

In fact, their whole wedding was a low-key affair. They spent thirty pounds on sausage rolls and a beer keg and that was it.

In the pictures, everyone is staring at Mum's boobs. Dad, the vicar...everyone.

But I suppose it was the Eighties. See-through lace and lots of cleavage were the fashion in those days.

Thursday, 11th August

Didn't I just cut Daisy's finger and toenails yesterday? They've already reached slasher proportions.

How do people cope with three children? That's sixty finger and toenails, not even counting your own.

Mum offered to help me, but I don't trust her with a pair of scissors.

She can't even cut a loaf of bread straight.

The Oakley Arms is famous for its thick cheese sandwiches.

Friday, 12th August

Mum and Dad drove me to Aldi today because (yet again) my car wouldn't start.

Dad drove there; Mum drove back.

Dad drove 5 mph under the speed limit, put his face right up against the windscreen and cut the engine out to save petrol going down hills.

Mum sped up at amber lights, beeped the horn constantly and ate M&Ms/swigged Gaviscon while overtaking vehicles she deemed 'too fucking slow'.

Saturday, 13th August

Daisy's toes are poking holes through her socks.

Nick really does need to start contributing to his daughter.

I left a humiliating message on his answer machine asking for cash.

Half an hour later, I got a call from Penny Castle (his solicitor) asking me to 'desist any financial requests until after the maintenance hearing.'

Penny lives in Great Oakley too. In a three-storey townhouse with two white cats. She shouts at the kids in legal speak, 'Please REMOVE your ball from the perimeter of my property ...'

I told her that I couldn't stop Daisy growing while we waited for the hearing. 'She needs clothes now,' I said. 'Not in six months' time.'

'Perhaps you could borrow the money from a family member,' she suggested. 'I'm sure your solicitor would be happy to draw up a loan agreement.'

I asked her what the legal speak for 'fuck off' was. Then I hung up.

Didn't really want to do Oxford Street shopping on my own, but Laura was studying, and Brandi was doing her manicure exam.

Getting the tube with Daisy was no fun at all. No one helps you on the steps like they do in the village.

In Great Oakley, you can hardly walk down the street without someone cooing over your baby. But in London, it's like everyone is annoyed with you.

I probably shouldn't have used the big Silver Cross baby carriage with the massive wheels.

It was Mum's idea. She told me I'd have more room for the shopping.

She was right. But it's been in the garage since Brandi was a baby. So it was full of spider's egg sacs, and the wheels squeaked.

Mum said, 'No one will get in your way pushing *that* beast along,' adding that it was 'the Rolls-Royce' of baby carriages, and could 'fit four babies and a pound of potatoes'.

I tried Mothercare first, but there was nothing on sale. And I need to economise.

So I went to Primark.

I've always wondered why half the clothes in Primark are on the floor.

Now I know.

It's because women with ridiculously huge Silver Cross baby carriages push their way through the aisles and knock everything off the hangers.

They didn't have anything in Daisy's size – it had all sold out.

So I decided to go back to Mothercare.

Halfway back down Oxford Street, I realised I'd accidentally shoplifted three pairs of neon socks. They were hanging off different parts of the stroller.

Went all the way back to Primark to hand them in.

Security asked me why I'd come back since I 'got away with it'.

Wandered down New Bond Street past all the designer shops.

Saw this AMAZING brown tote bag that Laura would just LOVE for Christmas.

Then a car pulled up beside me.

I started to apologise for the size of the baby carriage and how it wouldn't all fit on the pavement.

But then I shut up because Alex Dalton was in the car.

He was wearing a black suit and glaring at me.

'We saw you walking,' said Alex. 'Can we give you a lift?'

His little sister Jemima was in the back.

I nodded at the baby carriage and said, 'Thanks, but this was made in the days of horses and carts. I don't think it'll fit in your car.'

'We'll walk you then,' said Alex. 'Jemima could do with the fresh air.' Then he pulled the car up on the curb.

'You've parked on a double yellow line again,' I said.

Alex pointed out that we were, in fact, a few feet from a Dalton Hotel, which meant he could park freely.

'The valet will take my car if it's still there in an hour,' he added.

I was torn between disapproval (rich people can park wherever they like) and being massively impressed (imagine being able to park ALL over central London!).

Jemima clip-clopped out of the car wearing a little madam outfit of blue jeans, flat knee-high riding boots, a lovely navy blue sweater and a jaunty little pink satchel slung across her body. Utterly adorable.

Alex asked if I was enjoying London.

I told him I hadn't really enjoyed London since I had Daisy.

Alex said he hated cities too.

'But aren't all your hotels in cities?' I said.

'Yes,' he said. 'I like the hotels. Just not the cities.'

Alex asked if I was going inside the bag shop.

'We're off to Mothercare actually,' I said, in a silly, high voice.

Jemima said, 'Oh we'd *love* to go with you.' Then she grabbed my hand and said I'd have to show her the way.

Alex walked beside us, hands in his trouser pockets, looking all serious.

When we got to Mothercare, Alex frowned at all the kids bouncing in the cots.

Jemima said, 'Can I –'

'No,' said Alex.

'But that little boy –'

'He shouldn't have that on his head AT ALL,' Alex barked. 'If you must go and play, there's a toy kitchen over there.'

Jemima scampered off and left Alex and me alone.

Daisy was crying a bit, so Alex got her out of the baby carriage.

149

'You're clever, that's the problem,' he told her. 'You're trying to take this all in. And giving yourself a headache.'

Daisy stopped crying and chewed his shirt collar.

I was impressed.

'I remember what Jemima was like,' said Alex, 'when she was little. She hated too much stimulation.' Then he said, 'I trust Nick Spencer is paying for this shopping trip.'

'Why do you always call him by his full name?' I asked.

'To set him apart from the Nicks I actually like,' Alex said.

Then he asked me who my solicitor was, and I told him it was Ted Grunty.

'Christ,' said Alex. 'The man who forged those planning applications?'

I told him that was never proved. Then Alex asked me how my training was going.

I said, slowly.

'Hopefully, you'll be able to keep up with me,' said Alex, his eyes crinkling into a smile.

I felt myself smile back.

Then Jemima decided to show us all the things she'd written on a little toy chalkboard.

I 'oohed' at her letters.

'They're not letters,' she announced. 'They're words. Look, 'ECZEMA'. And 'ARCHITECT'. Are you coming to afternoon tea with us?'

'Yes she is,' said Alex.

I tried to protest. I said I didn't want to interrupt their family time, and anyway I was meeting Laura in a few hours.

But Alex said, 'Jemima wants you to come and so do I.' Then he put Daisy in the baby carriage and said, 'Let me push that behemoth for you.'

And off we went.

We had afternoon tea at the Mayfair Dalton Hotel.

The fanciest hotel in all of London.

I've never seen anything like it.

I tried not to stare at the gold cherubs and silk walls, but I don't think I quite managed it because the bellboy said, 'Do mind the rug, madam.'

Daisy bounced up and down, trying to grab the antique oil paintings.

Jemima was, of course, a perfect little lady. Gliding through reception to the tearoom, smiling serenely at the waiting staff.

One of Jemima's school friends was having afternoon tea (how the other half live!), and Jemima wanted to sit with her.

'Do we know her family?' Alex asked.

Jemima had to give a long, complicated description of her friend's parents.

I asked Alex why Jemima needed cross-examination to sit with a little girl in a pristine sailor's dress, eating sandwiches with a knife and fork.

'That's just how we do things in our family,' he said.

We then ended up in the very weird position of talking about Alex's family and his upbringing.

He's not half as spoiled as I thought. He had a pretty tough childhood, actually. Boarding school. A lot of studying. No toys unless they were earned. I mean, it's not as if he went hungry or anything. But it didn't sound like a lot of fun.

Daisy fell asleep on my lap, thank God.

Alex was very gentlemanly and had the waiter run out to get me a straw for my cup of tea, so I didn't wake her.

And Daisy didn't wake – not even when I dropped a pistachio macaroon on her head.

When I burned my mouth drinking tea through the straw, Alex said, 'Perhaps Champagne would be better.' And ordered a bottle.

He knew all the staff by name and stuff about their lives and their families. And he didn't once seem uncomfortable to be stuck with me. All in all, it was an unexpectedly lovely afternoon.

At one point I said, 'Your staff in the Bond Street Dalton must get jealous. Because you know everyone's name here.'

He said he knew the names of his staff in every hotel he owned.

I was a bit blown away by that.

'You know your sisters' names, don't you?' said Alex. 'The people working in my hotels are my family too.'

Which I thought was pretty lovely.

We ended up talking about the Dalton New Year's Ball, and he asked me how I liked them since I'd been to every single one since they started.

I was a bit taken aback that he'd noticed.

'Of course I noticed,' he said. 'I notice you every year. Always have done. Why wouldn't I?'

'We know each other,' I said, 'but it's not like we're *friends*, friends.'

'You don't think we're friends?' he asked. 'What about when we were children?'

'Maybe as kids,' I said. 'But before the training this year…we didn't see much of each other, did we?'

I didn't tell Alex that I remembered all those summers together as kids. Or that us girls watched him as teenagers. That we giggled about tall, dark and handsome Alex Dalton.

Alex said, 'I've always seen you as a friend.'

We talked a bit more about the charity balls, and I asked him what the theme would be for this New Year.

He said his mother hadn't decided yet, but he was sure another humiliating auction would take place.

I blushed bright red.

Did he know I only got old-man bids this year? He wasn't in the room, but did someone tell him?

Then Alex said, 'Look, if you're going up against the Jolly-Piggott's', you really do need a decent solicitor.'

I said that Ted was fine. An old family friend.

Alex said something about misplaced loyalty. Then he said, 'Doesn't your daughter deserve the best?'

We looked at Daisy sleeping on my chest.

I said that Ted would do his best for us. Better than some super-solicitor we hardly knew. He'd go to the ends of the earth. He'd known me since I was a baby.

Then Alex said I should take Nick for every penny. He'd seen Nick, pre-wedding, in the City – bar-hopping and flirting with women. He said it was disgusting with a baby at home. And he wished he'd told me.

I told him I already knew Nick bar-hopped and flirted with women. I just didn't know he was sleeping with my bridesmaid.

Then it suddenly hit me that Sadie's baby will be Daisy's half-sibling, and felt like I was going to be sick.

I must have gone a bit white, because Alex said, 'Are you cold? We can get the fire lit. Let me take Daisy.'

But I just mumbled something about feeling ill and having a lot on my mind. I honestly thought I was going to throw up. I thanked Alex for a lovely afternoon and ran out like Cinderella at midnight.

He must think I'm such an idiot.

All I could think, wandering around London, was that Nick never loved me. All those years with him and he never even knew my favourite colour.

And yet Alex has noticed me at every Dalton ball I've ever attended.

Sunday, 14th August

Took Laura out for lunch to apologise for standing her up yesterday.

Planned to take her to Jamie's Italian, but Daisy started howling and WOULD NOT stop. So we ended up at Kentucky Fried Chicken where they have bottle warmers.

As soon as Daisy calmed down, I started blubbing. Going on about how Nick never loved me and I missed what was right in front of my face.

Laura got me a bargain bucket to drown my sorrows.

I gave Daisy a drumstick, then panicked because it was full of salt.

Laura reminded me that Mum gave us KFC when we were babies. And McDonald's too – there's a baby picture of me in a Ronald McDonald highchair dipping fries into a strawberry milkshake.

I told Laura about the afternoon tea with Alex. How nice it was, but what a twat I made of myself. Then I asked her how it was going with Zach.

She admitted she hadn't heard from him in a while. He's on a skiing trip. But there was some *Hello* picture of him at a ski lodge party with some girl.

'It's probably nothing,' she said. 'But, then again...'

We bought a copy of *Hello* so we could scrutinise the picture.

I had to admit the girl was pretty, but not in Laura's league.

'Zach doesn't care about pretty,' Laura insisted. 'He's not like that.'

After we'd looked at all the arm angles and Googled 'body language', we decided the picture was perfectly innocent.

'Just a friend at a party,' I said.

'Yes,' said Laura. 'But...I still wish I'd never seen that picture.'

Monday, 15th August

Mum and Dad went to IKEA today to buy a wardrobe.

They ended up buying half the shop.

Mum bought neon tea towels, a doormat with pink feet on it, hooks shaped like dogs wagging their tails and a load of meatballs for the freezer.

Dad bought drawer tidies, Tupperware and plastic boxes for all his screws.

Mum's added meatballs to the pub specials menu.

Tuesday, 16th August

Mum and Dad have spent all day trying to put together the IKEA wardrobe.

It's the first time I've heard Dad swear in years.

Mum was storming around the place shouting, 'If I ever see another Allen key, I'm going to shove it up someone's backside.'

She's taken meatballs off the pub menu.

Wednesday, 17th August

Daisy has started waking up again at night.

I know I should try and ignore her and teach her to settle herself.

But it's like there are two people in my head, arguing with each other. And the one shouting SHE COULD BE HUNGRY! always wins.

Thursday, 18th August

Daisy slept for twelve hours straight!

I woke up at five, worrying that she'd died.

Then I spent the next two hours going back and forth, checking her breathing.

She woke up at seven, all happy and well-rested.

I was red-eyed and irritable, just like always.

Friday, 19th August

Mum and Callum's birthday today.

Everyone says it's a coincidence that they were born on the same day, but I think God knows they're kindred spirits.

Mum celebrated by buying a giant trampoline for the garden.

It's the size of a swimming pool and takes Callum a full minute to bounce from one side to the other.

I'm a bit worried Callum might break a limb. I read somewhere that trampolines cause lots of childhood accidents these days. And Callum is one of those kids who leaps first and looks later.

I bought Mum a foot of hazelnut chocolate as a birthday present.

I used to buy her expensive bath products and lovely things for the home. But she always gives them straight to charity.

Chocolate is the only thing I can guarantee she'll be delighted by every time.

Gave Callum school things – pencil case, pencils etc. But he looked a bit disappointed, so I think next year I'll buy him a violent computer game.

Saturday, 20th August

Mum has broken her wrist on the trampoline.

Doctor Slaughter came round on an emergency visit. He looked in the fridge and told Mum off for having a salad drawer full of fun-size chocolate. Then he told her she'd have to go to hospital and wait in line.

Mum said she and Dad pay five times more taxes than most people AND have private healthcare, so she shouldn't have to wait.

Dr Slaughter said private health insurance didn't cover stupidity.

Sunday, 21st August

I will never understand Daisy's eating habits.

The only thing she'll eat off a spoon is bananas, porridge and angel delight (that last one is Mum's fault).

And yet she roams around the house eating leaves, stones, old dried-up hard food and bits of carpet fluff. She even tries to grab her nappy and eat it while I'm changing her.

How did human beings ever evolve from caves?

Monday, 22nd August

9 am

I've lost four more pounds! WOOOOOOO!

I'm going to celebrate with an Options Hot Chocolate drink, exotic mint flavour.

10 am

Exotic mint flavour tastes like muddy toothpaste. Even Daisy didn't like it. She made a face and spat it down her little ballerina outfit.

4 pm

Just got back from 'Little Tiddles Play Time' at the village hall.

Daisy tried to eat the big crinkly blanket all the babies were supposed to lie on.

Then, while I was changing her, she grabbed the nappy and hurled it across the room.

I used two packs of wet wipes to clean up, saying 'sorry, sorry' the whole time.

The woman who ran the group said, 'It's fine.' But I could tell she was annoyed. She was muttering about the big crinkly blanket being dry-clean only.

Tuesday, 23rd August

Ran all the way around the village three times today.

And *then* I ran along the trail into the woods, past the river and all the birds and boats.

I kept thinking about Alex – wondering if I'd bump into him.

But I didn't see him today.

I bet he'll make a really good time in the marathon.

Me – I just want to finish. But the more I run, the more I'm thinking… Maybe I will finish. Maybe I will.

It will get harder as the weather gets colder, though. I remember running in January – the chilly air really hurt my chest.

Wednesday, 24th August

A funny day today. Alex Dalton's solicitor called.

His name is Jeremy Samuels. He's one of those forthright, shouty men who make you hold the phone a little bit away from your ear.

'Alex said I should put my foot down with you,' he shouted. 'He said you were being very silly and saying you wanted to use some local fellow. But he's decided it's me you should be using, and he will foot the bill. Who is this local fellow, anyway?'

I told him it was Ted Grunty.

'Good Lord!' he yelled. 'The chap who forged all those signatures?'

Then he said, 'I'll have a word with Ted. He'll understand. All's fair in love and law. Then we'll go about getting you a settlement. Alex says you're a lovely girl – you deserve a decent amount.'

A lovely girl!

Did Alex really say that about me?

Amazing!

Thursday, 25th August

Althea and I met at the pottery café again today.

We probably should have learned our lesson from last time. Wolfgang and breakable things don't mix.

Within three minutes, he'd smashed a plate with baby handprints on it and a soup mug that said, 'I love you, Daddy'.

When everyone turned to stare, Althea snapped, 'He's just expressing himself. Why can't you give him the freedom to be himself too? I'll pay for the fucking breakages.'

Althea never worries about money. Wolfgang's dad is a famous keyboard player and earns loads in royalties. Which means Althea earns loads in maintenance.

They have a very open-minded relationship, are still legally married and sleep together sometimes.

I told Althea about the Jeremy Samuels phone call.

'Fucking hell,' she said. 'That's a big deal. Why would Alex Dalton go and do something like that?'

I told her I didn't know, but that Alex had said something about feeling responsible. Because he'd seen Nick flirting and bar-hopping.

'Rubbish,' said Althea. 'It's because he likes you.'

'Alex Dalton?' I said. 'I don't think so.'

But then Althea said that Alex was always watching me.

I told her that glaring and watching weren't the same thing.

Friday, 26th August

10 am

Supermarket shopping.

Daisy hates my cooking these days. She loves ready-made vegetable pouch meals, but I just feel like she should be eating something homemade.

Have found a website showing lots of delicious baby recipes, and am determined to cook something she likes.

11 am

Sometimes I miss London.

Our village co-op supermarket doesn't sell *anything*.

It had sold out of all fresh vegetables (except a few dirty carrots) and didn't stock tofu or lentils.

It had a massive range of Angel Delight (in flavours I never even heard of. Mint? Treacle?), Dream Topping and basically everything you need to make a trifle. It even sold ready-made trifles in the fridge section. But I didn't want trifle. I wanted healthy baby food.

I asked Pauline at the checkout when there'd be any fresh veg coming in.

She said, 'Oh Lord knows. I always shop at Tesco.'

Saturday, 27th August

Went to Tesco.

Got ingredients.

Cooked and pureed Lentil Savoury Bake for Daisy's tea.

I made enough for the whole week and froze it in those little weaning pots.

Sunday, 28th August

Daisy wouldn't eat the Lentil Savoury. She spat it out then made retching noises at the spoon.

Mum tried to feed her too.

'Open up, you fussy monkey,' she barked. 'Your mum's spent all day cooking this healthy crap.'

When Daisy refused, Mum said, 'Well I can't say I blame her. It looks like something you'd find in her nappy. Why don't you give her one of those pouch meals?'

I finally cracked and gave Daisy a pouch of Banana Breakfast.

She ate the whole lot in under a minute, making smacking noises and sucking hopefully at the empty packet.

I don't want to throw away all my carefully prepared Lentil Savoury. But at the same time, it does look disgusting.

I'll throw it out tomorrow.

Monday, 29th August
Summer Bank Holiday

Mum threw out my Lentil Savoury Bake.

I am absolutely furious!

She'd just come back from Iceland (to buy frozen pizzas, mini Kievs and chicken nuggets 'for Callum' – but she eats them too) and needed to make room in the freezer.

I need to start thinking about getting my own place. It's impossible to eat healthily here.

Mum has this special popcorn recipe where she can get a whole pack of butter into the pan.

Tuesday, 30th August

Got a mega-period today. Ten months without any period at all and then it's like ten months at once.

Lucky I didn't throw out those jumbo sanitary towels.

I'd forgotten about periods. That, at least, was one good thing about being pregnant.

Wednesday, 31st August

Althea phoned today. She'd seen Nick and Sadie shopping in Harrods.

Apparently, they were at the oyster bar drinking Champagne.

Sadie looked quite pregnant, but still thin apparently.

I was really pissed off. I'd hoped that Sadie would have puffed up like a sumo wrestler by now. And Nick never took me to fancy places like Harrods.

Apparently, Althea asked Nick (in a big loud voice) if he'd paid any child support yet.

She's a good friend.

But then Wolfgang got 'collared' by a security guard, and she had to leave.

The staff at Harrods don't share Althea's view about freedom of expression.

Thursday, 1st September

Little Callum's first settling-in day at school today.

The kids were allowed to wear 'whatever they felt comfortable in', so Callum chose his Spiderman costume and Mum's feather boa.

He clung to our hands the whole way to the school.

It was hard leaving him.

He just looked so little.

But then he got in a fight with another boy in the playground, so we knew he'd be OK.

Saturday, 3rd September

Some nights I think I can run forever. And some nights I can barely do ten minutes without hating it and swearing to myself and wishing I'd never promised Daisy I'd do the marathon.

Tonight was one of those nights. I only managed one jog around the village once, then staggered home.

Sunday, 4th September

Brandi cooked the family tea tonight, in honour of Callum's first day at school tomorrow. Also, she's practising because she has a crush on the man who hosts Master Chef. She did us nachos with squeezy cheese sauce and salsa – all from jars and packets.

For dessert, she made us a tower of ginger-nut biscuits stuck together with squirty cream.

Mum and Callum loved it. Although Callum was bouncing off the walls by the end. We sent him outside to jump on the trampoline before bed.

Mum asked if I'd heard anything about Nick paying maintenance.

I said I hadn't, but told her about my new solicitor courtesy of Alex Dalton.

Everyone was impressed.

'Alex must like you,' Mum decided.

I told her I wasn't in his league.

Mum hefted her boobs up in her Lycra bodysuit and said, 'Men don't care about leagues. They care about sex, beer and sport. In that order.'

Dad frowned and said, 'What about wildlife? And star constellations? And die-cast models?'

Mum said, 'All men except your father.'

Monday, 5th September

Little Callum started school today. I can't believe it. He looked so grown up in his uniform. Today is his first full day.

Brandi held it together, but I had tears in my eyes. It's true – they grow up so fast.

Somehow, Callum managed to vandalise his uniform before he'd even got to the school gate.

Brandi was really proud. 'He's such a little dude.'

It was really strange going back to Oakley Primary as an adult. Everything looked tiny.

I remember my first day at school so well. Our teacher, Mrs Bat, had an attack of nerves and forgot the alphabet.

Callum went tearing across the playground and into the classroom without a backwards glance.

We saw him through the classroom window, charming a little blonde girl. Then he chivalrously pushed another boy off the computer so the girl could have a turn.

I think it's safe to say he'll be fine.

That's Callum – he takes life in his stride.

Brandi was upset on the walk home. 'One day, he won't need me any more,' she sobbed. 'Not today. But one day.'

Weird to think of Callum needing anyone. If there were a nuclear war, the rest of us would die, but Callum would be all right somehow. He's the toughest little kid I know.

Wednesday, 7th September

It's amazing, but tonight I really loved running.

And I can run for ages. I'm still pretty slow. But that's OK. It's not as if I'm planning on *winning* the marathon.

I feel so much lighter after I've run. I don't just mean weight-wise. I mean…just in my heart.

Thursday, 8th September

Daisy had a cold today and WOULD NOT NAP.

Rocked, patted, jiggled and eventually shouted. Nothing worked. In the end, I bundled Daisy in the stroller and went for a run around the village.

When I got back, she still hadn't fallen asleep. But I had managed to run six miles.

Result!

Friday, 9th September

It poured with rain today, so I took Daisy to the village library.

They were doing a 'Reading Rocks!' event, and loads of the village kids were there – including Jemima Dalton.

She is such a sweet, polite little girl. She said, 'So nice to see you again,' then helped Daisy find a book to chew.

Jemima couldn't take part in the reading event because she'd already read all the books in the library.

I apologised for rushing off the other day and asked her to thank Alex again for the afternoon tea.

'Thank him yourself,' she said. 'He's right behind you.'

I jumped out of my skin, and Jemima laughed and said, 'Only joking. But he'll be coming soon. You like him, don't you?'

'He's a very nice man,' I said.

She gave me a knowing smile.

I pretended I needed to change Daisy's nappy, then sprinted to the toilet, splashed a load of water on my face and wiped yesterday's mascara from under my eyes.

I casually returned and carried on reading to Daisy. But I kept checking the door to see if Alex was coming.

A few minutes later, Alex arrived.

I pretended to be surprised to see him.

Jemima said, 'But I just told you he was coming.'

I went all red.

Alex knelt down to blow a raspberry on Daisy's stomach, and asked me if Jeremy Samuels had been in touch.

I said I'd been meaning to thank him and told him he was right about me needing good representation.

'I usually am right about things,' said Alex, adding that he'd seen me running around the village and that my form was improving.

I wanted to ask which day he'd seen me.

Was it Monday, when I'd been wearing Laura's sleek, black running gear and powering along swigging from a runner's water bottle?

Or Wednesday, when I was staggering along in stained elephant trousers, panting like an old horse and muttering, 'I fucking hate running'?

I told Alex that the colder the weather, the less faith I had in myself to finish the marathon.

'Isn't it about time I started training you again?' Alex asked.

I felt myself nodding vigorously.

Alex gave me that wry smile and said he'd come by my parents' house at 8 pm tomorrow.

'Are you sure you don't mind?' I said. 'Coming right into the village…away from the fancy bit.'

'Perhaps I'm not as fancy as you think,' said Alex.

Then he marched outside to his silver Rolls Royce.

Saturday, 10th September

7 pm

Daisy in bed.

Alex is coming over in an hour.

What the fuck am I going to wear??!!!

Laura and all her runner robot Lycra are in London. And there's no point asking Mum or Brandi for clothes. Unless I want to go jogging in high heels, neon and seven layers of spray tan.

Why oh why didn't I think of this before, when the shops were open?

At the moment, my options are:

♦ Nick's old Abercrombie and Fitch T-shirt. Bad memories there. And anyway, it makes me look fat.

♦ Leggings with big saggy knees.

♦ Dad's bright white tennis kit from 1980 something.

I seriously need to update my wardrobe.

I'm in this horrible no man's land where I don't have the figure for tight T-shirts that show my tummy when I lift my arms (and I STILL have that weird brown pregnancy line under my belly button. Will it EVER go?), but I'm too young to wear big billowy Monsoon tops with flowers all over them.

7.50 pm

Decided that the best thing to wear is Dad's tennis kit. It's the cleanest, anyway.

Oh, fuck it – the doorbell.

That must be Alex.

Sunday, 11th September

Seeing Alex on the doorstep yesterday was…well, just weird. Good weird, but weird nonetheless.

I mean, I've seen him loads of times around the village. But actually calling at the back door where the family come in…

He was all silent assassin again – arms crossed, black T-shirt and dark grey joggers. Very serious-looking.

'Have you come to repossess the house?' I said.

He gave his quirky little smile and said, 'Did you think we were playing tennis?'

I told him my running gear was in the wash and said I hoped I looked OK.

'You look perfect,' he said. So I forgave him instantly.

Then he asked about Daisy and my parents. And whether the pub was doing well.

I said yes. It's the only pub in the village. So it always does well.

We went jogging along the waterfront.

I kept saying, 'Go ahead if you need to. I don't want to slow you down.'

But he stayed by my side the whole time. Even though it was obvious, he could go much faster.

We jogged for over an hour, not really saying much. Well – I couldn't say much, I was too busy wheezing.

If Alex hadn't been there, I'd have stopped after ten minutes. I so wasn't up for running in the dark and cold. But I couldn't stop with him there. It would have been too embarrassing. So on I went. And weirdly, as soon as I stopped thinking that I *could* stop, it got easier.

When we got back to the Oakley Arms I was all flushed and sweaty – my hair all frizzy around my face.

I thanked Alex for the run, and he said, 'I'll be here again tomorrow. Same time. We'll do ten miles. Make sure you're ready.'

Monday, 12th September

Another run with Alex last night. We did ten miles. Just like he said. Didn't talk much. But it was nice. Just running together.

Tuesday, 13th September

The whole village is talking about Alex and me.

I'm trying to make out like it's no big deal. But secretly I'm MEGA happy.

I get butterflies in my stomach whenever Alex calls at the pub.

And also, I'm running further than ever.

Friday, 16th September

Alex and I went running EVERY night this week.

EVERY NIGHT!

At times it's hideous.

Alex is incredibly strict and doesn't go easy on me.

'Come on!' he barks, as he bounds around me. 'Keep up! Push yourself. PUSH yourself!'

But I have to admit we're getting amazing results. I've run further and faster than ever. There are definitely times when I want to kill Alex and myself. But they're getting fewer.

I've been so full of energy in the day that I've even run with the stroller sometimes. Just on a whim. Daisy always looks a bit shocked. Like I'm shoplifting her or something.

Saturday, 17th September

Helen phoned today.

She'd heard about Alex and me running around the village.

'You're barely out of your wedding gown,' she said, 'and you're out in public with another man.'

I told her that since Nick got my bridesmaid pregnant, I could go out with whomever I liked.

'Nobody knows Sadie was *with* Nicholas prior to the wedding. Or that she was pregnant so soon after. And I think it best we keep that on a low level. No sense in causing a scandal.'

God!

'When Sadie has the baby it won't be hard to work it out, will it?' I shouted.

I could almost feel Helen wince down the phone. 'There's *no* need to swear.'

And then she said how important Nick's reputation was in his *profession*.

'He's not a priest, Helen,' I said, 'he's an actor. A bit of scandal might do his career some good.'

'BUT IT WOULDN'T DO ME ANY GOOD!' she snapped.

Then she talked about men being men, and said Nick's father had been the same.

I said Nick's dad sounded like a bastard.

She got annoyed then and threatened to 'end this conversation if you can't be a grown-up'.

I told her that since she phoned me, I didn't mind in the slightest if she ended the conversation. In fact, I'd prefer it if she didn't phone me up and tell me what to do.

I said, 'I'm not engaged to your son any more. I'm not living in your apartment any more. And I don't have to be nice to you any more. So if I want to go jogging with Alex Dalton, I bloody well will.'

'You're only doing this to get at Nicholas, aren't you?' she said.

'Oh get a life, Helen,' I shouted and hung up.

Mum, Dad and Brandi gave me a round of applause.

Callum said, 'Who was *that* headache?'

He sounds so much like Brandi sometimes.

'The evil stepmother,' said Mum.

'Did she ask about Daisy?' said Dad.

'No,' I said. 'Not once.'

Sunday, 18th September

HORRIBLE thing happened with Callum this morning.

Brandi and I were in Mum and Dad's living room, when suddenly Callum's Darth Vader costume caught on fire.

His black cape was literally a ball of flame.

I managed to throw Callum to the ground and roll on top of him while holding Daisy aloft in the other hand.

I thought I was crap at yoga, but it turns out I'm pretty bendy in an emergency.

Brandi was quick too. She shook up a bottle of Coca-Cola and used it like a fire extinguisher.

Luckily Callum was just fine. He has nine lives, that kid.

We both shouted at Callum for the next half an hour. It turns out he'd found an old lighter in the garden.

Brandi was really upset with herself for letting Callum get the lighter. But it wasn't her fault. Callum had hidden it under his Darth Vader armour.

Monday, 19th September

Apparently, Alex and I running together is now *officially* the gossip of the village.

This is according to Mum, who is almost certainly the one spreading it.

Let them talk.

It's perfectly innocent, much as I wish it weren't.

While we were running last night, I told Alex I'd updated my Facebook status to 'single'.

'God, is that what Facebook is all about?' he said. 'Telling everyone whether you're in a relationship or not?'

It turns out HE'S NOT ON FACEBOOK!

I always wondered why I could never find him. (Yes – I did try to cyberstalk him when I was younger.)

Then he said I was 'far too good for Nicholas Spencer'.

My knees go all weak when he looks right at me. Which isn't all that good when I'm running.

Tuesday, 20th September

Did a 'bad mother' thing today.

Needed to get the forms filled in for all the legal stuff with Nick.

Put Daisy on her baby gym while I was doing it, thinking she'd be safe. But somehow she managed to pull my handbag off the sofa, unzip it, pull out a share-sized bag of Cheesy Doritos, open the packet (HOW?) and eat a load of tortilla chips.

I had a heart attack thinking about all the salt.

Spent an hour obsessively Googling 'baby salt death', with Daisy crying in my arms.

It turns out a baby died from eating cereal!

And cereal can't be half as salty as Doritos.

Panicked.

Took Daisy to Accident and Emergency.

After a few hours, two midwives came to see me.

They laughed when I told them about the Doritos.

Then they told me all the salty things they'd given their babies.

Pretzels. Bacon. Chicken chow mein.

'And they turned out just fine,' they kept saying.

Midwives are strange. One minute, they tell you to sterilise everything. The next minute, they're making fun of you for being overly cautious. You just can't win.

Wednesday, 21st September

Went through the bin bag of stuff from the old apartment today. The one Nick packed up for me.

I really should have gone through it ages ago, but there have been so many more important things to do – like stopping Daisy sticking her fingers in plug sockets.

Silly Nick. He put the knick-knack coffee tin in there, which has his emergency credit card in it. The one Helen pays off.

I spent a long time staring at the credit card, wondering if I should take it on a big spending spree.

But no. I will be mature. The courts will (eventually) order him to give me money.

Saturday, 24th September

Ate takeaway Chinese with the family tonight – chicken chow mein, egg-fried rice, chicken in black bean sauce, prawn crackers, spicy battered beef and Chinese chicken curry.

Little bit of a splurge is OK right now because I'm losing loads of weight.

Still, it'll be a job to squeeze into my running gear tonight.

Blah.

Better get ready. Alex will be here soon.

Sunday, 25th September

Oh good God in heaven.

Did fifteen miles with Alex, which I think is amazing in itself (although Alex had already done five by the time he picked me up).

When we got back to the waterfront, Alex said, 'Fifteen miles. I think that deserves a drink, don't you?'

I agreed, wanting to add, 'And five packets of dry-roasted peanuts.'

Usually, I would have said, 'Dad will give us a free beer at the Oakley Arms.'

But I felt weird about drinking at Mum and Dad's pub.

I was pleased when Alex said, 'I was thinking the Yacht Club. It's right over there. The wine's very good.'

'I didn't know you drank wine,' I said. Because I've only ever seen him drink whisky.

'I don't,' he said. 'But you do. White wine. And Guinness. Not together. Obviously.'

'How did you know that?' I asked.

'Observation,' he said.

I've only ever been to the Yacht Club for private parties (you have to be a member to drink there), so it was nice to go on a normal night.

The whole place is basically one long panoramic window built into pale, Swedish-style wood, so we had an amazing view of the river and all the boats bobbing in the water.

Alex was right about the wine – it was delicious. I mean, not that I really know much about wine. But it definitely tasted better than the stuff at Mum and Dad's pub.

For a while, we sat watching the river, me drinking white wine, and Alex sipping some dark-coloured whisky with a Scottish name.

Then we started talking.

I found out that Alex spent part of his childhood in Shanghai, Singapore, Bahrain and a whole load of other places. Which explains a lot – namely why he and Zach weren't around for most of the village events, but would magically appear at the Dalton

174

charity balls with fantastic suntans.

I asked him how it was, growing up in lots of different places. He said it gave him an education.

I asked if Jemima liked staying in Great Oakley.

Alex said, 'Of course. Why wouldn't she?'

'I just thought… I mean, you Daltons are well-travelled,' I said. 'I thought Great Oakley might seem too small for her. She might want to live in London eventually.'

Alex said Jemima loved Great Oakley.

As we were talking, fireworks went off along the river, in honour of some village celebration or other.

I thought of the burn on Alex's arm and said, 'You must hate fireworks.'

'Loathe them,' he smiled. 'But that's our secret.'

'We didn't have to go running tonight,' I said. 'You could have cancelled.'

'Fireworks don't bother me any more,' said Alex. 'Although I'd never let Jemima stay in Great Oakley on Bonfire Night. So I suppose I still carry a few scars.'

I was a *teensy* bit drunk at that point – all that running had burned out the contents of my stomach. So I said, 'There were so many rumours about that fire. No one knows what to believe.'

Alex's expression didn't change at all. 'Great Oakley likes its rumours,' he said. 'Tell me. Would this be the rumour about my father setting our house alight for insurance purposes? Or the rumour that he left me in there to burn?'

I felt awful then. Because it's true – they were the rumours.

Alex took a sip of whisky and said, 'When the house was on fire, my father got me out. And Zach. So you see, Mr Dalton Senior isn't all bad. And no – it wasn't an insurance job. A firework set the stables alight, and the fire spread to the house.'

'So how come you got burned?' I asked. 'No one else was hurt.'

I knew I'd gone too far then, because Alex looked out at the boats bobbing in the water and said, 'I'll tell you another time. Let's talk about something else.'

So we did. We talked about growing up in the village, and the woods and the fishing stream and all the things we both did as children.

I teased Alex about being the stuck-up rich kid, and he teased me for being a chatterbox and wearing too many bright colours.

He said, 'You were always the curly-haired blonde girl with the big voice and the bright pink cycling shorts.'

Of all the things he could remember…those cycling shorts!

And then he asked me if I remembered the rope swing.

'The ten-foot-high one?' I said. 'The one that kid got knocked unconscious on? Of course I do. It's still there, isn't it?'

'Do you remember the day I wouldn't get on it?' Alex asked.

I said yes.

I remember that day very well, actually. Some older boys teased Alex for being a wimp. You could see he was about to get into a fight, so I helped calm things down.

'My father beat me with a tennis racket that morning,' said Alex. 'So hard I couldn't sit down. That's why I wouldn't get on the swing. But I wasn't about to tell those kids that. I would have fought all of them first.'

I was completely shocked. First, that his dad did that to him. And second that he was telling me, of all people.

'That's…shit,' I said.

Because I couldn't think of a better way to say it.

'Do you remember the four-leaf clover you gave me?' Alex said.

I laughed and said, 'I remember.'

Fancy him remembering.

When the fight was kicking off, I found this perfect four-leaf clover and gave it to him. I told him it was lucky and he mustn't break it by fighting.

It worked – Alex calmed down, and the other kids left.

Alex said, 'I kept that clover. You didn't know that, did you?'

'You did?' I said. 'Why?'

'It's my lucky mascot,' he said. 'And probably saved me getting beaten up. When you can barely walk, fighting is never a good idea. I've never told anyone that before.'

'About not wanting to fight?' I said.

'No,' said Alex. 'About the tennis racket.'

I felt like the whole room got really quiet. Like there was no one else around. Just the two of us.

Then Alex leaned forward and kissed me.

It was amazing. Just AMAZING.

Like being swept away.

Then Alex pulled back, and he said, 'I shouldn't have done that.'

'Why not?' I asked.

'You and Nicholas Spencer,' he said. 'I don't think it's over. You have unresolved issues.'

I was all breathless, but managed to say, 'What's to resolve? He ran off with my bridesmaid.'

'But you'd still get back together with him,' he said. 'Wouldn't you?'

'I don't know,' I admitted. 'We have a baby.'

'That's the trouble,' said Alex.

We sat holding hands for…I don't know. Maybe twenty minutes or something. Looking at each other. Not saying anything.

And then, bloody Helen came bobbing up to the table. I'd forgotten that she and Henry drink at the Yacht Club sometimes.

She said in her horrible shrill voice, 'Alex. What a pleasure to see you. I've just been talking to your mother about arrangements for the New Year's Eve Ball.'

Then she pretended to look all surprised to see me. 'Juliette!

Goodness, I didn't expect to see you here. Where's *baby* Daisy? Have you left her to the wolves?'

She was wearing a Vivienne Westwood suit that made her look like Cruella de Vil.

Henry was swaying beside her, clearly extremely drunk.

I told Helen that Daisy was with Mum. And Helen said, 'Well I suppose your *mother* knows all about babies. She's had enough of them.'

Alex didn't take his eyes off me. He kept a firm grasp of my hand and said, 'Good evening Mrs Jolly-Piggott. My solicitor, Jeremy Samuels, sends his regards. He's representing Juliette now. So any comments you have to make, make through him.'

Helen's mouth fell clean open.

Then she stammered that she thought Ted Grunty was representing me, and why wasn't she told about this new development? She shouted at Henry for not passing correspondence on to her. Then she said, 'Well! I suppose legal matters and socialising don't mix. Isn't that what they say? So. Anyway, Henry and I were just getting a drink.'

'It looks like Henry has drunk enough for both of you,' said Alex.

I started giggling. Once I start giggling, I can't stop. And I didn't. Not when Alex led me out of the Yacht Club, or up the little roads back to my parent's pub.

I was still giggling when we reached my front door.

'You've got to stop that now,' said Alex.

I asked why.

'Because otherwise, I can't kiss you goodnight.'

I was suddenly all serious. I said, 'Goodnight, Alex.'

'Goodnight, Juliette.'

He stood watching me for a moment, with that little smile of his. 'I'm usually so in control,' he said.

And then he kissed me again.

It absolutely took my breath away.

He was so sexy. So warm. So dangerous. So…everything. And I didn't want it to end.

When Alex pulled back, I was left all giddy and silly, holding onto the front door.

'I'll see you tomorrow for training,' said Alex.

I think I must have said OK. I remember nodding dumbly, at least.

'Eight o'clock,' he said. 'Be ready.'

Am now shitting myself.

It feels like I'm in an alternate reality.

What next?

Afternoon

How can time be going so slowly? When will eight o'clock be here?

Late afternoon

Too nervous to eat.

I just can't stop thinking about Alex.

This is madness.

Daisy slept soundly last night. Yet I was wide awake – crazy infatuated like a teenager.

Oh, this is ridiculous. I'm a mum now. A single mum. I don't have silly romances. None of this makes sense.

It was just kissing. Just stupid, drunken kissing.

Oh my God!

What am I going to say to Alex? Are we going to pretend like it didn't happen? Will he want to forget all about it?

Or…or…

6 pm

Crazy storm outside.

It's like the world knows something is happening. And all this energy is just flying around the sky.

179

7 pm

Alex just rang the pub.

'Juliette?' he said.

And I sort of squeaked 'Yes.'

I knew it was him, but I said, 'Um…who is it?'

He laughed and said, 'You know who it is. We can't run tonight. It's treacherous out there. But can I see you?'

God – I couldn't speak then. It was like my whole throat had closed up.

See me? Why? To tell me last night was a stupid mistake?

I managed to say OK, and he said he was coming straight over to pick me up.

Am now DOUBLE shitting myself, waiting for his car to pull up.

Monday, 26th September

Last night, Alex arrived ten minutes after he phoned.

I met him at the front door, and he held an umbrella over me.

We went to his Rolls Royce, and he turned up all the heaters and felt my fingers.

'You're freezing,' he said. 'Don't your parents heat that pub of theirs?'

Which actually they don't, most of the time. Dad is very conservative with things like heating. And Mum doesn't feel the cold because of all the Chicago Town pizza she eats.

Alex said he'd been thinking about me. And about last night.

I felt all nervous then. In the pit of my stomach. I felt like he was about to give me the Dear Juliette speech.

'Shall we go for a drive then?' I squeaked.

He gave me that quirky smile of his and said, 'Unless you'd prefer to take the bus?'

'I wouldn't mind,' I said. 'I like the bus.'

'Christ – how can you?' Alex replied. 'It's so *slow*.'

The storm had cleared up by then, and the stars were out.

Alex drove us through the village, past the maypole green and all the boutique cottage shops.

Then we went up the farm track by Bluebell Woods.

Alex parked the car up right by the stream – the one we used to play in as kids. By the rope swing.

'Whenever I see that rope swing I think of you,' he said, 'Do you know that?'

'Since when?' I asked.

'Since always.'

My heart was beating so fast.

Alex was watching me so intensely. I could hear him breathing, and I could hear my own breathing too – really fast, like butterfly wings.

And then Alex kissed me again, one hand in my hair and the other on my cheek.

We kissed for a long time.

I rolled down the car seat, so we tipped back, and then he was on top of me, kissing me so fiercely I could hardly breathe.

I started stripping off my clothes, and he grabbed my hand to stop me.

'Juliette –'

But I said it was OK. Totally fine. That I was a grown up. He didn't need to protect me from myself, I knew what I was doing.

Then he said, 'Oh to hell with it,' and helped me out of my top.

I unbuttoned his shirt, and let my hands feel his chest and back. His skin was amazing – I just couldn't get enough – and being against his bare chest was heaven.

I remember him stroking my hair and kissing my eyelids, my lips, my neck...everywhere.

Before I knew what was happening, he was inside me. Staring into my eyes.

All those times with Nick – they were nothing. Nothing at all.

With Alex, it was like floating around the clouds.

Afterwards, we just lay there for the longest time, half-naked, gazing at each other.

Then I started worrying about Daisy and said I should get back.

Alex helped me get dressed. He asked me if I was OK. If I was comfortable.

That sort of broke the magic, and I felt a bit awkward.

I tried to break the ice by joking, 'We couldn't have done *that* on the bus.'

'What's happening?' Alex smiled. 'I'm usually so in control.'

I didn't know what to say to that. So I didn't say anything.

Alex started the car.

We drove for a few minutes in silence, and then Alex said, 'You know, this car means a lot to me.'

'Is that why you hate buses so much?' I said. 'Because you're in love with this car?'

It was meant to be another joke, but Alex said, 'I do love this car.'

'It's just a thing,' I said. 'How can you love a thing?'

'To me, it's more than a thing,' he said. 'It's a symbol. Of who I am. I bought it when I turned over my first million. Without trampling over people. Without underpaying the staff. Without blackmailing the competition. I proved that I wasn't my father. So it means something to me. About what I am and what I'm not. And it's *not* flashy.'

'Well it is a *bit* flashy,' I said. 'I mean, you're the only person in the village who has one.'

'It would be a bit hard for anyone else to have a car like this,' he said. 'It was made specially for me.'

When Alex dropped me at the pub, he said, 'Wrap up warm in

there. No more cold hands. I can't see you tonight, but I'll come round tomorrow.'

I sort of lingered for a few seconds. Wanting to kiss him goodbye or something. But then Mum shouted, 'That SODDING waste pipe is blocked again.' So I just said, 'Bye.' And ran inside.

What is happening? Is this really real? Could Alex and I...oh God, I don't even want to think that. Just enjoy the moment and the memory. Don't hope for more – you could be horribly disappointed.

Tuesday, 27th September

Morning

Nick just called, asking if he could see Daisy. He even had the nerve to ask if we could talk 'about us'.

'What us?' I asked him.

'Oh don't be like that,' he said. 'Come on – you owe it to Daisy not to write us off.'

I told him he could arrange visitation through my solicitor and hung up.

Afternoon

Helen just called, asking if we could arrange for Nick to see Daisy.

Told her I had to go because Alex Dalton would probably be calling for me soon.

Bit childish I know. But wanted to let her know I'm not sitting around waiting for Nick.

Evening

Have now come crashing down to reality.

Alex hasn't called. Or showed up for running.

I've been watching the news to see if a hurricane has hit a Dalton hotel. Or similar disaster that would mean Alex leaving the country in a hurry.

But nothing.

Feel pretty low and stupid and humiliated.

When a man doesn't call after sex, it's because he isn't interested. End of story.

Feel like such an idiot for getting it SO wrong. Again. Stupid. Stupid, stupid, stupid.

Wednesday, 28th September

No call from Alex.

Yesterday could have had some weird, random explanation (sudden death of relative, embarrassing diarrhoea virus). But two days in a row…

Feel angry, in a way.

I mean, all that talk about rope swings. Doesn't he know how vulnerable I am? I've just been dumped by my fiancé – it's pretty shitty of him to sleep with me if he's just going to disappear.

Sad day all round really.

Thursday, 29th September

Nick called again today.

He asked if he could see Daisy, adding, 'Jules, *please* can we talk? Things aren't going well with Sadie.'

I should have told him to go fuck himself, but all this stuff with Alex has messed with my head.

Nick ended up coming to the Oakley Arms. Which means he must have been pretty desperate to get away from Sadie. He hates Mum and Dad's pub.

We sat in the saloon pub with all the regulars staring at us.

Nick was wearing a leather jacket that was ten years too young for him, and sunglasses indoors. He threw himself into a booth and

184

said, 'Fucking hell, this pub *still* doesn't serve Peroni?'

Luckily, none of the family was serving. If Brandi had been behind the bar, she would have smashed a pint glass over his head.

Nick looked awful actually. Pale. Sad.

'I want you back, Jules,' he said, leaning dramatically onto his elbows. 'Please come back to me.'

'But you're living with Sadie,' I pointed out. 'She's very pregnant.'

'It doesn't work,' he said. 'Two actors together with only one bathroom. She spends hours in there. Hours. And she's always on at me about flushing the toilet. Anyway, I'm not one hundred percent sure the baby's mine.'

He said Sadie had slept with a director around about the time she got pregnant.

I told him it sounded like he and Sadie deserved each other.

'Christ,' he said. 'I'm not that bad, am I?'

It was too dark for Nick to take Daisy out (he arrived two hours late because he couldn't work out the Sunday train timetable), so he ended up playing with her at the pub. He threw her up in the air and said, 'Say, Nick! Say, Dadda!'

When he left, I thanked my lucky stars for how things turned out.

Spending time with Alex has done me a favour really. It's made me see there are better men out there than Nick. Even if those better men aren't interested in an actual serious relationship with me.

Friday, 30th September

Have spent the last half hour watching the window for signs of Alex or his car.

I don't know why I'm torturing myself. It's already been days. It's pretty clear what's going on. Alex is staying away, so I don't get the wrong idea.

Stupid hope.

Going to bed now.

Saturday, 1st October

No Alex again.

Sunday, 2nd October

Told Laura about Alex and me.

She knew some of it – news of us at the Yacht Club was already circulating the village.

She also knew that Nick had phoned, and come to see me.

I asked Laura if she'd had sex with Zach yet, and she replied, 'Of *course* not.'

She said she had real feelings for Zach. And she wasn't going to ruin things by having sex before she knew he felt the same way.

Althea made me feel a bit better.

She said sex was empowering. And that any man who ditched a woman after sex was the sort who'd never empty the dishwasher or replace the toilet roll.

I said Alex probably pays someone to empty his dishwasher and replace his toilet roll.

'But he's a right snooty bastard anyway Jules,' she said. 'Why would you want to hook up with someone like that?'

I told her that he wasn't that bad, once you got to know him.

And it's true.

On the surface, Alex looks all cool and aloof. But the real him is kind and thoughtful and decent.

I miss him.

Monday, 3rd October

Daisy's birthday tomorrow.

My maternity pay has been successfully transferred to my new bank account, so I can finally pay my way.

Also, found a stash of department store cash coupons so bought Daisy some bits and pieces.

Just a few things.

A baby princess outfit. A rag dolly and alphabet blanket. Mini ballet shoes and tutu, baby tiara, personalised dressing gown with her name on it, personalised hooded bath towel (that came half-price with the dressing gown). A silver christening bracelet and necklace. And then a few toys – Noah's ark playset, pull-along horsey, V-tech baby walker (that's pretty much an essential – every baby seems to have one). And then some bath things – splash fun dolphin, Mr Bubbles penguin and a baby grooming kit.

Dad lectured me about how spoiled babies are these days. He grew up with one broken train set and a single football boot, both of which he had to share with his brothers.

Tuesday, 4th October

Daisy's birthday.

Should have been a lovely day, but got all worked up about Nick not calling. I thought at least Helen might call on his behalf. But nothing.

Nick sent presents – a robot dog that you can train with your voice and an ankle-length velvet dress (I know Helen chose that last one because it's hideous). But that's not the same as actually seeing Daisy in person.

Waited until 8 pm, then phoned Nick to say he was a shit bag who missed his daughter's birthday.

Nick whispered that today had been difficult.

In the background, I could hear Sadie screeching that she wanted '*Fresh* fucking grapefruit juice, not the crap from concentrate.'

I think Daisy liked my presents. She got a bit irritated in the baby princess outfit and kept pulling off the bracelet and necklace. But she gave the walker a good chew and butted her head against the Mr Bubbles penguin.

Mum bought Daisy a Swarovski crystal pacifier that lit up different colours. And a big frilly baby bonnet with roses all over it.

Brandi made a birthday cake covered with bright red ready-roll icing.

Laura got Daisy a lovely tasteful dress, tights and shoes from Marks and Spencer.

Althea gave us a rainbow cardigan and some jangly bells on a stick.

All in all, I think Daisy had a good day. Luckily she's too young to know that her dad has shacked up with the bridesmaid.

Wednesday, 5th October

So tired today.

I didn't even have the energy to stop Daisy chewing my iPhone.

Thursday, 6th October

Daisy is sleeping through the night. But I can't sleep. I can't stop thinking about Alex.

It's really lucky I don't have his number. Because I'd have texted him by now. And that would have made me look really desperate and ridiculous.

I'm not eighteen any more. I don't need to know why, why WHY a man isn't calling.

I know why men don't call.

It's because they're not interested.

And anyone who says otherwise is kidding themselves.

Friday, 7th October

Decided to throw myself back into dieting and getting fit and the marathon.

Saturday, 8th October

Food today:

+ Breakfast – One home-blended strawberry and yoghurt smoothie with oats and pumpkin seeds (mess all over kitchen).

+ Lunch – One Slim Girl spinach and kale soup (123 calories, tasted like burnt grass).

+ Mid-afternoon – Weird sugar frenzy – eight of Daisy's apple-juice and oatmeal cookies. But strong-willed enough to leave the last two.

+ Tea – Cheese and beans on toast with Worcester sauce and (fuck it, I'm already over my calories) half a tub of Häagen-Dazs (didn't mean to eat half, but kept trying to get the surface perfectly smooth and got carried away).

9 pm

Ate last two cookies.

Sunday, 9th October

Went for a run with Laura this evening.

Laura was all vibrant and full of energy, even at 8 pm in the freezing cold.

I wore my fat girl's running outfit – great big baggy sweatpants and one of Nick's old T-shirts. It's just the mood I'm in right now.

Laura wore sleek black sports leggings and a skin-tight Lycra vest.

We ran along the street, me huffing and puffing, Laura bouncing along like a gazelle.

By the woods, I got all emotional and had to stop.

Laura was very supportive. She'd already run five miles to 'warm up' so she was on an exercise high. She kept talking about 'ideal conditions' for training and that this temperature would be just like the Winter Marathon.

It was freezing.

But then I remembered what I'd told Daisy. Wiped the tears away and carried on running.

I'm going to do this.

Monday, 10th October

Alex has disappeared off the face of the planet. It's like he was some crazy dream. Did I imagine the whole thing?

Haven't lost any weight this week.

Maybe I've mucked up my metabolism and now can never lose weight. Maybe I'll have to eat rabbit portions forever more to stop myself becoming a big heifer.

Told Althea I might be in love with Alex.

She gave me a big lecture about love being a feminist issue and how society uses romance to control women.

Then she went on about her new boyfriend and how he's given her the best oral sex ever. And he didn't freak out when Wolfgang chewed a hole in his canvas rucksack, so she thinks he might be partner material.

Tuesday, 11th October

Alex, Alex, Alex!

I really miss him today. Not just because I fancy him. I liked going running with him. He was a friend.

I feel like someone's died. Stupid, I know. There must still be some hormones flying around. When did I get so dramatic?

Got the tube to Oxford Street and bought myself a McDonald's big breakfast and a vanilla latte with whipped cream from Starbucks.

Went back to the pub and sobbed to Mum about what a terrible mother I was. A bad role model for Daisy. Not in control of my eating habits.

Mum told me to get a hold of myself. She said she was ordering the Domino's pre-Christmas special – a giant pizza with roast chicken, beef and cranberry sauce – and did I want one.

I gulped, 'Mighty Meaty please.'

Ate pizza.

Felt much better.

It's amazing how much happier you feel when you're not hungry.

And truth be told, I have lost a lot of weight recently.

Wednesday, 12th October

Bad night with Daisy. Very, very tired this morning.

Daisy woke up happy and smiling like last night had never happened.

I said, 'I don't know what you're smiling at.'

Then she said, 'Mama.'

Her first word!

I cried.

My little girl!

I've never felt so proud.

Thursday, 13th October

Decided to write today off as a failed diet. 'Damage limitation' or something like that.

It was all rainy and miserable, and I ended up eating half a packet of cream crackers with big slices of cheddar cheese.

Still, I did manage to go out for a run. The first really good one since Alex stopped coming.

I ran for HOURS! Amazing. I'll have to remember to eat cream crackers and cheese before the marathon.

Friday, 14th October

Did some shopping in the village this morning.

Bumped into Clarissa while I was coming out of the chemist.

I had a box of suppositories in my hand called 'Anusoids'. Why do they give them names like that? Why can't they call them private tablets or secret medicine?

Clarissa gave me that 'Oh, you're really not coping, are you?' smile of hers.

'Has Nick been in touch?' she asked. 'I hear he and Sadie are making a go of things. Living together...'

Bad news travels fast in this village.

'I've barely seen him,' I said. 'Nor has Daisy.'

She gave me lots of pitying nods, then told me how lucky she is to have her husband. He brings her glasses of water while she's breastfeeding and ready meals from Marks and Spencer's when she's tired.

Then she asked if I'd seen Alex lately.

I said no.

'I heard you two go running together,' she said. 'Was that just a rumour?'

I said we had gone running. But I hadn't heard from Alex in weeks. And then stupidly, I added, 'I miss him, actually.'

Clarissa raised her eyebrow and said, 'Look. Friend to friend, I saw Alex a few days ago. At the Yacht Club. Talking to Rebecca Castle. You know – Penny Castle's daughter?'

Ugh.

I mean yes, yes I know that Alex and I were never going to happen in the real world. But felt like I'd been punched in the stomach.

After Clarissa left, I caught sight of myself in the chemist window and realised I had toothpaste in my hair.

Secretly, I quite like embracing the 'I'm so sleep-deprived I can't be bothered' look. But toothpaste is a step too far, even for me.

Mums like Clarissa, with full make-up, styled hair and conservative yet fashionable clothes first thing in the morning ruin it for all the rest of us.

Saturday, 15th October

Hoped it would be rainy today so I could take Daisy to the soft play area. That way, I could sit around drinking tea while she chewed soft toys.

But it was sunny, so I had to take her out.

It was all right actually. Went to the play park. Cold, but sun shining. Felt better than I have in ages.

I think bumping into Clarissa sorted me out a bit.

Just like the thing with Nick, sometimes knowing a door is closed makes you feel better. It hurts, but at least you know you can't go back. You have to move forward.

So am turning the page, re Alex. Feel better today. Lighter. And ready to move on.

Sunday, 16th October

More training with Laura. Hated it, but am making progress.

I am going to do this marathon.

I am!

Not because of a bet with Nick. Not to show Alex. I'm going to do it for Daisy. To show her women can overcome pain and humiliation and still reach the finish line.

Monday, 17th October

Mum took Daisy out to 'give me a break', so I decided to Facebook-stalk Sadie.

Sadie's wall was full of selfies, as per usual.

Look at me wearing this hat! And another hat! Look at me with this lovely-looking cake!

And then... Look at me in my new maternity coat with my *boyfriend*, Nick Spencer...

I checked her relationship status, and it said,

'In a relationship with Nick Spencer.'

Ouch.

Ouch, ouch, ouch.

But I didn't wallow in self-pity.

I really, truly don't want Nick back any more. I don't want things to be how they were. I was too good for him.

It still hurts, but Sadie is welcome to him.

Tuesday, 18th October

HAPPY BIRTHDAY, JULESY!!

Good things always happen on my birthday. And this year was no exception.

Mum made the traditional Duffy birthday breakfast (fried bread, fried eggs, black pudding, sausages, hash browns, potato smiley faces, toast, chips, baked beans with butter mixed in them, crispy bacon and then Mum's special extra – brown sauce mixed with pork scratchings).

After breakfast, I was looking on Facebook for my shower of birthday love and found a new Facebook message.

From Alex.

There was no profile picture of him, just that little question-mark face thing.

I thought it must be a joke at first. Brandi messing around or something.

The message said:

Happy Birthday, Juliette.

I read and re-read the message, my heart yammering away.

Then I shouted, 'Brandi? Is that you doing this on Facebook?'

Brandi shouted back that she definitely was NOT on Facebook because she was 'having a shit'. Although I know full well, she uses Facebook while she's on the toilet.

My fingers got all shaky then. And I wrote back, 'Thank you.'

Then I got another message saying, 'How are you?'

'I'm fine,' I wrote. 'Is that really you, Alex?'

'Yes it's me,' came the reply. 'Alex with the flashy car.'

So then I knew it was really him.

So, my fingers REALLY shaking, I wrote, 'I haven't seen you for a while. How come?' And clicked send.

I waited, praying he'd reply because if he didn't, I'd feel like a complete idiot.

After seven minutes (yes – I was counting) I got a reply: 'I heard you were talking things through with Daisy's father.'

Whoa!

My heart was absolutely pounding when I read that.

I don't think I've ever typed a reply so fast.

I wrote that I'd only seen Nick once, but there was practical stuff to sort out with Daisy. And yes, Nick and I had talked on the phone the day after our car drive, but I'd told him to arrange things through my solicitor.

'I heard there was a little more to it than that,' Alex wrote. 'I was told the two of you were working on a reconciliation.'

'According to who?' I messaged.

'You mean "whom,"' he replied.

'Well tell whomever it was that they're talking out of their arse and have it completely wrong,' I wrote.

'I will happily tell Helen Jolly-Piggott exactly that,' he replied.

I was absolutely furious! That fucking interfering bitch.

I took a few deep breaths and wrote, 'You shouldn't listen to gossip. Especially coming from Helen.'

'You're quite right,' he replied. 'But when you expect to hear a certain piece of news, sometimes you get it.'

I told him Nick and I were totally finished, and although I respected him as Daisy's father (sort of), there was no way I'd ever get back with him. Not now. Not after our night together.

Alex wrote, 'Do you have plans for your birthday?'

I wrote back, no. Everyone I know was working or studying or in Cornwall teaching their son the value of shells.

And *then* Alex wrote, 'How about I take you out?'

I wanted to reply, 'YES PLEASE' in big, block capitals, but I tried to be 'message cool' to steal one of Brandi's phrases, and just wrote, 'That sounds really nice.'

'I'll pick you up tonight,' he wrote. 'Eight o'clock.'

'Are we going running then?' I asked.

'No,' he replied. 'I'm taking you out for your birthday.'

And then he came up as 'offline'.

Felt so happy I thought my chest might explode.

Spent a few minutes dancing Daisy around the bedroom.

Then I started to get paranoid.

What if Alex is only taking me out so he can sleep with me again? What if I'm just some easy single mum target he's using for sex? How did he know Nick phoned, and why didn't he call before that?

Called Laura. She told me I was beautiful and funny and she always suspected Alex liked me. Zachary thinks so too, apparently.

Felt better then. But am now panicking about going out tonight.

Where's Alex going to take me? What should I wear?

Brandi offered to give me a makeover and pummelled my body with salt scrub. She dabbed the bleeding bits with t-gel, but I know there'll be scabs.

I refused to let her fake-tan me, so she did me a facial instead.

It took twenty cotton wool balls to get my face clean. She shouted at me for not removing my make-up properly, saying, 'Did you know that every night you leave make-up on, it ages your skin by seven days?'

Honestly! She gets all this scaremongering crap from people who sell cosmetics. If what she said were true, I'd look sixty years old.

I stupidly let her wax my eyebrows and fill them in with black pencil. When she'd finished, I looked like a blonde Cleopatra.

While we were arguing over my eyebrows, there was a knock at the door.

In my panicky state, I thought it was Alex – calling four hours too early.

I screamed, 'Hide me! He can't see these eyebrows!' And tried to climb into the airing cupboard.

But then Mum shouted up that it was a delivery man. With a great big pink box.

For a moment, I thought it might be a present from Nick. A big sorry gift. Begging for me to forgive me and take him back.

He never remembers my birthday, though.

Brandi read the card and was like, 'NO! You will NEVER guess who this is from. You will never guess!'

It was from Alex.

He hadn't put any kisses in the card or anything. It just said, 'This is for tonight. Alex.'

No 'love' or anything like that.

My stomach did a load of lovely somersaults.

I must have been giggling or squealing or something, because Mum said, 'Calm down, Cleopatra. And let's find out what it is.'

It was a beautiful dress in pink silk.

Stunning. Just stunning. Sort of vintage 1940s, with a big skirt and tight waist.

And there were matching shoes – grey ballet pumps made from swirled silk.

Mum went on about how 'me' it was because I love 'all that vintage crap', and how Alex must have been paying attention.

Brandi Googled the dress label and confirmed it was from a very expensive designer.

Then Mum got out her shoebox of diamante and talked about adding a *bit* more sparkle. But I wouldn't let her.

The dress was absolutely perfect. So perfect I was sort of scared to try it on. I mean, what if it didn't fit? It was a European dress size, which I think equated to a UK size 12, which I was certain wouldn't fit.

Everyone knows men are usually terrible at knowing women's dress sizes.

But it did fit. Perfectly.

And I realised – fucking hell, I really am looking better after all this running. I've lost weight, and my legs are much more svelte. A better shape. And everything is just more…held in.

I didn't want to take the dress off, but Daisy woke up, and I was worried it would get covered in dribble. So I laid it carefully back in the box ready for tonight.

I'll be honest, I am totally shitting myself.

I'm just so nervous. It was never like this with Nick.

Oooooo! Need a wee again!

Wednesday, 19th October

Should have been the most amazing night ever.

But it wasn't.

Stupid Nick.

Alex picked me up at eight o'clock on the dot.

I was pretty much ready. He only had to shout at me twice to hurry up.

A driver took us into London in this big wedding car thing. In fact, it was fancier than my wedding car.

And Alex looked a lot better than my groom – black suit, white shirt, black bow tie.

I got even more nervous, thinking – fucking hell, we're going somewhere really fancy.

Alex said I looked 'stunning'.

The whole drive, he wouldn't tell me where we were going. He got quite stern about it actually. When I kept asking.

London was frosty and felt magic. The streets were sparkling, the sky was dark, and the air smelt of roast chestnuts.

FINALLY, we stopped outside the London Coliseum, which was covered from top to bottom with long, straight strings of fairy lights.

Alex told me we were seeing *Swan Lake*. Which is a ballet.

He said I'd love it and he was right.

It was beautiful.

Of course, it helped that we had our own balcony. And a bottle of Champagne.

When I asked Alex how the ballerinas stood on their toes without swearing, he told me they spent their whole lives practising discipline and restraint.

I said that seemed a bit sad. That they gave up so much just to look beautiful for other people.

Alex squeezed my hand and whispered, 'They retire before they're thirty. And spend the rest of their lives eating boxes of Godiva chocolate. Don't feel too sorry for them.'

We held hands the whole way through. And then, just near the end, Nick rang.

SOO embarrassing.

MC Hammer – *Can't Touch This* blaring out across the auditorium.

I ran out to take the call in the stairwell.

Nick was all slurry and drunk, telling me I should be at home with Daisy.

I asked him how he knew I was out.

He said he'd phoned the pub and Mum had told him.

I said it was my birthday.

'Is it?' he replied.

Then he said he wanted to see me. And that he wanted things to be how they were.

Why does life happen like that? When I *wanted* him to beg for forgiveness, he didn't. And now I'm moving on, he says everything I wanted to hear months ago.

Nick got all teary and angry, and I ended up hanging up on him.

Then I rang Mum and checked everything was OK with Daisy.

I heard Mum say, 'Spit it out, Daisy! Spit it out! Oh, you've swallowed it …'

I shouted, 'WHAT HAS SHE SWALLOWED!'

Mum said it was just something brown she'd found on the floor and it would 'all come out the other end'. Then she told me I used to eat gravel as a baby.

Panicked for a bit. Phoned back and made Mum put Daisy on the phone. Daisy was making her usual noises, so felt better.

When I got back to the balcony, Alex didn't look at me. He didn't take my hand again either.

He was quiet in the car on the way back.

Just as we were arriving at the village, Alex said, 'Look, if you want to make a go of things with Daisy's father, I'm not going to stand in your way. It's the right thing. For Daisy to have a family.'

'I don't want to make a go of things with Nick,' I insisted. 'Not any more.'

'And yet you take calls from him at nine o'clock at night,' said Alex, not looking at me.

Just to make things worse, Nick was WAITING OUTSIDE the Oakley Arms.

He looked pretty drunk, swaying around with a can of gin and tonic in his hand.

Alex's jaw went all hard and twitchy, and he said, 'Sleep well' in this really formal voice like he was reading the news.

And off he went. Not so much as a goodbye kiss or anything.

As soon as Alex was gone, Nick came lurching towards me doing his big smouldering puppy-dog eyes.

He'd been waiting on the doorstep 'for hours' apparently.

'What would Sadie think if she saw you here?' I shouted.

He said he couldn't give a fuck what 'that high-maintenance cow' thought. Apparently, Sadie won't even let him sleep in the bed any more. She says he farts in his sleep.

Then Nick said we had a child together and shouldn't we try to make things work?

I asked why the sudden change of heart.

'Maybe I'm jealous,' he laughed. 'Your mum told me who you

201

were out with. You know I hate Alex Dalton.'

Eventually, I said Nick could sleep on the sofa. He was way too drunk to get home – I have no clue how he even got here in that state. He can't read a train timetable at the best of times.

At some point, Nick got into bed with me and started pulling the moves.

It was all so familiar I almost found myself going along with it. I mean, Nick was pretty sexy when we first got together.

Luckily, I was awake enough to push him away.

Nick acted all innocent and hurt.

'Come on Jules,' he said. 'You know you want to. I want you back, Jules. I made a mistake. A stupid mistake. We're good together. You know we are.'

Then he said he just wanted to spend the night in bed with me. Like old times. And he wouldn't try anything. He was lonely and blah, blah, blah.

I was so tired. So like an idiot I let him stay.

This morning, Brandi came bursting in and saw us together.

'This is SO not what it looks like,' I told her.

I have to admit it did look bad.

Nick was stark naked.

He must have flung off his clothes at some point in the night.

I shook Nick awake and told him he needed to leave.

God, he reeked of booze. He pulled his underwear on and asked if I wanted to grab a bacon sandwich with him at the village deli.

I told him to sod off.

He checked his watch and said, 'Actually, no time anyway. Sadie's going to freak. Can I give Daisy a kiss goodbye?'

He picked up Daisy and gave her big smacking kisses.

Daisy stared at me like, 'Mummy, who is this madman?' Then she started howling and reached out her little arms towards me.

'She's probably a bit tetchy,' said Nick. 'First thing in the morning. Like Daddy, aren't you? Daddy hates mornings too. Love you Daisy boo.'

Then he left, promising to see us soon.

What on earth was I thinking, letting him sleep in the bed with me? What on earth was I thinking?

I just pray that Alex never finds out.

Thursday, 20th October

WHY hasn't Alex called?

CALL ME, CALL ME!

Friday, 21st October

Once again, today started well and ended terribly.

I worked up the courage to Facebook Alex and thank him for the other night.

He replied, 'You're welcome.'

And then, even more courageously, I said, 'So are we going running tonight then?'

I didn't want to go into all the Nick stuff via Facebook message, but I was pretty sure face-to-face I could explain everything better.

He wrote, 'Juliette, I don't want to get in the way of your family. Nicholas Spencer is Daisy's father.'

I wrote back a long reply saying I honestly wasn't interested in Nick. And that I'd moved on. That Daisy and I were better off without him, and please could we talk in person?

Alex wrote, 'I think you need time. And space.'

I wrote that I'd had plenty of time and space. And that I really needed his help with running. That I ran so much better when he was with me. And that the marathon was REALLY soon.

203

'I'll pick you up at eight,' Alex replied.

But it felt all sort of stern and formal. I knew I had some explaining to do.

Alex showed up at eight on the dot, just like always.

While I was doing my calf stretches in the garden, I tried to explain that Nick had come round *totally* uninvited last night.

I said, 'About Nick coming over last night –'

But Alex cut me off with his hand and said, 'That's none of my business.'

Very unluckily, Brandi picked that moment to come clattering down in skeleton leggings and Ugg boots, bleached blonde hair in a big messy bun.

'Jules didn't *do* anything with Nick,' she said. 'You can sleep in a bed with someone without anything happening.'

Thanks, Sis.

Alex's face went really stern.

I think Brandi knew she'd said the wrong thing, because she added, 'I've slept in LOADS of guys' beds and not done anything. Sometimes you just need somewhere to crash.'

And Alex's jaw started twitching. He looked at me – a mixture of anger and disappointment. I felt about a foot tall.

Brandi gave me a hapless shrug as if to say, 'Well there's no pleasing some people.' Then she tottered off to her pink Mini and gave us a friendly toot as she left.

'I think you've done enough stretching,' said Alex. All cold and formal.

So we went running.

We ran for miles, Alex always a little bit ahead.

Sometimes he'd turn around and bark, 'Keep up.'

Towards the end, he pulled right away from me.

He's never done that before.

I shouted at him to slow down, and he told me that I needed to work on my self-discipline. That I needed to push myself through the pain barrier.

'Can I try that tomorrow?' I said.

'No,' he barked.

'*Why* are you pushing me?' I asked. 'Is it because Nick –'

'I've heard enough of that man's name today,' he barked back.

And then we ran on in silence.

When we got back to the pub, I said, 'Are we running tomorrow?'

'I've trained you as much as I can,' said Alex, hands on hips, not meeting my eye. 'The rest is up to you.'

Then he left.

Saturday, 22nd October
Still no word from Alex.

Sunday, 23rd October
Nick keeps calling me.

But now I want Alex to call.

Monday, 24th October
I've been Facebook-stalking Alex, but there's really nothing to see. He never puts up pictures or status updates or anything.

Althea is pleased as anything that Nick wants me back. She thinks it's a good opportunity to torture him.

'Karma,' she said. 'I told you it would come around.'

'Doesn't karma mean that I *shouldn't* torture him,' I said, 'because the universe will do it for me?'

'No,' said Althea, 'sometimes you have to step in.'

Then Althea told me she'd heard a rumour about Sadie.

Apparently, she's getting fat now.

So maybe karma really does exist.

Tuesday, 25th October

Marathon not far off now. Just a few weeks away.

I should be thinking about running and timings and carbs. Plus the weather – there are rumours it might snow. (Is there such a thing as running gloves? Must Google it.) But all I can think about is Alex.

Wednesday, 26th October

Maybe I'll see him at the marathon? Maybe he'll call and want to meet at the starting line? Maybe, maybe, maybe.

Thursday, 27th October

Checked Facebook about fifty times today, but Alex hasn't messaged.

Althea thinks I'm having rebound syndrome and don't really fancy Alex at all.

She could be right I suppose.

Friday, 28th October

Laura called off her studying to come running with me tonight.

I dragged myself ten horrible, awful miles. By mile nine, Laura was so sick of me moaning that she banned me from talking at all.

It was different with Alex. Maybe I was too embarrassed to moan. Or maybe it was just so exciting being with him. I don't know. But the miles used to fly by.

I have no idea how I'm going to do those twenty-six miles.

Wait – twenty-*seven* miles.

Saturday, 29th October

Mum, Dad, Brandi and I watched *Chariots of Fire* this evening.

I had tears in my eyes at the end of the movie.

I will do this! I will finish! Even if it snows on marathon day.

I will make Daisy proud.

Sunday, 30th October

Marathon TWO WEEKS AWAY!!

Why am I so nervous? It's not like I'm running in the Olympics or anything. But I really am shitting myself.

Mainly because I might see Alex.

Monday, 31st October

Halloween

Brandi and I took Callum 'trick-or-treating' tonight.

It was pretty embarrassing.

Callum pounded on doors, stuck out his bucket and said, 'Give me sweets or I'll silly string you.'

Luckily, most people thought it was funny. Except for one old lady who Callum threatened with shaving foam.

Mum decorated the pub with spray cobwebs and dangling rubber spiders. Then she moaned because no one was drinking her 'Witches Brew' – a mixture of all the pub spirits that haven't been selling.

I'm not surprised no one was buying it – it smelt like boozy toothpaste.

In the end, Mum and Brandi drank most of the 'Witches Brew'. Then they got up on the bar and danced to the Monster Mash.

Tuesday, 1st November

I think training is getting harder – probably because of the cold.

This was a fucking stupid thing to sign up for. But I'm happy about all the running. It's been really good for me.

Wednesday, 2nd November

Mum is ALREADY putting up our Christmas decorations.

We have two Christmas trees every year – one in the house, one in the pub.

Mum makes sure both trees are so covered with tinsel, flashing fairy lights and various tacky ornaments you can't see the branches.

Her favourite ornaments are all from our summer holidays – a mini bottle of Ouzo (Greece 2000), a pink plastic couple having sex (Spain 1991), and a hanging wooden penis (Cyprus 1995).

Mum was annoyed because the village supermarket won't sell real trees for a few more weeks. The pub one is plastic, so she's put it up already, but she'll have to wait to do the house one.

Thursday, 3rd November

The village supermarket still isn't stocking Christmas trees, so Mum demanded that Dad go into the woods and cut down a real one.

Dad was happy to do it, saying it was 'a very frugal move' and 'an excellent way to mind the pennies'.

He went into the woods with his handsaw this morning and didn't come back until after dark.

When we saw the tree, we understood why it had taken so long – the trunk was like a telegraph pole.

All the branches were covered in cobwebs and dead leaves, but Dad said it only needed 'a little wash and brush up'.

The tree wouldn't fit in the family room without the top bending against the ceiling, so we've put the Christmas fairy back in her box.

Had a nice time hanging the Christmas decorations.

While we weren't looking, Callum ate one of the playdough decorations he made at nursery last year – sequins and all.

He won't do it again though. It was salt dough, and he drank three pints of water, then wet the bed. That'll teach him.

Saturday, 5th November
Fireworks Night

Funny feeling in my stomach this afternoon.

Maybe it's all the fireworks going off and the smell of bonfires. But it just feels like something is about to happen.

We let off a few fireworks in the garden (why don't Catherine wheels *ever* spin round?), and Callum burned himself on a sparkler.

I don't really want to go for a run tonight.

I'm absolutely stuffed.

Mum made her usual bonfire tea of hot dogs, jacket potatoes, piles of grated cheese, butter, coleslaw, mayonnaise, chocolate cake and a big bowl of Haribo sweets.

Still, have to go running. REALLY don't fancy it, but I've got to get in all the practice I can.

Sunday, 6th November

God! Nick turned up at eleven o'clock last night and threw stones at my bedroom window.

He was totally drunk, slurring about, 'Do you remember me doing this when we first got together?'

I shouted that I did. And that's why my bedroom window now has a new pane of glass in it.

Monday, 7th November

Things are starting to get Christmassy.

A few teenagers were on ladders around the village today, putting up Christmas decorations – the usual flashing tinsel bells and stars.

They strung fairy lights around the church tower and were decorating a huge, wobbly tree in the graveyard.

Even with my train-wreck of a life right now, I still love Christmas.

Good things always happen at Christmas.

Tuesday, 8th November

More freezing cold marathon training.

Ugh.

Lungs burning. Fingers freezing, even in gloves.

I fucking hate running.

Wednesday, 9th November

Took Daisy for a late night walk along the waterfront tonight.

On the waterfront, people were drinking cups of mulled wine and calling out 'Merry Christmas!' as we walked past.

Christmas gets earlier every year, but who cares? I'd be happy if Christmas started in September.

I put Daisy in a little snowsuit with reindeer ears, so all the old ladies went, 'Awww' and tried to give her mince pies.

I politely declined, though. Everyone knows Iris Skinner's mince pies are two parts booze to one-part raisin.

Thursday, 10th November

God, I hate running right now! Can't wait for this marathon to be over.

Blisters as big as 50p coins.

Friday, 11th November

Blisters as big as sherbet flying saucers.

Ow, ow, ow!

Saturday, 12th November

Big night tonight – turning on the village Christmas lights.

Unfortunately, the teenagers had arranged the lights to spell out 'Santa isn't real' along the High Street. They also arranged a big, flashing penis and a pair of boobs on the church tower.

It wasn't obvious until the lights were turned on.

The old ladies selling mince pies in the churchyard didn't know where to look.

Sunday, 13th November
Remembrance Sunday

Woke up to find Dad at the kitchen table with Granddad's medals and photos. He was wearing a poppy in his buttonhole and looking teary. I asked if he was missing Granddad.

'More than words,' he said.

Then he talked about the photos, which were all of Granddad in the Second World War. Granddad was one of the few soldiers who enjoyed it. He liked the camping and fresh air. And he always was a big fan of tinned meat.

We had a little cry for Granddad and then we wore our poppies and watched the memorial parade on TV.

Callum thought it was hilarious (old people dressed up like Medal of Honour on Xbox!).

Monday, 14th November

The Christmas carol bus drove around the village today, full of singing children dressed as elves.

I still get excited by the free lollypops they throw out. Caught my favourite flavour too! Strawberry.

Daisy managed to get hold of two lollypops and refused let go of either, sucking the plastic wrappers on both of them alternately.

When I tried to prise one out of her hand, she tried to bite me! Really hope she doesn't turn out like Callum. I love him, but he's hard work.

Mum can never turn down a free lolly either, and Dad likes a carol, so we all watched the bus drive past and joined in singing with the kids.

Dad's voice goes operatic when he sings, no matter how silly the songs are.

Mum sings every song like a rowdy pub sing-along. She kept forgetting herself and singing the rude-word versions.

Tuesday, 15th November

To take my mind off the marathon, I helped Althea make her Christmas presents.

Althea doesn't believe in 'buying plastic crap'.

This year, she's got into welding. I arrived to find her in the garden, showing Wolfgang how to use the welding gun.

Wolfgang was clapping his hands with delight at the orange

sparks. He did have a welding mask on, but it was a little big for him – covering not only his face but most of his torso.

Althea had already made a load of wrought-iron Christmas wreaths, and had moved on to welding Christmas-tree decorations.

I pointed out that wrought iron is too heavy to hang on Christmas trees, but Althea explained they were 'concept pieces' – to show the weighty financial burden Christmas puts on the common man.

Althea is a good businesswoman because she's already sold three of the wreaths to her neighbours. I just hope they have some really strong nails.

Wednesday, 16th November

Went shopping in the village today for marathon supplies – Lucozade sport, glucose tablets and gummy bears.

The church ladies were all on ladders, trying to fix the rude Christmas decorations. They'd managed to make the boobs look like a big Christmas bow, and they'd turned the penis into a fairly convincing Christmas tree.

Thursday, 17th November

Marathon two days away.

Am shitting myself now.

Friday, 18th November

Had my last supper – a huge plate of spaghetti bolognaise. Apparently, you're supposed to load up on the carbs before a marathon.

Since I was loading, I had sticky-toffee pudding too.

And a large packet of peanut M&Ms.

Saturday, 19th November

MARATHON DAY!

Woke up at 5 am feeling really nervous.

Annoyed, because then I couldn't get back to sleep.

Daisy woke up at 6 am.

It was cold.

Frost on the ground.

I didn't bother moaning because I knew Dad would start telling me about 'frost inside the windowpanes' and 'proper winters' when he was a kid.

When he was little, they had one outside toilet that froze over in winter. Apparently, it was very important not to poo directly on the ice. You had to pee first to defrost it.

Had an energy drink for breakfast and three strawberry energy bars.

Ended up completely wired, jiggling on the spot and telling Daisy I was going to win the marathon.

When I said bye, I got all teary and weirdly hormonal.

Like I was going away to war or something.

Mum told me she had a box of cold hot dogs ready for the halfway mark.

I told her it was a sporting event, not a 1970s wedding.

She said, 'Beef jerky then?'

Dad was all dressed up in his 1980s marathon gear, ready to cheer me on. String vest, royal blue shorts with rainbows around the pockets and his London Marathon medal.

He ran the London Marathon in 1986 in just under four hours. His time would have been better, but he stopped to take photographs of all the London landmarks.

I asked him if he'd be cold in just shorts, but he insisted this was 'all too exciting' to worry about the temperature.

At the start line, there was an awesome atmosphere. Just awesome.

Huge holly wreaths hung over the twisty tinsel start line.

Loads of people were in costumes – quite a few were Christmas-themed.

A little bit premature maybe, but who doesn't love Christmas?

There were at least twenty Father Christmases (which is really going to confuse the kids) and various elves, snowmen etc.

Everyone was smiling and shivering. And sort of secretly pushing forward and trying to get in the best position.

You could tell half the runners were hyped-up on glucose. One guy dressed as a giant snowman was so twitchy he started accusing people of 'invading his area' and bumping them with his big padded stomach.

I kept thinking about Alex.

Stupid. In a crowd of thousands. And anyway, I knew he'd be right near the front with the decent runners.

When the race started, everyone was all smiley.

Then after a mile or so, everyone stopped smiling.

After five miles, everyone had on their marathon faces: pain, misery and anguish.

And on we ran. And on. And on.

I felt so sorry for the people in costumes. You could tell they were really suffering – especially the ones with Father Christmas beards and padding.

It was so much harder than in training.

And SO cold. My lungs were absolutely burning, and my fingers were bright red.

The crowd do cheer you on and cheer you up. But marathons are still horrible and gruelling, and only professional athletes or maniacs should attempt them, let alone in winter.

By the time we crossed Tower Bridge, every step was agony.

All I could think was, 'I want to stop, I want to stop!'

I wasn't thinking about pacing myself or anything, just running and running.

At the halfway mark, I saw Mum, Dad, Laura, Brandi and Althea.

Dad was waving a Union Jack flag.

Mum was eating a mince pie. She went mental when she saw me.

'WOOOOOOOOOOOO JULES! WOOOOOOOOO JULIETTE! COME ON GIRL! SHOW THEM WHAT YOU'RE MADE OF, DO YOU WANT A PORK PIE?'

My eyes welled up when I saw Daisy.

Mum had put pink leg warmers and baby trainers over her snowsuit.

Dad was all manic-eyed. 'Are you enjoying it? It's amazing, isn't it? What the human body can do.'

He was still in his shorts and vest, jogging on the spot and blowing on his fingers.

I told him it was the worst thing I'd ever done in my life. I said my body wasn't made for running, but gentle walking and massages. I said I would never, ever run another marathon as long as I lived and made him promise not to let me do it again.

'Only thirteen miles to go,' Mum said.

Dad corrected her: 'Thirteen and a half!'

Laura told me to think of Daisy and how proud she'd be.

'She doesn't care,' I said. 'She doesn't have the slightest clue what's going on.'

'Then do it for you,' said Laura.

'I don't care about me either!' I said. 'I just want to stop. This is awful. AWFUL! There is no way I can finish. No way.'

Laura put a calming sisterly hand on my shoulder and said, 'You can do it, Juliette Duffy.'

'I think I might sit down and eat a hot dog,' I said.

'No.' Laura was adamant. 'You have to keep going.'

I started crying and said I couldn't do it. I said my chest hurt. And my ears hurt. And my boobs hurt. And I kept seeing people on stretchers who'd slipped on the ice.

'Juliette Duffy, you can do this,' said Laura. 'I'll run with you. Come on.'

She hopped under the safety barrier, grabbed my hand and pulled me back into the race.

The next five miles were bad.

I felt every step, and my lungs burned.

But Laura was with me. And she gave me strength somehow.

Then some stupid jumped-up usher noticed Laura wasn't wearing an official bib with her name on the back. He blew a whistle at her and shouted, 'PEDESTRIAN! REMOVE YOURSELF FROM THE RUNNERS AREA IMMEDIATELY!'

So Laura had to go.

God, the marathon is so emotional!

We both had tears in our eyes.

'I can't do this, Laura,' I said. 'I can't do this on my own.'

'Juliette Duffy, you are going to finish,' said Laura. 'I will see you at the finish line.'

All I had left then was pain and hopelessness. No, Laura. No strength left. And no more gummy bears.

It was horrible. Awful.

I looked around and saw nothing but misery – all the runners looked so unhappy.

I started thinking, 'Why on earth am I putting myself through this? Why put myself in such pain? Why don't I just stop?'

Then someone shouted out, 'Come on, Juliette!'

And someone else yelled, 'You can do it, Juliette!'

And the crowd started clapping for me.

It was such a beautiful thing. All these strangers willing me on.

And miraculously, I carried on running.

One step at a time.

Slowly, the miles went by.

And step by horrible step, I made the twenty-five-mile mark. Then the twenty-sixth. And suddenly I could see Buckingham Palace up ahead.

I knew I could do it then. No matter how much pain I was in, I could manage the last little bit.

But just as I was turning into Piccadilly, the man in the snowman suit came careering into me. There wasn't even any ice or anything, but I lost my footing.

I fell down and felt my ankle twist under me.

God, it hurt.

I tried to stand but I couldn't. At least not without crying.

I had a crazy idea that I might crawl over the finish line.

While I was mulling it over, a crowd gathered around me – generally elderly or overweight people. People who were never going to make a good time.

Someone gave me a bottle of tropical Lucozade and a handful of Mentos.

And then, through the crowd, came Alex.

I thought I was seeing things at first. But no – it really was him.

He was in black running gear with barely a drop of sweat on him.

He pushed everyone out the way and said, 'Juliette. Get up. Can you get up?'

I told him I'd hurt my leg and that I should probably just sit here until the marathon finished.

He told me not to be ridiculous.

I asked why he was here with all the slow people.

The runners around me looked a bit annoyed then, and someone muttered, 'Knowing your limits and setting a good pace is something to be celebrated …'

Alex said he'd been shadowing me to make sure I finished.

'But you'll get a shit finishing time,' I said.

'I've run plenty of marathons,' he replied.

I went all pink and said, 'Thank you. For caring.'

'I've always cared,' said Alex. 'That's the problem.'

I wanted to tell him about that night with Nick – that it wasn't what it looked like. But my ankle was throbbing, and I just couldn't think of a good way to arrange the words.

And anyway, there's a part of me that thinks if it's meant to be, it's meant to be.

Mum was seeing someone else when Dad met her (actually two someone else's). But Dad was so certain she was the one for him he 'moved heaven and earth' to show her he was the right one. He even sold his very rare collection of *Roy of the Rovers* comics, so he could afford to take her to Stonehenge.

Alex tried to help me up, but I really couldn't walk. I mean, it was agony. I cried and told him I couldn't do it.

'Come on,' said Alex. 'You're going to do this.'

Then he put my arm around his lovely, hard shoulder and half dragged, half carried me along.

Everyone was staring as we went down Piccadilly.

Alex looked so stoic and handsome and determined. When we crossed the finish line, everyone was cheering.

I was laughing and crying, more out of relief than victory.

My family and Althea were waiting by the big Winter Marathon trucks.

They looked pretty surprised to see Alex carrying me.

Mum said, 'Have you run out of energy, love? Do you want a mini Scotch egg?'

Alex shouted at a steward to get me a chair.

I sat down, and Mum put Daisy on my lap. I burst into tears when I saw her.

'I did it!' I said. 'I finished! I can't believe it! Don't ever let me do that again. Don't EVER let me do that again.'

Alex started bossing people around – asking for paramedics and a stretcher.

Then he said, 'Look, I'll leave you with your family. The ambulance is on its way. If you need anything, call me.'

Then he gave me his business card and sprinted off into the crowd.

It was all a bit chaotic after that.

The paramedics came over and (irritatingly) told me it was 'nothing serious', and they'd 'seen much worse'.

'But it really hurts!' I moaned.

They said it would be fine with a bit of ice on it.

Mum asked if a cold bottle of Coke would do the job.

They said yes, and offered to drive us home in the ambulance. Dad said they shouldn't 'waste resources'. So we ended up borrowing a wheelchair and going home on the train.

Quite nice being disabled. Everyone smiled and let me go first.

Sunday, 20th November

My ankle is MASSIVE. It's nearly as big as Mum's.

Doctor Slaughter says it'll be fine in a few days. Then he checked the fridge and shouted at Mum for having a shelf full of chocolate mousse and Jaffa Cakes.

Monday, 21st November

I miss Alex.

There. I said it.

Thought maybe I should message him and explain about Nick. But Brandi said no – explaining only makes you look guilty.

'I should know,' said Brandi. 'I've cheated on *loads* of my boyfriends.'

'But I didn't do anything with Nick,' I insisted. 'Nothing happened.'

'Wow,' said Brandi. 'You're *really* good. I totally believed you just then.'

Tuesday, 22nd November

I'm getting quite used to sitting around, especially since Mum has filled the house with mince pies.

She always buys a packet from every supermarket to 'consumer test', so there were 36 mince pies in the cupboard, plus various novelty Christmas items:

+ Turkey and cranberry flavour Pringles
+ Star-shaped cream crackers
+ White Mars Bars
+ Mince-pie ice cream

Wednesday, 23rd November

Alex still hasn't messaged or anything. And I think Brandi's right – trying to explain will just make me look bad. I mean, I've tried already. He doesn't want to listen. Maybe this is just his way of letting me down gently.

Is it too early to send a happy Christmas text message?

I have his number now…

No.

If this year has taught me anything, it's that men will invariably do what they want. If Alex wanted me, he would have been in touch by now.

I've had enough humiliation.

Time to move forward.

Thursday, 24th November

Did Skype link-up with Uncle Ralph and Aunty Yasmin.

They hadn't had their Thanksgiving lunch yet, and Aunty Yasmin was panicking about the turkey.

Uncle Ralph had bought a regular chicken from the supermarket, and Aunty Yasmin thought it could be full of dangerous growth hormones that would give them all cancer.

Aunty Yasmin's singing lessons are really paying off – at least in the volume department. I think everyone in LA must have heard her shouting at Lolly for rollerblading on the marble floor.

Friday, 25th November

Mum went to B&Q and bought a load of new Christmas lights today.

She bought waving Santa, jumping Santa, Santa's sleigh, three flashing Christmas gift boxes, Rudolph reindeer and eight free-standing reindeer – all made of tube lights.

The front of the pub is already covered in neon Christmas lights, so she's set the new ones up in the back garden.

Now a rumour has gone around the village that there's going to be a Santa's grotto at our pub. We keep getting little kids knocking on the door with letters for Father Christmas.

Saturday, 26th November

Took Daisy to see Santa at Harrods department store.

Mum would have hated the Christmas decorations – they were simple, tasteful white fairy lights twinkling along bare wood branches. Not a neon fairy or wooden cock in sight.

Harrods was Althea's treat – she'd booked it for us months ago.

Althea is totally anti-establishment, but she loves anything creative, which includes seasonal stuff.

For the Harrods trip, Althea dressed Wolfgang as a punk Christmas elf, with safety pins through his green elf ears.

When it was our turn to see Santa, Althea warned the door elf that Wolfgang was 'quite sensitive' and tended to bite when angered.

The lady elf reassured us that Santa was very good at putting children at ease. Then she led us into the grotto, where a big, jolly Santa welcomed us.

Wolfgang shouted, 'Fat! Fat!'

Santa chuckled politely and gave Wolfgang a toy truck to snap in two.

Daisy wouldn't take her dolly present. She pushed it away and said, 'No, no!'

Wolfgang tore off the cab compartment and a wheel from his truck and gave it to Daisy.

She chewed the wheel happily.

Wolfgang really can be a kind little boy sometimes. I think Santa was a bit annoyed though, because Wolfgang tore his knitted present sack apart.

Monday, 28th November

Althea and I took the kids to Bethnal Green playgroup today.

We had to get there really early because London playgroups are like nightclubs – once they're full, they're full, and then it's one in, one out.

Today was especially busy because Santa was visiting.

Stupidly, Santa asked Althea if she'd planned her Christmas dinner yet.

Althea shouted at him about 'assumed gender stereotypes' and 'teaching my son that a woman's place is in the fucking kitchen'.

Santa cowered against his cotton-wool throne.

One of the kids said, 'Mummy, if Santa goes to prison, will we still get presents?'

Tuesday, 29th November

Trying very hard not to think about Alex.

Ankle much better.

Feeling very festive and Christmassy.

Brandi and I went to Starbucks and bought ourselves gingerbread lattes in red cups.

Then we went home and wrote out all our Christmas cards. Well – I did. Brandi got bored and persuaded Dad to do it for her.

Dad loves anything tedious, so he was more than happy.

We had a nice afternoon together, drinking tea, eating Christmas shortbread and writing Christmas cards.

Thursday, 1st December

I can't believe it. I absolutely CANNOT believe it.

I've lost 20 pounds.

I've spent all morning turning sideways in every mirror, lifting up my top and admiring my tummy region.

Brandi said, 'Wow, I didn't know your stretch marks were *that* bad.'

I considered celebrating with a white-chocolate Christmas Mars Bar, but NO! I am going to maintain.

Maintain, maintain, maintain.

Saturday, 3rd December

Called Althea, re weight loss, and she said, 'Right. We're going to get you some new skinny-girl clothes.'

I told her I had other financial priorities.

'Didn't Nick say he'd buy you new clothes if you finished the marathon?' she said.

I told her Nick never honoured his bets.

She asked if I still had Nick's credit card. The one Helen pays off.

'Yes,' I admitted. 'But it doesn't seem fair to use it.'

'Maybe he'll have to cancel his flight to "somewhere sunny",' she said.

I told her the credit card was for emergencies.

'No offence,' said Althea, 'but your wardrobe *is* an emergency. If you wear that big grey woolly-elephant dress again, I'm going to throw up.'

I started talking about doing the right thing and being the better person, and she said, 'Nick made a bet with you. So now he has to pay up. He cheated on you and left you alone to bring up a baby. What are a few clothes after everything he's put you through? You've been totally humiliated.'

She is right, I suppose. I mean, I can't even buy a Kit Kat in Great Oakley without the checkout lady saying, 'Go ahead, love. You deserve a little treat after everything you've been through.'

Finally, Althea persuaded me by saying, 'Look, you're going to need new clothes when you start working again. Think of it as an investment. No one is going to hire you in those old stained leggings of yours.'

Sunday, 4th December

Have just spent all morning giggling.

Althea insisted we go to fancy Sloane Square and hit all the designer stores.

London is still all magical and twinkling.

The Sloane Square trees were hung with huge, beautiful snowflake lights, and a 50ft Christmas fir towered over us tiny shoppers.

Railings were strung with pretty little lights, and the shop windows shone with Christmassy displays.

Whenever a sales assistant asked if we needed help, Althea said, 'What costs the most in here?'

I really haven't bought any clothes since I was pregnant with Daisy, so it was all a bit strange.

In Chloe, the sales assistant was a gushing type who kept saying 'lovely'.

'Can I help you lovely ladies?' 'Have you seen the lovely things back here?' 'I think this would look lovely on you.'

Althea grabbed a load of clothes for me to try on, and the assistant said, 'Oh you've made a lovely choice!'

I tried them on. And the assistant was right – they were a lovely choice.

I really am looking pretty thin, too. I mean, I don't think my stomach will ever go back to how it was. But I'm looking fit and healthy.

When we got to the cash register, I freaked out.

I told Althea I couldn't pay with Nick's card. 'And anyway,' I added, 'Helen's the one who pays it off. She didn't make the bet with me.'

'She was the one who raised an irresponsible shitbag of a son,' Althea pointed out.

I twisted the credit card in my hands, really not sure if I could go through with it after all.

'If you can't do it,' said Althea, 'give me the credit card and I will.'

The sales assistant asked, 'Is everything OK?'

Althea explained that my ex-fiancé cheated on me with my bridesmaid. And that we would be using his credit card.

The sales assistant narrowed her eyes, snatched the card and said, 'Paying by card? Lovely!'

I ended up buying a whole new wardrobe. And we also bought Daisy a pink cashmere twinset, baby pearls made of rubber, and tights with little pretend-high heels onto the feet.

Then Althea forced me into a swanky hairdresser's, and I got a beautiful new haircut. Layers that made my curls really bouncy, and some really lovely, subtle blonde highlights.

After that, we went to Fortnum & Mason for a Christmas afternoon tea – three silver tiers of turkey and cranberry sandwiches, star shortbread biscuits and filo pastry mince pies.

I told Althea that Nick would shit himself when the bill came through. And Helen would be furious.

'When will that be?' Althea asked.

'In January,' I told her.

'Yes,' said Althea. 'Serves them right.'

Then we started giggling and couldn't stop – until Daisy tried to blind herself with a silver fork.

Monday, 5th December

Christmas songs on the radio.

It's the most wonderful TIME of the YEAR!

Even when shitty things are happening, you've got to love Christmas.

Nick rang this morning and asked to meet me in London

tomorrow.

For a moment, I thought he'd somehow found out about the credit card. Silly me. As if Nick would ever check the statements ahead of time.

Actually, he wanted to talk 'about us'.

I'm going to meet up with him.

He's still Daisy's dad.

And if I'm totally honest, I'm enjoying him chasing after me. I feel I should be allowed to milk it for a little bit.

Especially since Alex hasn't called or messaged.

Tuesday, 6th December

Just been to the Christmas cake sale at Callum's school.

Nothing cost more than 20p, so I bought a chocolate sponge, six mince pies and a jar of iced shortbread biscuits all for £2. Result!

Callum won a prize for his 'technical bake' – a pile of biscuits and squirty cream made to look like a snowman.

Wednesday, 7th December

Callum's nativity play at the school.

Brandi is very proud because Callum got the part of God.

Seeing him perform, it's fair to say he can project his voice. Some of the old ladies were wincing and covering their ears when he shouted down from heaven.

Luckily Daisy slept soundly in the stroller, even when Callum beat the drum so hard it had to be taken off him by the teacher.

Thursday, 8th December

Whoa.

What a day.

Met Nick at 'Vodka!' this afternoon – a swanky bar full of men with neckerchiefs and women with shiny leather boots and tasselled handbags.

It was like the bar that Christmas forgot. There were no decorations, and everyone looked serious and miserable.

They didn't do Diet Coke, so I had to have some perfumed lemon drink that tasted like bath water.

Nick was late of course.

So I spent half an hour trying to stop Daisy smashing the glass coasters.

While we were waiting, this drunk guy from Manchester started talking to me. He was so drunk, he could only manage one word in three.

'You...lovely-looking girl...on Saturday? Nice...lager tops... and then the policeman said...not my broken glass, mate...'

When Nick finally showed up, he had that wet-eyed smiley look that told me he'd already had a few drinks.

He did a double take when he saw me and said, 'Wow. You look amazing.'

I was wearing a silk dress, cashmere coat and suede knee-high boots. And I did look nice, even if I do say so myself.

I didn't tell Nick that he'd paid for my outfit.

Nick ordered a double Monkey Shoulder on the rocks, then slurred at me about how fantastic the other night had been.

I told him off for being late. Daisy was getting near shitty hour and would soon be crying inconsolably.

She'd already started grizzling like a fire alarm running out of batteries.

Nick gave me his dazzling Nick smile – the kind of smile he used in the old days. When we first got together. He said, 'Look, listen. Are we really going to do all this legal stuff? Solicitors and all of that? I want you back, Julesy. I want my family back. I've been such an idiot.'

He told me that after Daisy, he thought he'd had some kind of mid-life crisis, not feeling like he'd made it as an actor, not knowing how 'babies work'.

'I thought I'd settled down too soon,' he said. 'That I needed more passion. Excitement. Sadie gave me all that. But it's meaningless. Empty. Because it's all about her.'

He took my hand and said, 'Look, I know all this shit has been horrible for you. But when you think about it, it's kind of worked out for the best. Because being with Sadie has shown me what I had all along. I needed to see that. Otherwise, I would have been bar hopping for the next twenty years. I'm ready now, Julesy. I'm ready to be a proper father. And husband. If you'll have me.'

Everything I wanted to hear. Six months ago. But thank God, I'm stronger now.

Nick grinned at Daisy and said, 'What do you think, Daisy boo? You think that's a good idea? Mummy and Daddy together again for Christmas? Good idea? Yes?'

He held my hand to his chest and said, 'Didn't you love me once?'

I admitted that yes, I had loved him once. But I said I'd moved on now. I was making a new life for myself.

'But what about our family?' he said. 'Don't you want the best for Daisy? Don't you want a family?'

Daisy's little hand reached out and grabbed my finger.

She gave me the sweetest, loveliest little smile.

And I thought *I'm what's best for Daisy. I'm her family. Nick is just a side dish. As long as Daisy has me, she'll be just fine. Families come in all shapes and sizes.*

I told Nick I didn't think it was best for Daisy, us being together. Then he got cross and said if things went to court, he'd be financially 'well out of pocket'.

'How about we put all that legal shit on hold?' said Nick. 'Then we can figure out when you're going to move back in. Maybe you should be the one to break the news to Sadie. She gets pretty violent with me...'

I realised then that Nick is just totally deluded. Always has been.

So I told him that it was a mistake, me coming to meet him. And that from now on, if he wanted to speak to me, he needed to do it through my solicitor.

Nick didn't answer. Just scowled at his drink.

I walked out with my head held high. Would have been a perfect strong woman moment. Except on the way out, Daisy grabbed some woman's beige cashmere coat and rubbed her nose back and forth on the lining.

When I got outside, it was snowing. Really heavily. Big, fat snowflakes tumbled from the sky by the bucketload, and the pavements were already covered.

The privet hedges and black railings around Soho Square had turned white, snow twirled in the sky under bright yellow Christmas lights, and London looked like a magical scene from Harry Potter.

For a moment, my head was full of poetic words about the majestic soft, swirling flakes.

Then I tried to push the stroller through the layer of snow and started swearing.

'Stupid, fucking...these wheels... Come on! Stupid pushchair!'

It took me a full ten minutes to get to the top of the street.

Then I saw Sadie.

She must have been on her way to see Nick.

It was one of those horrible moments where we both saw each other at exactly the same time, so neither of us could do anything other than keep walking forward.

Except I wasn't really walking. I was doing a sort of 'shove, lift, shove, lift' thing with the stroller in the snow.

Sadie looked awful. Pasty skin, spotty and pudgy-looking. She definitely didn't have the pregnancy glow any more.

The smock maternity coat she wore was all bobbled around the stomach. Her hair was limp and thin. And she was lumbering along in Ugg boots, knees turned out. I've never seen her in flat shoes before. She's got quite short legs really.

Sadie pretended to see something across the street and made a little waddling detour.

She really is a terrible actress. Very unbelievable. No wonder she only gets parts by sleeping with directors.

By the time I got to the train station, the snow was a blizzard.

I was covered. So was the stroller.

I was so worried about Daisy getting cold.

And then I discovered all the trains were cancelled.

Double shit.

Rang Althea, wondering if she had any bright ideas.

Althea is like an encyclopaedia of London transport. She always knows which train station you can detour from, or whether a bus would be better.

She told me London transport was 'fucked up', including trains, buses and taxis.

Apparently, the roads around Great Oakley were blocked too.

I phoned Laura, and she said to stay put, and she'd come to meet me. But in the meantime, I should try and book myself a hotel.

After dragging the stroller to every hotel around the station and finding them full (I even tried the King's Cross Dalton and humiliatingly name-dropped Alex and Zachary), I sat on a bench in King's Cross with a howling Daisy in my arms, wondering what I was going to do.

More and more people bundled into the station, covered in thick snow. It really was coming down. And it was *freezing* cold. Daisy's cheeks were a sort of bluish colour. She had a snuffly nose and kept doing little fairy sneezes.

A band of church carol singers started singing at the coffee kiosk, I think in a bid to cheer us all up. But actually, the low tones of 'Silent Night' had an eerie Armageddon quality.

To be honest, I was feeling a bit scared. People were getting angry, shouting about the end of days. And some teenagers smashed WH Smith's window.

I tried to call Laura again, but the signal was down. The whole network was jammed. I texted to say I was still at King's Cross but got no reply.

Daisy and I sat and waited – me eyeballing the train timetables like a crazy woman. But the same message kept flashing up over and over:

'Happy Christmas! All Services Cancelled.'

I cuddled Daisy inside my coat, but I was still worried about the cold.

I knew things were bad when the Red Cross turned up with blankets – threadbare ones that looked distinctly Victorian orphanage.

I always thought I'd be dignified and polite in an emergency. But as soon as I saw the Red Cross man, I started yelling, 'Over here! OVER HERE! HEY! I HAVE A BLOODY BABY; I NEED A BLANKET MORE THAN HE DOES!'

Then a deep voice behind me said, 'Juliette. Here. I have a blanket for you.'

I turned around.

It was Alex, in a black wool coat and leather gloves, black hair dusted with snow. He was holding a fluffy beige blanket that looked

233

a lot warmer than the Red Cross ones.

'What are *you* doing here?' I said.

He wrapped the blanket around Daisy and me. 'Your sister told Zachary you were stuck,' he told me. 'And he knew I was in the area. I'm taking you to the King's Cross Dalton.'

'But it's full,' I said.

Alex said, 'Not for me it's not.'

The hotel was like being in a Christmas movie – huge roaring log fire and big, thick carpets.

Lots of people were pretending to read newspapers. I got the feeling they weren't actually staying in the hotel but had snuck in to hide from the storm.

Daisy fell asleep as soon as she felt the warmth of the fire.

Alex took us to the Royal Suite on the top floor.

It was four times the size of the apartment I'd lived in with Nick.

I kept saying thank you, but Alex got annoyed and said, 'I heard you the first time. And the fourth.'

Then he asked about Daisy – whether she'd be OK sleeping in a strange place.

I told him she'd be fine. In fact, once I saw the suite, I decided she probably wouldn't want to go home.

One bedroom (yes – there was more than one) was made up with a cot and a load of fancy baby things. Organic cotton wool, brushed cotton baby gros, herbal baby shampoo...

Daisy woke up and looked a bit scared. I could tell she was getting ready to howl, so I started bending my knees and shushing her.

'Here,' said Alex, taking her. 'Let me. You must be exhausted.'

'Don't be offended if she cries,' I said. 'She doesn't like new people when she's tired.'

'I'm not a new person,' said Alex. Then he put Daisy on his shoulder and within a minute she'd fallen asleep again.

After Alex had laid Daisy in the cot, he asked if I wanted supper.

'Is supper like tea?' I said.

He looked confused. 'Tea? As in a cup of tea?'

'No. *Tea*,' I said. 'The meal you have in the evening.'

'Oh, you mean dinner?' he replied.

'No.' I shook my head. 'You have dinner at lunch time, don't you?'

'That would be lunch,' said Alex. 'Dinner you have in the evening.'

'What's supper then?'

'*Informal* dinner,' he replied.

I still don't quite get it ...

But anyway, *supper* turned out to be beef stew with dumplings, a cheese board and a chocolate fondant pudding. Under big silver dome things.

Before the food arrived, Alex poured me a glass of brandy.

'You should have one too,' I said.

'No.' Alex crossed his arms. 'I should be going.'

'Oh go on,' I said. 'It's so nice to see you.'

Which it was. I really have missed him.

He poured himself a brandy. 'I'll stay with you while you get used to the place.'

We stood by the window and watched the snow falling.

London was totally still and silent. No cars. No people. Just soft, white flakes falling on tiles and red brick.

I've never seen the city so beautiful. All the sharp edges gone and everything soft and white. Snow twirled past the windowpane while Alex and I watched it dancing.

We were standing almost shoulder to shoulder, and I could feel this sort of electricity between us. I so badly wanted him to take my hand. I even nearly put my hand into his. But the sensible part of me knew that wasn't a good idea.

We stood for a long time.

Then Alex asked why I hadn't thought to check the weather

235

forecast before coming to London.

I told him I was meeting Nick.

'Didn't *he* think to check the weather?' said Alex.

I told him he was mistaking Nick for someone considerate.

'Listen, about Nick –' I began.

Alex held his hand up and said, 'Let's not go there.'

'Please.' I said. 'Just let me explain. You and I were close before –'

'There's nothing to explain,' said Alex, sounding all cold and formal. 'I wish you well. I wish Daisy well. And I hope we can be friends. I still value your friendship. But closeness…is not a good idea.'

Then he said he had to go. The hotel was swamped, and he needed to help out, but he told me to call room service if I needed anything.

Felt really sad when he left. Because I could tell, he'd sort of closed himself off from me. He was all cold and distant. And I realised how much I missed the old Alex. The one I went running with.

Still. I made the best of things.

Ate all the stew, cheeseboard, fondant pudding. Drank quite a bit of brandy. Watched *The Real Housewives of Orange County* on the great big flat-screen telly. And generally had a nice time, except I couldn't help wishing Alex had stayed.

Friday, 9th December

Daisy slept in until *half past* seven this morning!

Must be something to do with the big thick hotel curtains.

Had fresh croissants for breakfast, courtesy of room service. (Daisy made a real mess of hers – it took AGES to pick croissant crumbs out of the thick-enough-to-lose-your-shoes carpet).

Before we left, I asked the receptionist if Mr Dalton was around so we could thank him. But she said he'd left earlier this morning.

Alex had arranged a car to take us back to Great Oakley.

Apparently, he'd been very insistent about putting the baby seat in the back. And having water and food in the car, in case there were any delays on the road.

Then the receptionist went on about how thoughtful Alex was and how she loved working for him. 'He's a wonderful employer,' she said. 'Always thinking of other people.'

Yes. So thoughtful. Except he thinks that closeness isn't a good idea.

The car ride back was lovely. But all I could think about was Alex. And at times, what Alex looks like with no clothes on.

Saturday, 10th December

Will NOT text Alex or anything stupid like that.

I've tried to explain about Nick. He doesn't want to hear it. And as Althea says, that should tell me everything I need to know.

'If a man doesn't trust you, forget it,' she said. 'Move on. Find someone better.'

The trouble is, right now I can't think of anyone better than Alex.

Oh well. It's all for the best. I mean, I can hardly imagine us sharing a life together. What would Alex make of the giant wooden penis hanging on our Christmas tree?

Sunday, 11th December

Still haven't done my Christmas shopping.

I used to be so organised.

It's like my brain has been stolen and replaced with Nana Joan's.

Which reminds me – Nana Joan!

Need to arrange getting her to the pub for Christmas dinner.

Monday, 12th December

Because so many kids think Santa's Grotto is in our back garden, Dad put his Santa suit on today and let the kids in for some free (only slightly out-of-date) packets of Doritos.

He was the most efficient Santa I ever saw, getting the children in an orderly queue and giving them all exactly one minute and thirty seconds to tell him what they wanted for Christmas.

Then Mum came out with a big bowl of pick-and-mix sweets and let them all go mad on Callum's big trampoline.

When the kids left, we had baked cheese with cranberry bread, lit the coal fire and sang carols for Callum and Daisy. It would have been a perfect family moment, except that Callum switched the word 'Christmas' for 'poo' in every song.

Tuesday, 13th December

I think Daisy has more teeth coming through because she woke up four times last night. It was like she was three-months-old again. Trouble is, I've got used to a not-bad night's sleep now. So had to drag myself through today.

Couldn't face braving the shops for Christmas presents.

Saw Nana Joan instead.

The manager at Nana's care home is very progressive and has banned tinsel from the building. She's persuaded a local artist to do modern, minimalist decorations.

The lounge area was hung with stainless-steel stars and reinforced glass icicles.

There had been a complaint about the decorations though, because mad Doris tried to attack another resident with a giant plastic snowflake.

Nana was in good spirits but won't come round for Christmas

dinner. She's got a dodgy stomach and is 'farting like an old horse'.

These days she mainly eats bananas and humbugs so has constant bowel trouble.

I told her nobody would care if she farted.

She said, 'This isn't just *farting*, love. It's tribal drums. Anyway, the care home is holding a séance on Christmas Day. I don't want to miss it. I'm looking forward to talking with your granddad.'

Wednesday, 14th December

Christmas shopping is SOO stressful.

Ended up on Oxford Street, ramming the crowds with the stroller, trying to fling whatever I could into my bags for life (Remembered them! YESSSS!).

I wondered if I should buy Alex a present. Sort of a thank you for everything he's done for me this year. But what do you buy a man who owns fifty hotels? So I decided just to buy for family and Althea.

The shops were REALLY busy, so cleared my head with a cup of coffee and a jumbo chocolate teacake.

Two hours later, I still hadn't bought anything. And the shops were looking bare.

Ran into British Home Stores and filled my basket. All logic left me, and I just bought whatever I could lay my hands on.

In the end, I bought:

◆ Bottles of beer called things like 'Old Fart' and 'Geriatric' (most stupid purchase ever, since parents own a pub and get really good-quality beer at trade price).

◆ A walking stick full of jelly beans (like Callum doesn't get enough sugar).

◆ A 'grow your own' Venus flytrap.

- A little vending machine of Cadbury's chocolate miniatures (Mum will be happy at least).
- A mojito set (one glass, one mini bottle of Bacardi, one sachet lime flavouring – £25. Feel a bit ripped off.).
- A foam moustache on a lolly stick.

Afternoon

Got the train home with lots of other sweaty, irritable shoppers.

Daisy cried the WHOLE train journey.

We got stuck in a tunnel for half an hour due to cable being stolen from the train tracks.

Daisy SCREAMED in the tunnel. No amount of cuddling or shushing would calm her down.

Everyone looked pretty annoyed, except one hippy man who said, 'It's OK. She's just saying what we're all thinking.'

Got home and realised I STILL had to wrap everything.

ARG!

It took an hour.

Daisy kept trying to eat the Sellotape.

Thursday, 15th December

Too cold to go out today, so picked up Nana Joan and we all sat around the pub eating Christmas cake and drinking sherry.

Nana Joan made the Christmas cake, so the ready-roll icing Santa looked a little sinister. Nana's hands aren't as steady as they were, so Santa had snake-like slits for eyes and a furious mouth.

Also, I found a screw in my slice of cake, and Mum found a piece of tinsel. Nana's eyesight isn't what it was either.

Friday, 16th December

Should I send Alex a Christmas card?

Saturday, 17th December

Lovely Laura back home!

Zach came to the pub this evening to see her. They sat in one of the cushiony booths by the Christmas tree, sharing a bottle of red wine and holding hands.

Mum wanted to offer them a free 'Christmas' shot of whisky, but I persuaded her not to ruin their romantic moment.

Laura was all giddy and happy when she came upstairs. Zach had bought her a *diamond* tennis bracelet as a Christmas present, which she was wearing with pride. But now she's worried because she only bought him a charity subscription to UNICEF.

Sunday, 18th December

Christmas films on telly!

Watched *Herbie*, *Gremlins* and *Ghostbusters* with a big tin of chocolates, while Dad and Laura walked Daisy around the village.

Mum has no preference when it comes to mixed chocolates, so she ate all the coffee creams and the ones with old nuts inside, leaving me with strawberry creams and toffees.

Hooray!

Monday, 19th December

Wonder what Alex is doing for Christmas? Oh, stop it, Juliette. Just stop it.

Tuesday, 20th December

Last chance to send Alex a Christmas card. But he hasn't sent me one. So fuck it.

Wednesday, 21st December

Christmas card from the Daltons. A generic one, signed by Alex, Zach, Catrina and Jemima, and addressed to the 'Duffy family'.

Oh well. What did I expect?

Thursday, 22nd December

Mum's bought a sexy Santa outfit. It would be obscene, even on a regular-sized woman, but Mum's huge boobs make it positively pornographic. She's wearing it while she serves behind the bar.

Dad and the regulars gaze at her adoringly whenever she leans forward to pull a pint.

Friday, 23rd December

Probably should catch up again with Nick, see what he's doing for Christmas. But he's a grown man. If he wants to see Daisy, he can make the arrangements himself.

Saturday, 24th December

The usual Duffy Christmas Eve tradition – glass of sherry while putting candles in the window for everyone we love who has passed away.

We all had a cry for my two granddads, Aunty Karen, the baby Mum miscarried before Brandi and our old childhood dog, Pastry.

After that, we put Callum to bed eighteen times. Getting him under the duvet was like trying to wrestle a puppy into one of those doggy outfits.

In the end, Mum had to sit on him until he fell asleep.

Sunday, 25th December
Christmas Day
Morning

Christmas DAAAAAAAY!!

Mum woke me up at 5 am, wearing her Christmas elf pyjamas and singing 'Rudolph the Red Nose Reindeer'.

She's always the first one awake. Then she gets grumpy because we won't let her open her presents until everyone else gets up.

Callum woke up next, delirious with happiness because his stocking was full of presents from Santa.

He kept saying, 'I can't believe it. I wasn't a good boy at all.'

We all ended up opening our presents around the dining table and eating smoked-salmon and cream cheese bagels amid a sea of wrapping paper.

Dad got Mum a doormat that said:

BEWARE OF THE WIFE

Mum had tears of joy in her eyes, and she and Dad held hands fondly over the mat. Then she went out to replace the existing doormat, which says:

OH SHIT NOT YOU AGAIN

After that, we all watched *The Snowman* and comforted Dad because he always cries at the end.

Afternoon

Leetle bit merry.

As Mum says, it wouldn't be Christmas without a pint of chocolate liqueur.

Nearly phoned Nick first thing, for Daisy's sake. Spirit of Christmas and all that. But then I thought...well, he knows my number.

Then spent all morning feeling annoyed that he hadn't called.

But Mum made everyone Christmas cocktails with her secret ingredient (two shots of vodka), and suddenly I didn't care about Nick so much.

As usual, Dad made the Christmas dinner (Mum always gets too stressed and starts screeching at everyone to get out of her fucking kitchen).

At first, he was humming 'Joy to the World', checking all his kitchen timers and sharpening his knives.

Then he realised Laura had bought organic vegetables from the farm down the road and they were covered in mud and rotten bits.

He stopped humming 'Joy to the World' and started trying to de-mud the veg with his electric sander.

Then Daisy pulled the tree over, and Callum jumped on it.

Brandi and Mum had to serve in the pub between 12 pm and 2 pm, and got drunk on sherry mixed with energy drink.

But it was all OK in the end.

Christmas lunch, as usual, was out of Dad's 1970s cookbook *Frugal Meals* – bronzed turkey, little sausages in bacon, roast potatoes, parsnips and Brussels sprouts.

Dad hates 'all this modern chef splash of this and that nonsense', and measured everything, so our plates looked identical.

Two slices of turkey breast, three potatoes, two parsnips, six Brussels sprouts and 200ml of gravy each.

As usual, Mum moaned about 'pathetic portion sizes' and 'why not just serve me a big plateful and then I won't have to get up?'

Dad smiled at her adoringly and made *his* usual Christmas

speech about how he loved Mum more every year.

Ate lots. Drank lots. Nice day.

Monday, 26th December
Boxing Day
Blurrg.

Lovely fizzy Christmas feeling all gone. Just tidying up wrapping paper and feeling fat.

Zachary called round to take Laura on a woodland walk today. Meaning I have no one sensible to talk to.

Althea is still with her mum in the Caribbean. They go most years and have a barbeque on the beach.

She's sent me a postcard of a Rastaman drinking Red Stripe. It says, 'Enjoy bronchitis, suckers!'

Tuesday, 27th December
Dad is forcing us to eat Christmas leftovers.

So far today we have eaten:

+ Turkey and Brussels sprouts omelette
+ Turkey and Brussels sprouts sandwiches
+ Turkey and sliced Brussels sprouts on crisp bread with mayonnaise.

By teatime, Mum said she was 'sick of turkey' and wanted to throw all the leftovers out. But Dad gave her a lecture about wasting food and starving children.

He boiled the turkey carcass and made a disgusting soup.

When the soup was ready, the whole kitchen smelt like dead animal. Dad finally admitted he was 'sick of turkey too', so we ended up getting fish and chips.

Wednesday, 28th December

Althea back today. She called, wanting to know if I needed moral support for the Dalton New Year's Eve Ball.

I hadn't even thought about the ball. I suppose I'd just decided I wasn't going. It's just all too humiliating. I don't want to look like I'm chasing around after Alex. And of course there'll be the charity auction. No fun if you're single.

The Jolly-Piggotts might be there too.

'But you've lost a fuck-load of weight, and you're looking fabulous,' Althea bellowed. 'To the ball, Cinderella. To the ball!'

I have to admit I am looking extremely slim – even after a Christmas of mince pies and Mum's constant Iceland buffet food (SO un-Christmassy this year. Spring rolls?? Spicy samosas??)

Also, I don't want Alex to think I'm hiding from him.

I gave in and told Althea I'd go.

Which turned out to be the right choice. Because she'd already bought our tickets.

Thursday, 29th December

Will it look a bit desperate if I go to the ball?

Friday, 30th December

Dalton New Year's Eve Ball tomorrow.

Maybe I won't go after all. I'll just feel disappointed when Alex is all cold and talks about 'friendship'.

I'm not quite over him yet. And I've had enough disappointments this year.

I can just stay at home with Daisy. She's making all these lovely little babbling noises now. Ba ba ba! So cute. What better way to spend time than with my little girl? Who needs a fancy party when you have all the love you need at home?

Saturday, 31st December
New Year's Eve

Brandi woke me at 7 am this morning – 'IT'S THE FUCKING NEW YEAR'S EVE BALL TODAY!!! WE NEED TO START GETTING READY!'

I told Brandi I didn't want to go, but she said, 'Don't be fucking stupid. You're a single mum. You need to find a boyfriend.'

She dragged me into her bedroom and gave me a face mask that burned my cheeks. Then she tried to paint my toenails neon pink. I asked if she had any grey nail polish (very fashionable right now).

'Why'd you want to look like a corpse?' said Brandi.

We settled on a French manicure.

It did look pretty nice.

Maybe I will go…

Oh, to hell with it. I'll go.

5 pm

Nervous about the ball.

Does everyone know Alex and I have slept together? Has he told anyone?

Strange to think we could have a night like that and it just go nowhere.

But I've learned this year that life rarely goes the way you want it to. You just have to roll with the punches.

6.30 pm

Have been buffed and preened to within an inch of my life.

Didn't let Brandi do my make-up, so I don't look like a drag queen. In fact, I look pretty nice. Even Mum said so. Although she kept wanting to 'add more sparkle'.

Mum said Brandi looked a 'knockout' and asked me why I couldn't show off a bit more of what God gave me.

We're meeting Laura there. She's already in London with Zach.

OK, OK, time to go.

Right. Chewing gum. One last cuddle with Daisy. Has she left any spit trails?

Check, check, check.

Sunday, 1st January
New Year's Day
Morning

Oh. My. God.

The Dalton's New Year's Eve Ball.

When we arrived, Nick was right by the door, clutching a double whisky and looking decidedly worse for wear.

He must have been waiting for me, because as soon as I walked in, he said, 'Jules. We should talk, Jules. Do you want a drink?'

It almost made me feel sorry for Sadie. She must be close to giving birth now.

I said hello. May as well keep things civil. But I told him I'd get my own drink.

He kept giving me puppy-dog eyes from across the room.

Ugh.

Then Helen came over, while Brandi and I were at the bar.

Brandi stopped yelling, 'SHOTS! SHOTS! WE WANT SHOTS!' and said, 'What the fuck do *you* want, you headache?'

'I'd like to speak to Juliette alone if you don't mind,' said Helen, all formal, like she was reading the news.

Brandi and I exchanged looks.

Then Brandi barked, 'We do fucking mind actually.'

But I said it was OK. I'd hear what Helen wanted to say.

Helen led me to the side of the bar and said, 'Nicholas is very unhappy. He feels he's made a mistake. He had a family, and now he's lost it.'

'Lucky he's got another family now then, isn't it?' I said. 'Let him make his mistakes with Sadie.'

'I know you're upset,' said Helen. 'But would you consider giving Nicholas another chance? For my sake?'

I had to laugh at that. 'After the DNA test? And freezing my bank account? And ignoring Daisy for the last six months. For *your* sake?'

'Then do it for Nicholas,' said Helen. 'He wants to be a good father. He just…needs a little practice.'

'You don't even like me, Helen,' I snapped. 'You've never liked me. Why on earth would you want Nick and me to get back together?'

'A mother always wants her son to be happy,' said Helen. 'And Sadie *is* a little erratic. Nick needs stability.'

'Tell him to find some other idiot to mother him,' I told her.

I could see Nick across the room, looking all hopeful and expectant.

God! Did he really think I was that stupid? And that *Helen* of all people could talk me into going back to him? It was clear, by the double whisky in his hand, that he hadn't changed a bit. Not one bit.

Then he had the nerve to come over.

'I miss you,' he said, with a big, soppy drunk grin on his face.

Through the crowd I noticed Alex, wearing his usual immaculate black suit, hands in his pockets. He caught my eye, then noticed Nick and turned away.

'I'll leave you two to talk,' said Helen, looking all smug and pleased with herself, and disappearing into the crowd.

I told Nick I had nothing to say to him.

'But I *miss* you.' He put a heavy, drunk hand on my arm. 'Please

Julesy. Just tell me what to do. How can I win you back?'

I shouted at him to get off me.

Then Alex came striding over. 'Everything OK, Juliette?'

I told Alex, yes. I had everything under control.

But Nick shouted, 'Fuck off, Dalton. I'm talking to my fiancée.'

The nerve of it! His *fiancée*!

I screamed at him that I was no more his fiancée than he was a successful actor. And that he needed to take his hand off me or I would break his nose.

'But Jules, I love you,' Nick implored.

'Well I don't love you,' I shouted.

'You do,' he insisted.

'No I don't,' I yelled, trying to pull my arm free. 'Not any more.'

'Take your hand off her,' said Alex, his voice very low.

Nick noticed the look in Alex's eyes and dropped his hand.

'Juliette,' said Alex. 'Can I talk to you?'

Alex led me out of the ballroom, into an empty conference suite.

He took a jug of iced water, dipped a napkin in it and sponged my arm, which was the tiniest bit red. I mean absolutely nothing to make a fuss about.

I told him I was fine.

'So you don't love Nick Spencer,' said Alex.

'I told you I didn't.'

'No,' he said. 'You never said you didn't love him.'

'You didn't give me a chance,' I shouted. 'I tried to explain. You wouldn't listen.'

'I'm listening now.' Alex pulled two chairs from the long conference table and offered one to me.

We sat opposite each other.

'I've had enough of being messed around,' I told him. 'I tried to tell you before. You didn't want to know. What's so different now?

You've had months to talk to me. If you really cared, you would have listened ages ago.'

'The last thing I want to do is mess you around,' said Alex. 'I care about you. Isn't that obvious?'

'Actions speak louder than words,' I snapped. 'What's obvious is you didn't call.'

Alex rolled up his sleeve, held out his scarred forearm and said, 'Do you know how I got this burn?'

I looked at the twisted skin, and said, 'When your house burned down. When we were teenagers.'

Alex said, 'I went back into the fire. After my father dragged me out.'

'Why?' I asked.

'I'd left something in my bedside drawer.' Alex took a silver coin box from inside his suit jacket and flicked the lid open.

Inside the box was a four-leafed clover frozen in see-through plastic.

I felt too stupid to ask the question. But Alex answered for me:

'The one you gave me. My lucky mascot. I went back into the house for it. That's how much it meant to me. And then a burning door fell on my arm. After that, firemen pulled me free. So you're right. Actions do speak louder than words.'

I felt a lump in my throat. But I quickly swallowed it down.

'You've left me hanging for months. If you really cared, you wouldn't have done that.'

'I was protecting myself,' said Alex. 'A survival mechanism. Selfish, I know. It comes from my father.'

'So what's changed?' I asked.

'I saw how you looked at Nick Spencer tonight. It…changed things.'

'I don't know, Alex.' I shook my head. 'This is still all just talk.'

Then the conference-suite door banged open, and Brandi

251

stumbled in.

'Jules!' she yelled. 'Auction time! You promised you'd go up with me.' She winked at Alex. 'You can bid on her you know. It's allowed.'

Alex rested his elbows on his knees and said, 'Bartering for women isn't really my thing. But Juliette – you go and make my mother some money.'

I touched Alex's scarred arm and said, 'I care about you too, Alex. I always want to be your friend. But words aren't enough.'

He took my hand and held it. Then he nodded and let go.

In the ballroom, Brandi and I climbed on stage with the other girls.

Fat Doug Cockett was striding back and forth, trying to get more 'ladies' to join us.

He asked Althea to come up, but she refused. She barked that it was all 'fucking sexist bullshit' and she'd never be part of 'some capitalist cattle market' unless the men got bid on too. Then she said she'd like to see *Doug* get bid on.

Doug looked a bit frightened and started the auction pretty quickly. He did his usual boring speech about 'lovely girls', and then reminded everyone it was a cash-only auction. 'So no loot, no lady!'

Ugh.

Then the bids started.

I was lot number five.

When it was my turn, Doug put his arm around me.

'JULIETTE! Juliette Duffy – let's see if we can do any better for you this time, love.'

He did this big, embarrassing speech about me having a hard year, but looking 'pretty damn fine tonight' and 'scrubbing up well'.

'Let's begin at fifty pounds, shall we, chaps?' he said. 'Unless anyone wants to go higher?'

To my horror, Nick stuck his hand up.

'One hundred pounds.'

Nick gave me this hopeful smile.

I couldn't believe it.

'Shouldn't you be saving your money for when Sadie gives birth?' I shouted, but my voice was lost on the noisy, echoey stage.

Doug boomed into his microphone, 'Well, there's a turnaround! Juliette and Nick making a go of it for the New Year. Here, here!'

For one horrible moment, I thought Nick would be the winning bidder. But then Althea's hand shot up.

'One hundred and fifty pounds!'

Good old Althea.

Doug chuckled, 'A *lady* bidding. Well, all in a good cause I suppose. Nick? Care to raise your bid?'

I was shaking my head at Doug, hoping he'd get the hint. But his drunk eyes were glazed and unseeing.

On stage, Brandi grabbed the microphone from Doug and shouted, 'Two hundred pounds!'

Doug looked a bit confused. He said, 'I'm not sure the auction girls should…' But then he took one look at Brandi's face and said, 'Um…yes, well I suppose. Ah…all in a good cause. Any other bidders?'

On Doug's other side, Laura leaned towards the microphone and said, in her lovely polite voice, 'Two hundred and twenty pounds and fifty pence.'

Everyone laughed.

Nick pulled a wad of notes from his wallet and waved it in the air. 'Five hundred pounds. Cash.'

'FIVE hundred pounds!' boomed Doug. 'Quite right, sir. Well met.'

There was silence.

No one else carries big wads of cash like Nick does. He's such a flash idiot.

'Well, ladies and gentlemen,' Doug shouted. 'I have FIVE

HUNDRED pounds for Juliette Duffy. Going once. Going twice.'

Then Alex's voice boomed out, 'I bid my Rolls Royce.'

There was a stunned silence.

Everyone turned to the doorway.

'Mr Dalton?' said Doug. 'Are you making a bid?'

'My car,' said Alex. 'My Rolls Royce. I bid my Rolls Royce for Juliette.'

The room was totally still.

Doug chuckled and said, 'You're not making a joke, are you?'

'I'm not joking,' said Alex.

Doug blinked at him for a moment, then said, 'Uh…Nick? Care to match that bid? If you can?'

'He can't,' said Alex.

There was a ripple of laughter.

I stared at Alex, not quite believing what was happening.

'Well then,' said Doug. 'I suppose…Juliette Duffy. Sold to Alex Dalton. For one Rolls Royce.'

He banged his hammer.

I was frozen to the spot.

Alex strode up on stage. He threw his car keys at Doug, took my hand and said, 'Is that a big enough action for you?'

I felt a big silly grin spread across my face and nodded.

'You know I hate these auctions, don't you?' said Alex. 'Only for you would I do this.'

He led me down the stage and through the crowd.

Everyone was clapping and cheering.

Nick was swaying and blinking with bewilderment.

When I passed him, he said, 'Julesy. Babe. Please. You can't leave with him. Come on. We have a baby together.'

I stopped.

'Sorry about all this, Nick,' I said. 'I just go with my heart.'

Alex and I ended up on the top floor of the Bond Street Dalton, in the Empire Suite.

Below us, London sparkled and twinkled through panoramic glass.

I said, 'Am I dreaming?' or something tacky like that.

'You're not,' said Alex. 'I might be.'

We lay on the bed and talked and talked.

About growing up in Great Oakley. About stuff we remembered. The woods. The rope swing.

Alex wanted to know everything. What my perfect day would be, my favourite superhero, my favourite food…everything.

It was five in the morning before we fell asleep. And then Alex woke me at six.

'I'm taking you home to see Daisy,' he told me, propped up on his elbow, looking all first-thing-in-the-morning ruggedly handsome. 'I can't believe you're here. It's surreal.'

I told him it was surreal for me too. But good surreal.

I wanted to enjoy the moment. But I found myself asking, 'Can you really see us being together, Alex?'

'Yes,' he said. 'Can't you?'

I asked what his family would think. His mum in particular.

He laughed. 'My mother hates any woman under forty. I doubt you'll be the exception. If I cared about my mother's opinion, I'd never do anything. Anyway. Listen – someone once told me that life isn't about avoiding the storms. It's about dancing in the rain.'

Thank you for finishing my book.
If you have a minute, please review
on Amazon and GoodReads.

Suzy xx

What to read next?

BOOK 11:
The Bad Mother's Detox

Here's a taster...

The

BAD
MOTHER'S
DETOX

SUZY K QUINN

Lightning
Books

Sunday, 1st January

New Year

Afternoon

A time to take stock.

Last January, I was living with Nick in London.

We were engaged.

Things weren't perfect.

Nick's mum was always letting herself into the apartment, criticising my parenting and eating fishy salads at the breakfast bar. Nick was drunk half the time, and panicky when left alone with Daisy.

Also, getting Daisy's pram into the tiny executive lift was a nightmare.

But I honestly thought Daisy would grow up with two parents living together.

I was wrong.

Now I'm staying at my parent's pub in Great Oakley, with Daisy in a travel cot, while Nick plays happy families with my former best friend, who will give birth to their child any day now.

Last year, Nick and Sadie's affair felt awful. I wallowed. But then I got on with it. I even ran a marathon. Now I'm stronger. I've learned that life doesn't end because your ex-boyfriend and ex-best friend are shitheads.

And now Alex and I…well, things are looking up.

Can't stop thinking about the Dalton Ball.

What a night.

Nick was SO shocked when Alex and I headed upstairs together.

'Julesy. Babe. Please. You can't leave with him. Come on. We have a baby together.'

Hilarious that after getting my best friend pregnant, Nick thinks he can have a say in my love life.

Nick STILL hasn't paid any maintenance for Daisy.

And it's been six months since we split up.

BLOODY Nick.

I suppose I shouldn't be surprised.

Everyone warned me not to settle down with a charming, bit-part actor. But pre-Daisy I was young and stupid.

In my early twenties, Nick's puppy-dog eyes and charismatic personality felt romantic. Then Daisy came along, and I realised charm means nothing. Responsibility is everything.

Nick's new baby is due any day, so it's not a great time to talk finances. But that's not Daisy's fault.

Sent Nick a text message:

Hope you are well. We need to sort out maintenance.

If you keep sidestepping this, I'll have to take you to court.

Sorry.

The text message wasn't strictly true. I don't hope he's well, and I won't be sorry to take him to court. But social nicety is hard-wired into me.

Nick hasn't replied yet.

Knowing him, he probably won't answer.

Denial is his favourite way of dealing with problems.

Monday, 2nd January

Alex Dalton called late last night.

'How are you?' he asked. 'Did you catch up on sleep after New Year's Eve?'

I pictured Alex in one of his marble-floored hotel lobbies, black suit and white shirt, jet-black hair, gleaming jawline. Like an aftershave model, but a heterosexual one.

'I'm OK,' I said. 'Just a bit of family drama.'

'Is Daisy all right?'

'Fine.'

Silence.

Then Alex said, 'I want to see you. But I'm flying out to Tokyo for work. I'll keep the trip as short as possible. I hate leaving, but a lot of people are relying on me.'

'How can you be working already?' I asked.

'There's no such thing as a holiday in the hotel trade,' said Alex. 'We have big plans for the Dalton Group this year. Do *you* have any New Year's resolutions?'

'Just one,' I said. 'I want to stop Daisy eating biros.'

'Come on now, Juliette,' said Alex. 'There must be something you want.'

Yes – many things.

+ Unstained clothing.
+ Leaving the house before 9 am.
+ Eight hours' uninterrupted sleep.
+ Financial support from Daisy's father.
+ And a lovely cottage with roses around the door.

But I'd count myself very lucky just to have unstained clothing.

Tuesday, 3rd January

Mum's been arrested again.

It was the usual charge – disrupting the peace.

She was drinking tea with the policemen, playing cards and sharing out her sausage rolls when I picked her up.

The police were cheerful too, letting Daisy crawl into the empty cells and jangle their handcuffs.

Mum asked me about the Dalton Ball on New Year's Eve.

Under different circumstances, I would have shared my evening of drama. However, the police station wasn't the place to relive a romantic encounter, so instead I lectured Mum about proper grandmother behaviour while she signed her release papers.

I could tell she wasn't really listening, because when I'd finished the lecture, Mum said, 'Can we stop at the Co-op on the way home? I fancy some Findus Crispy Pancakes.'

Wednesday, 4th January

Visited Nana Joan this afternoon with the shopping she wanted – bacon, pork chops, frying steak and beef kidneys.

Her care home has a strict vegetarian policy these days, so Nana makes a little on the side selling contraband meat.

Nana took one look at my tired face and fired up her portable grill to make bacon sandwiches.

She's not supposed to have Calor gas in her room, but the staff let her get away with it because it saves arguments at meal times.

Daisy got really excited about my bacon sandwich and kept making grabs for it. Foolishly, I let her have a bite, and she crammed half the sandwich in her mouth before I could stop her, then clamped her little lips closed and stubbornly refused to let me pry them open.

Was concerned about salt content, choking, etc., but Nana told me not to worry.

'Our family are born with unusually large gullets,' she said. 'Your mother used to scoff whole Eccles cakes, and no harm ever came to her.'

Cleaned Nana's portable grill in the en-suite shower room, using Fairy Liquid from the shower rack.

Then I helped Nana with her mobile phone. 'It doesn't ring any more,' she complained. 'There's something squiffy with it.'

It turned out to be an easy problem to solve.

Nana had confused her phone with the temperature controller. The diagnosis was a relief for Nana because she'd been sweating at night for months.

Told Nana I'm a bit worried about Daisy re walking.

The NHS website says babies start walking *around* the age of one, but Daisy hasn't even taken her first step yet.

'Daisy is fifteen months old,' I said. 'Surely she should be able to walk by now.'

Althea's little boy, Wolfgang, walked at eight months – although it proved to be a nuisance. Althea was forever arguing about the price at soft play and eventually resorted to bringing Wolfgang's passport everywhere.

'But Daisy is walking right now,' Nana insisted. 'Look at her go.'

'She's not walking,' I said, as we watched Daisy pull herself up on the rise and recline chair. 'She's cruising.'

'Cruising?' said Nana. 'Isn't that something you do on a ship?'

'It's when children hold onto furniture,' I said. 'But it's not the same as walking. I wish she'd take a few steps.'

'She's probably just lazy,' Nana reassured me. 'Your mum was the same. She only bothered walking if there was cake to be had. The rest of the time she'd sit and whack your Uncle Danny with her rattle.'

Nana asked if I'd seen Nick recently.

'I saw him on New Year's Eve,' I told her. 'He asked for a second chance.'

'Steer well clear,' said Nana. 'He's a good-looking waster, that one. Has he paid you any money for Daisy yet?'

'No,' I said. 'Not a penny.'

'Better sort that out,' said Nana Joan. 'He'll have another baby soon, won't he?'

'It's not that simple,' I said. 'As far as Nick's concerned, Daisy and I are staying with Mum and Dad, so he doesn't need to take care of us.'

'Don't the government just *take* money from absent fathers these days?' Nana asked.

'Not in our case,' I said. 'Most of Nick's earnings are undeclared. And he gets pocket money from his mother – there's no tax bracket for that. If he doesn't pay up, we'll have to go to court.'

Nana asked about the New Year's Eve Ball. 'I hope you wore something that showed off your figure,' she said. 'I used to have a natural cleavage like yours. These days, I need yards of sticky tape.'

Nana is what you call a 'glamorous granny'. Even in her eighties, she wears leopard print, Lurex and Wonderbras.

Told Nana that Alex Dalton and I 'got close' at the New Year's Eve ball.

I don't really know how else to describe things with Alex.

I mean, I suppose we were already 'close'. Alex trained me for the Winter Marathon last year. And we had a few romantic moments while that was going on. But now…it feels like we're sort of, possibly, seeing each other.

'About time,' said Nana. 'Look at you. All your own curly hair and a lovely bosom. It's no wonder you've been snapped up.'

'Our lives are different, though,' I admitted. 'Alex is a Dalton. His family owns half of London.'

'Opposites attract,' said Nana. 'Your grandad liked wholemeal bread. Whereas I stick to white sliced.'

But the truth is, I have baggage with a capital B.

Actually, a capital N.

Nick.

Thursday, 5th January

Nick phoned at midday, sounding terrified.

Sadie is in labour.

Nick and I aren't exactly on friendly terms, but I sensed he was desperate for support, so I let him rattle on.

'How long does it last?' Nick asked. 'Sadie's going mental, and we're only an hour in.'

'Don't you remember my labour?' I said. 'It was over twelve hours.'

'Twelve *hours*?' Nick screeched. 'Daisy didn't take that long to come out, did she? That's *all day*.'

I couldn't help adding, 'You know my friend, Althea? Her labour took five days.'

To be fair, I think Althea strung her labour out a bit.

She had a big hippy love-in with candles and hummus and cushions, and shouted down any midwife who talked about 'speeding things along'.

Also, a yogi came to bend Althea's womanly figure into 'baby-friendly' positions, and weave her thick, curly black hair into 'love braids'.

Baby Wolfgang was 'breathed' into the world, with the occasional bellow of 'Om Shanti'.

'They won't let Sadie into the hospital yet,' Nick sobbed. 'I can't handle this shit, Jules. You know how sensitive I am.'

'Funny to hear you describe yourself as sensitive,' I said.

'Immature and self-absorbed are the words I'd use.'

In the background, I heard Sadie screech, 'Put on my Ellie Goulding album, you *useless twat*.'

Felt a bit sorry for Nick then, but not that sorry.

When Nick got Sadie pregnant, my world fell apart. But like Althea said, 'Karma will get him. Wait and see.'

She was right.

Friday, 6th January

Nick and Sadie have had their baby.

A little boy.

Actually, *really* little – only 5lbs 10oz.

Daisy was 8lbs, and the midwives said things like, 'big strapping legs' and 'a great pair of lungs'.

Daisy has a half-brother. Such a weird thought.

I wonder if the baby looks like Nick, with dark, flirtatious eyebrows and blue eyes. Or like Sadie, with a big moon face and porcelain skin.

Nick and Sadie's baby was born last night by C-section.

Nick phoned in the early hours of the morning to tell Daisy about her new brother. He was glowing with new fatherhood, telling me about little baby Horatio and his massive balls.

'You've called him Horatio?' I said. 'Like Penelope Dearheart's dog?'

Nick went quiet for a moment. 'Well we can't change the name now,' he said. 'Mum's ordered an engraved silver tankard.'

Sadie's doing well apparently (not that I asked) but has got a bit possessive – hissing at anyone who comes near 'little Horry'.

Nick sounded slurred, so I'm guessing he'd managed to sneak some whisky into the labour ward.

No surprises there.

At Daisy's birth, Nick won the prize for worst birthing companion ever, drunkenly screaming, 'What the fuck is that?' at all the wrong moments.

Even the midwife asked if I'd prefer he waited outside.

Saturday, 7th January

Nick phoned at 3 am, asking if I could put his 'little girl' on the phone.

'I'm not going to wake Daisy,' I told him. 'It's the middle of the night. Why didn't you ring in the daytime?'

'Come on, Jules,' said Nick. 'The baby wants to say hello. He's Daisy's *brother*.'

Wow.

Brother.

'Did you get my text message about maintenance payments?' I asked.

Nick didn't answer, which I took to mean yes.

'Sort it out,' I said. 'Or I'll take you to court.'

Sunday, 8th January

Alex just called.

He's cutting his Tokyo trip short and flying back next weekend specially to see me.

And in possibly the weirdest post-coital conversation ever, he asked if I would attend Mass with him and his mother at Westminster Cathedral.

Once I'd ascertained Alex wasn't trying to purge me of sin, I asked why he wanted me to meet his mother.

'Because you're an important person in my life,' said Alex.

'OK,' I managed to say. 'Yes. I'd love to come.'

Hung up before I started blubbing girl tears.

Think I must still be tired from New Year's Eve. That's the trouble with having children. You never get a chance to catch up on sleep.

But I felt so emotional. *Meeting Alex's mother …*

Nick *never* introduced me to his mother.

I met Helen by accident when she let herself into our apartment to give Nick a pair of Gucci loafers she'd picked up at Selfridges. Helen screamed in shock when she saw me, having had no idea I'd moved in with her son.

Not *totally* happy about Westminster Cathedral as a venue.

I might spontaneously combust at the door.

Need to sit down with Dad for a quick Christianity recap.

He has rubbings from all the famous cathedrals and can recite great chunks of the King James Bible by heart.

I haven't been to a proper church service since mine and Nick's wedding-day fiasco. And before that, not since school when we all used to snigger at Mrs Blowers, singing in her funny falsetto voice.

Monday, 9th January

Just phoned my old employer, Give a Damn, to find out when I can start work again.

Left a message, but got the distinct feeling it had fallen into a black hole of messages that will never get listened to.

Will keep trying.

Like the idea of using my brain again, but feel guilty about Daisy.

Then again, I feel guilty about living with my parents, and I need a job to solve that problem.

I suppose guilt and motherhood go hand in hand.

Tuesday, 10th January

My adopted cousin, John Boy, turned up on the doorstep this morning, wearing a huge military rucksack.

He left the army last year after losing half his leg in Afghanistan, and said he'd come to 'learn the pub trade'.

John Boy has gelled, black hair, a pencil moustache and lots of tattoos – plus Harley Davidson stickers over the fibreglass part of his prosthetic leg, and a Nike trainer on his metal foot.

Technically he's a war hero, although he didn't lose his leg in combat – it got blown off when he jumped from the tank for a roadside wee.

Still. We're all extremely proud of him.

After losing his leg, John Boy spent a long time in hospital, having fistfights with anyone who used bad language in front of the nurses.

Mum ushered John Boy into the living room, where he pulled out presents from his rucksack:

+ A jumbo tin of Quality Street for 'the ladies' (Mum, Brandi and me).

+ Army-ration lamb-stew sachets for Dad's countryside hikes.

+ Twenty Afghani pirated DVDs for Daisy and Callum (most of which contained moderate to frequent bad language and violence).

Once he had distributed gifts, John Boy started doing push-ups on the floor, clapping his hands between each one. For more of a challenge, he made Callum sit on his back.

After eating all the green triangles, Mum asked, 'Are you glad to be out of Afghanistan, John Boy?'

'Not really,' he said, switching to one-handed push-ups. 'I miss the lads. The punch-ups. The ten-mile desert runs. Staying awake all night on watch. But it wasn't meant to be. The physio said sand

269

and prosthetic legs don't mix.' Then he looked sad and said, 'They won't have me back now anyway. Not with half my leg missing.'

'You've been living with Trina, haven't you?' said Mum. 'What happened? Did she kick you out again?'

'We had a bit of a barney,' John Boy admitted, grabbing Callum in a headlock and ruffling his hair. 'You know what Mum's like.'

We all exchanged 'yes we do' looks.

Aunty Trina works in a hospital laundry and is obsessed with germs. She has cleaning products to clean cleaning products. Also, she's deeply religious and carries three different bibles in her handbag.

These days, Aunty Trina wouldn't be allowed to adopt, but she and Uncle Danny got John Boy in the 1980s before psychological evaluations came into it. All they had to be were homeowners and non-smokers.

'What did you fall out over this time?' Mum asked.

John Boy said Aunty Trina had thrown away his special-edition, luminous-orange Adidas trainers.

'I admit, I shouldn't have retaliated,' he said.

Apparently, John Boy phoned the local curry house and told them Aunty Trina wasn't really an OAP.

'She won't get free papadums with her main any more,' said John Boy. 'I'm not sure she'll ever forgive me.'

Wednesday, 11th January

Just had a heated phone call with Nick re maintenance.

'Daisy and I can't live above Mum and Dad's pub forever,' I said. 'I'll be going back to work this year, and it's time you supported your daughter.'

Nick said he was *trying* to be a better dad, a better *person*.

'Why don't we just get back together?' he said.

'Jesus Nick, you've just had a baby with someone else,' I said. 'What on earth are you talking about? Think of your son. And *Sadie*. Cut the bloody theatrics and send me some money.'

'I can't do that Julesy,' he replied. 'It has to be legal and shit. We need to come to a proper adult agreement.'

'But only one of us is a proper adult,' I said.

'I *am* an adult now,' Nick insisted. 'Living with Sadie has changed me. You can't have two irresponsible people in the same house, or there would never be any toilet paper.'

Agreed to meet in person tomorrow to 'sort things out'.

I know exactly how the meeting will go.

Nick will try and charm his way out of paying up.

I will shout at him.

Then we'll have to go to court.

Thursday, 12th January

Met Nick in Hyde Park.

It was FREEZING.

Luckily, I'd bundled Daisy into a snow romper suit, ski gloves and boots, thermal hat, and scarf. She was more padding than baby.

For a change, Nick was on time. He swaggered into the park wearing tight black jeans, Ugg boots, a leather jacket, Afghani scarf and sunglasses.

Baby Horatio was with him, wearing tinted sunglasses and tucked under a Mulberry blanket. He was held aloft in one of those futuristic pod prams, like an offering to the gods.

'You've dyed your trendy beard,' I said.

Nick stroked his facial hair. 'Oh. Yeah. Someone said it looked ginger, so I used Just for Men.'

'Where's Sadie?' I asked.

'Doing Instagram shots back at the apartment,' said Nick. 'You know – trying to get into mummy modelling.'

'Doesn't she need Horatio for that?' I asked.

'He throws up too much to get a good picture,' said Nick. 'We've nicknamed him Regurgatron.'

'How can Sadie do mummy modelling without a baby?' I asked.

'She Photoshops him in afterwards.'

Nick looked so tired. Drained. Like life had beaten him. He certainly wasn't glowing with new fatherhood, and the excitement of Horatio's massive balls had obviously worn off.

I suppose anyone would be tired, living with Sadie.

'How's your mother?' I asked. 'Slaving away over a hot witch's cauldron?'

Nick said he didn't know.

Apparently, Helen isn't talking to him right now.

'She keeps going on about a credit card bill, but I don't know what she's on about. I hardly ever go shopping in Sloane Square.'

Had a quiet smirk to myself, remembering my Sloane Square shopping spree last year courtesy of Nick's 'family' credit card.

Serves Helen right.

Anyway, as Althea said – Nick did offer to buy me clothes if I ran the marathon. So it was only fair.

Nick watched Daisy with tears in his eyes.

'She's walking,' he whispered. 'And I missed it. Daddy wasn't there.'

'She's not walking,' I corrected. 'She's just hanging onto the pram. It's called cruising.'

'Isn't that what gay men do outside nightclubs?' said Nick.

Daisy took one look at Nick's brown, beardy face and started crying.

'I love you, Daisy boo,' Nick simpered. 'It's *Daddy*.'

'Nick, you're a stranger to her,' I said. 'You hardly ever visit. How would you feel if a beardy stranger picked you up?'

'That's very hurtful,' said Nick. 'There's no need to knock the beard.'

Then Horatio started crying and threw up cottage-cheese sick over his Mulberry blanket.

Nick went white. 'Christ,' he said. 'Sadie's going to kill me.'

He ran off in search of a dry cleaners.

I told him I'd text over my bank details.

Friday, 13th January

Woke up this morning to find little Callum hiding under my bed wearing a gremlin mask.

I nearly screamed the house down.

I have a love-hate relationship with my mischievous nephew.

Callum is a great kid, but he can also be 'challenging'. In other words, a little shit. Some people say he lacks a father's firm hand, but my little sister Brandi is pretty strict, screeching at him morning, noon and night.

Anyway, Callum said he was playing a 'Friday the 13th trick'.

'You're getting confused with April Fool's Day,' I told him when my hysterics had worn off. 'Friday the 13th is just unlucky.'

Callum thought about that. 'I won't bet on the footie today then,' he said.

'You're betting on football matches?' I asked. 'How? You're five years old.'

Apparently, Callum's primary school has its own highly sophisticated bookmaking system, using Match Attax cards and keepie uppies as gambling currency.

Saturday, 14th January

Told Dad I'm meeting Alex and his mother at Westminster Cathedral tomorrow.

Dad's eyes filled with happy tears and he said, 'I always dreamed you'd discover the *true* meaning of love.'

Mum said, 'I'll say this for religion. It wears you down the nearer you get to dying. But if it's Mass, at least you'll get free biscuits.'

Daisy perked up at this. 'Biscuit! Biscuit!'

Dad looked stern. 'It's not only about biscuits, Daisy. It's about Jesus. Anyway, you get *wafers* at Mass.'

'Jesus biscuit?' Daisy asked.

Mum said, 'They probably sell Jesus biscuits at Aldi, Daisy. You get all sorts of weird confectionery there.'

Sunday, 15th January

Mass at Westminster Cathedral.

Managed to get Daisy into a nice dress, but she ruined the look by demanding her black swimming cap.

After half an hour of screaming, scratching and biting, Mum said, 'Oh let her wear it, love. She's going to church. Judge not lest ye be judged.'

So, I took Daisy to our nation's most famous cathedral dressed like a lunatic.

Met Alex outside Westminster Cathedral at 10 am, in a swirling crowd of well-dressed Londoners and wide-eyed tourists.

Alex wore his Sunday best, which was basically the same crisp, black suit and white shirt he wears all the time, teamed with a wool coat and leather gloves.

He pulled me into a long, serious hug, and told me he'd missed me. Then he held my face and looked right into my eyes with that

274

intense stare of his.

When Alex noticed Daisy, he smiled and knelt down to the Maclaren.

'That's a very fetching cap you're wearing,' he said, shaking Daisy's hand. 'My mother always says that ladies should wear hats to church.'

Daisy said, 'Biscuit?'

'Well I don't have any biscuits,' said Alex. 'But I did bring you one of these – if it's OK with your mummy.'

He pulled a packet of fruit yoyos from his suit pocket and turned to me for approval.

'She loves those,' I said. 'How did you know?'

'I asked,' said Alex. 'My PA has young children. Come on. Let me introduce the pair of you to Anya.'

'Anya?' I said. 'Your mother's called Catrina, isn't she?'

'Anya is what Zach and I call her,' Alex explained. 'It's the Hungarian word for mother.'

He stood then and pushed the Maclaren towards the cathedral.

Catrina Dalton was by the steps, laughing gaily and shaking hands with tourists like she was a visiting dignitary.

She wore a fitted pencil skirt, black high heels and a ruffled white blouse with a jewelled brooch at the collar.

Her white-blonde hair was in its usual French pleat under a swooping black hat, and her gleaming skin was stretched tight over sharp cheekbones. Heavy kohl lined her eyes, and her lips were bright pink with gloss.

I must admit, Catrina looks great for fifty-something, even if she does dress like someone out of Dallas. But then, she's had a lot of work done – including a fairly disastrous nose job that's given her Michael Jackson nostrils.

Alex waved at her. 'Anya. This is Juliette. The girl I've been telling you about. And her daughter, Daisy. You've probably seen her at our New Year's Eve balls and around the village.'

Catrina gave me a celebrity smile and a little gloved wave then turned on high heels and glided into the cathedral.

I felt like a rejected autograph hunter.

'I wouldn't swap her,' said Alex, 'most of the time. Come on. Let's get you two inside – it's cold.'

Alex parked the Maclaren, then led us into the magnificent cathedral.

I ended up squeezing onto a pew beside Catrina Dalton, hemmed in by Alex on the other side.

Catrina gave me another benevolent smile, eyes glazed and unseeing.

I smiled back, clutching Daisy.

Soon, the singing started.

I mumbled along where I could.

Alex didn't sing at all, which made me feel better.

'Why aren't you singing?' I whispered. 'Don't you know the words either?'

'I don't sing in public,' Alex said, taking my hand and squeezing it.

'Do you sing in private then?' I asked.

'No.'

'But you have a piano at your house.'

'I haven't played that in a long time.'

After the singing and some prayers, everyone lined up for wafers and Ribena from the priest.

I blurted out to Alex, 'We're not baptised or anything.'

Alex laughed. 'Nor is Anya. You don't have to go up if you don't want to.'

Behind me, I felt Catrina Dalton bristle. 'Alex! *What* are you saying? Of *course* I am baptised.' She pushed past us then and joined the sacrament queue.

Alex whispered, 'I shouldn't have said that. Anya has a certain image to uphold. It doesn't necessarily link to reality.'

Daisy noticed the wafers in the golden communion bowl then, and pointed excitedly at the priest, shouting, 'MUMMY! BISCUITS! BISCUITS!' Then she tried to clamber over Alex.

Alex held Daisy to stop her falling. 'It looks like Daisy wants to take the sacrament. Shall we go up?'

'OK,' I said. 'But we've never been blessed before.'

'You're blessed every day of your life,' said Alex, handing me Daisy. 'You have this little one. Look – just bow your head, hold out your hand and say Amen, then take a wafer for Daisy. It's not strictly allowed, but otherwise, I think you'll have a riot on your hands.'

'OK.'

As we approached the huge-nostrilled priest, I threw on my best religious smile. 'Good morning, Father.'

The priest looked down at Daisy. 'What colourful clothing!'

I bowed my head and held out a hand for the wafer, but while my attention was on the stone floor, Daisy grabbed five wafers from the priest's golden bowl and stuffed them into her mouth.

Then she reached for his giant cup of Ribena.

'Oh no, little one,' chuckled the priest. 'You can't have that.'

'Mine?' Daisy enquired.

'No, my child.'

'Mine,' Daisy decided, clamping both hands around the cup.

'Daisy!' I said. 'Daisy! NO Daisy! Naughty!'

'MINE!' Daisy shouted, so the word rang around the stone walls.

The priest pulled.

Daisy pulled.

Then Daisy, sensing she was losing the battle, sank her teeth into the priest's kindly fingers.

277

In slow motion, the chalice shot up into the air, splashing vivid purple Ribena over the stony floor.

The cup rolled noisily down the stone steps, coming to a stop by a frightened-looking old lady.

There was a stunned silence.

Beside me, I noticed Alex holding back a smile.

Then I heard Catrina Dalton's distinctive Hungarian accent: 'Good *God.*'

Daisy erupted into angry tears, landing a few well-aimed punches on the priest's arm before I could carry her away.

'NO man. OLLOCKS (bollocks) man!'

I hurried down the aisle and out of the cathedral, with Daisy howling over my shoulder.

On the hard, grey steps, I sat Daisy on my lap and dabbed her teary cheeks.

Then I heard Alex's leather shoes hitting concrete, and felt him sit down beside me.

'Juliette,' said Alex, eyes twinkling with amusement. 'How was your first holy communion?'

'Awful,' I said. 'I'm so embarrassed.'

'Don't be.' Alex took my hand. 'You were wonderful.'

'Something tells me your mother doesn't think I'm wonderful.'

'My mother doesn't usually pay much attention to other people. But I think you've made your mark.'

'By bringing a swearing child into her place of worship?'

'Anya's not as devout as she makes out. She wasn't brought up Catholic. She converted when she met my father. Come on – let me take you for lunch.'

After sandwiches and soup at a nearby deli, Alex bought us takeaway coffees, and we pushed Daisy along the Thames.

Late afternoon, as darkness fell, Alex called a driver to take us home. He spent ages checking Daisy's car seat and even made sure

I was strapped in properly too.

'It's OK,' I said. 'I know how to work a seatbelt.'

Alex looked serious. 'I like to make sure. I'd hate it if anything happened to you.'

We held hands the whole way home.

When we reached Mum and Dad's pub, Alex kissed me goodbye.

'We'll try again with my mother another time. OK?' he said.

'OK,' I said. 'Thanks for today.'

We smiled at each other.

Then Alex kissed me again and said, 'See you soon.'

Monday, 16th January

Just checked my bank account.

Predictably, there was no money from Nick.

Have arranged a 'last chance' meeting with him.

Alex has been texting from New York.

I get all giddy and excited when a new message arrives.

Alex always asks questions:

Where are you? What are you doing? Are you OK?

So different from Nick's former 'romantic' messages, which were usually pictures of himself in various 'amusing' poses.

Alex isn't happy that I'm meeting Nick tomorrow. He referred to Nick as 'Nick Spencer' and wrote he was 'disappointed' with my choice of companion.

But what can I do? I don't *have* a choice of companion. I'm stuck with Nick, for Daisy's sake.

Can Alex and I really work past one amazing night? I mean, really? I suppose anything's possible.

Will have to reread *Cinderella*.

Tuesday, 17th January

Met up with Nick again, this time at Taylor St Baristas near our old flat in Canary Wharf.

Correction, *my* old flat.

Now Nick and Sadie's current flat.

Nick started with the usual theatrics – sobbing that Daisy barely recognised him.

'If you want Daisy to recognise you, make a proper visitation schedule,' I said. 'No more of this "as and when" business. Think of your daughter for a change.'

'And how do I do that?' Nick demanded. 'Sadie keeps my balls in the bedroom drawer. The only reason she let me out today was because I'm wearing a geo-tracker.'

'Let's talk about maintenance,' I said.

'I offered you fifty quid a month—'

'No,' I snapped. 'You can afford more than fifty quid a month.'

'My income is complicated,' Nick wheedled.

'We can always prove your income in court,' I said.

'Can't we just get back together, Jules?' said Nick, sounding tired. 'I know I screwed it up. But I can't turn back the clock.'

'Forget it,' I said. 'Your focus should be on Daisy and your new family.'

'It *is*,' he insisted. 'But paying money is so final, isn't it?'

Then Nick tried to cuddle Daisy in her big snowsuit. She looked like an alarmed starfish.

'Look, Nick,' I said, taking Daisy before she cried. 'I'm being more than reasonable. I just want you to start paying up as of now. That's it. No back payments or anything.'

Nick got all actor-teary then, and said, 'You're right. I'm no good at being an adult. I fucked up…'

Blah blah blah.

Asked if he still had my bank details, and he said, 'Yeah, yeah. I'll sort it, OK?'

Wednesday, 18th January

Alex took me to the cinema last night in Leicester Square.

He was very gentlemanly, sending a driver to pick me up and helping me out of the car when I reached the busy city.

As we walked through the crowds, Alex held me tight and glared at anyone who jostled me.

'Did you wear your seatbelt in the car?' he asked as we headed into the cinema.

'Of course I did,' I laughed. 'What is this obsession with seatbelts?'

'Sorry,' said Alex. 'It's to do with my mother. She never wears one. It used to worry me to death as a child.'

'And now?'

'Now I know my mother is a law unto herself. So, I just have you to worry about. And Daisy.'

As we took our seats, Alex grilled me about meeting Nick. He wanted to know every detail – if Nick had arrived on time, what was said, if Nick had done anything 'inappropriate'.

I told him that Nick was his usual sidestepping, feckless self.

Alex said, 'I don't like you seeing him.'

We were silent for a bit after that.

Then my phone rang.

It was Mum.

I'd asked her only to call in an emergency, but our ideas about emergencies are different.

She rang three times during the film to ask:

+ Where I'd last seen Daisy's sleep blanket.
+ If I could sing Daisy a bedtime song down the phone.

* If I wanted to do Facetime, and see Daisy 'sleeping like an angel'.

The other cinema goers got a bit fed up with me – especially when I sang a whispery lullaby.

There were a few exaggerated huffs and sighs, and someone whispered, 'For goodness sakes!'

I felt I couldn't go to the toilet after causing so much disruption, even though I really needed to.

It got quite uncomfortable by the end because the film was nearly three hours long and had lots of underwater scenes. Plus, the man next to me had a particularly large slurpy drink.

Thursday, 19th January

Fucking bloody bollocking NICK!

OH, MY GOD, I was so blind with fury this morning that I put my dress on backwards.

Have just received a signed-for letter from Nick's solicitor, saying he is applying for RESIDENCY of Daisy.

This is absolutely outrageous.

After being absent for the best part of a year, not paying maintenance and getting my bridesmaid pregnant, Nick now thinks Daisy should live with him.

Why? WHY? What is he playing at?

He must know there is no fucking way ON EARTH he'll get residency.

The letter said that, prior to any court hearing, Nick and I must attend a Mediation Information and Advice Meeting (or MIAM).

MIAM looks a lot like 'maim', as in, to hurt or cause harm.

Couldn't those mediators have thought of a better acronym?

After mediation, Nick will apply for a Child Arrangement Order.

I'm so FURIOUS.

How DARE he?

Friday, 20th January

Rang Nick twenty times, but he didn't answer – the cowardly little shit.

I marched around to Helen and Henry's house with Daisy in tow.

Normally, I'd rather lick rats than visit my ex-mother-in-law, but I needed someone to shout at and decided she'd have to do.

Helen was on her way out, pulling red-leather driving gloves onto her sinewy hands. Her manic blue eyes looked startled when she saw me, and she tipped her head back to look down her long, bird-beak nose.

'I was just going into town,' she said. 'Whatever it is, can't it wait?'

I told her that no, it bloody well couldn't wait. And how dare Nick apply for residency when he's been an absent father and not paid a penny in maintenance.

Helen gave a patronising smile and patted the ends of her wiry black bob. 'He wants you *back*, Juliette. And a chance to father his daughter. How long are you going to humiliate him like this?'

'Humiliate *him*?' I exclaimed.

'Neither of you is perfect. You're both still *learning* to be parents.'

'Fuck off, Helen,' I said. 'I'm with my little girl EVERY DAY. Every single day. What does your son do?'

'Nicholas hasn't had a *chance* to be a father,' said Helen. 'You've kept his daughter from him.'

'What a load of bollocks,' I said. 'Nick didn't ring me for months after the wedding. And he hasn't paid a penny towards Daisy.'

'I'm not going to talk about finances,' Helen snapped.

'He's just doing this to dodge the maintenance issue, isn't

he?' I shouted. 'He lives in *London* for Christ's sake. What court would give an absent father residency *and* move a child from their location?'

Helen raised an eyebrow. 'As a matter of fact, Nicholas is moving closer to home. We're investing in a proper *family* home for him. Somewhere near Henry and I.'

I said a lot of bad words then.

Henry lumbered into the hall in his tweed jacket, buttons straining over his large belly, gingery-grey hair in strands over his bald head. 'What's all this?'

I said a cheery hello to Henry, then barked at Helen: 'You should be ashamed of yourself. AND your son.'

'I don't have time for this, Juliette,' said Helen, pushing on unnecessary sunglasses and strolling towards her Land Rover.

'Tell Nick he'll never get residency of Daisy,' I shouted after her. 'NEVER.'

Helen turned, gave me another patronising smile and said, 'Perhaps if you want to rethink your behaviour – these maintenance threats – then Nicholas will rethink his position too.'

Saturday, 21st January

Finally got through to Nick.

Asked him what the hell he was playing at.

'Desperate men do desperate things, Juliette,' he said.

'No one's stopping you seeing your little girl,' I shouted. 'But how on *earth* can you think this could be in Daisy's best interests? Putting us through a custody battle?'

'I want my family back,' he said.

'This isn't about what *you* want,' I said. 'Think of Daisy, for goodness sake. What's best for *her*?'

'When Daisy grows up, she'll thank me,' Nick insisted. 'She'll say, "Clever Daddy! Mummy was being silly, but you made me live with you, and then Mummy came back." You'll see.'

Ugh!

'You're a spoiled child, Nick,' I said. 'WE'RE NOT GETTING BACK TOGETHER!'

Sunday, 22nd January

Alex called.

He was in the First-Class lounge at Heathrow airport, about to jet off to Dubai, and wanted to tell me how much he was going to miss me.

Aw.

Told him about Nick wanting residency, and he was suitably disgusted.

'The man can't even dress his age,' said Alex. 'Why is he trying to play the father all of a sudden? He can't look after himself, let alone a child.'

'*Another* child,' I said. 'Sadie's had her baby.'

'Did the hospital check it for horns and claws?' Alex asked.

Which I thought was pretty funny.

'Why would Spencer want residency?' said Alex, in a pondering voice like a murder-mystery detective.

'He says he wants his family back,' I said.

Alex was silent for a long time. Then he said, 'I suspected as much.'

'Nick's a lot of hot air,' I said. 'You can never trust what comes out of his mouth.'

'You shouldn't see that man any more,' said Alex, his voice low. 'He's not to be trusted.'

'*What?*' I said. 'I have to see him. He's Daisy's father.'

Silence.

Then Alex said, 'I hate that he's in your life.'

More silence.

'Alex?'

'I have to go. It's getting busy here.'

It *did* sound a little noisy at his end. Someone was kicking off about the buffet lobster tails being 'F-ing tiny' and the caviar trough running dry.

Monday, 23rd January

Nick asked if he could come to the pub today to see Daisy.

Although I'm still furious with him, I agreed for Daisy's sake.

He is already over an hour late.

Just left an angry message saying that if he can't turn up on time, he shouldn't bother.

Have got the tea mugs ready for when Nick finally shows up. His tea will be in a rather rude mug.

Evening

Two hours late! AND Nick brought Helen with him.

I had to physically restrain Mum when she saw Helen on the doorstep. She wanted to squirt her with Callum's Super Soaker.

I screeched at Nick about responsibility and timekeeping and HOW DARE HE TAKE ME TO COURT, then slammed the door in his beaten-puppy face.

Oh god! I was SO FURIOUS!

Helen tapped softly on the door. 'Juliette. Be reasonable. Nick wants to see his daughter.'

'You'd never be late for a business meeting, Helen,' I shouted. 'What's your excuse about this one?'

'Good news,' said Helen brightly. 'Your joint bank account has been unfrozen and put into your name. So, you have access to funds. Can't you see how reasonable we're being?'

I shouted back: 'That's my own bloody money Helen – NOT A PENNY OF IT WAS NICK'S. TELL HIM TO PAY ME MAINTENANCE AND DROP THIS BLOODY COURT CASE!'

Silence.

Then I heard Helen mutter, 'She's obviously not seeing reason. Let's go and see if the café still has that nice soup on.'

Tuesday, 24th January

Alex called this evening from a balmy balcony in Dubai.

'I miss you,' he said. 'I hate being so far away.'

Told him I missed him too, then filled him in about yesterday.

'Well what did you expect?' said Alex. 'Nick Spencer didn't treat you respectfully before. Why would he start now?'

'Nick's just Nick,' I said. 'He's a mess – it's nothing personal.'

'Getting your bridesmaid pregnant isn't personal?'

'You don't have to be brutally honest all the time,' I said.

'Sometimes, the unvarnished truth is a kindness.'

'I'm fully aware I had a baby with the wrong person,' I said. 'You don't need to rub it in.'

'I'm not rubbing anything in. The last thing I want to remember is a woman I...care for deeply...is saddled with Nick Spencer for the rest of her life.'